THE BIG PUNCH

THE BIG PUNCH

Louis Maistros

CONTENTS

DALLAS, 1963

BALTIMORE, 1943

JACKSON COUNTY, 1963

BALTIMORE, 1943

For Elly

Well, this train rolls through the night
Its way is paved with light
Some people say this train is bound for hell
But I have been and back
And I can ease your mind
This train just goes in circles far as I can tell

DALLAS, 1963

H is beloved brains lay piled and sweating on the cool Texas pavement like so much steaming dogshit, still thinking.

Final sounds; a crack like an immense bone breaking, his woman's voice: SCREAMING.

MERCIFULLY: brain-reflex reading her screams as an expression of loss, a wail of grief at seeing the once beautiful head ruined by the assassin's bullet.

UNMERCIFULLY: the truth being that the lady's screams spring from a much baser emotion; revulsion. More mean TRUTH: a person of healthy mind can be expected to react no other way upon the surprise appearance of a strange, sticky glue plastered to one's cheek. A glue made up of warm blood, skull fragments, hair . . .

Still thinking.

Flashes of memory: strawberry ice cream melting: dripping sticky cool between waffle cone and palm. A nail he had stepped on as a child: his earliest memory of crying. The profound smallness of his young son's hand in his own. Vague feelings of having cheated and won, then lost, then won, then lost—but always of having cheated. A nagging sense of incompleteness. And then realization.

The big punch line to the bad joke of a life cut short is the sudden unexpected understanding of what's important and what's not; the terrifying realization that the life has been lived wrong. To an adult life in progress it's hard to reconcile facts; the simple things we cherished as children should have stuck but slid. The invisible but ever present TRUTH *(and truth and truth . . .)* gets its face shoved into the mud throughout a given lifetime, running home to mother time and again *(gonna tell on you)* only to eventually return in force with the coming of its tougher, more visible big brother, DEATH; not as small, not at all timid. Humble as a wrecking ball.

It was a long journey that brought the dying man to this place, Texas, and this final, brief understanding of TRUTH and DEATH were his only reward. As his suffering dissolved, though, so did the understanding. An understanding shared by no one.

His wife's screams outlasted those dumbly profound moments of the dying man's final thoughts easily, going on and on . . .

An old woman stared at the screaming mouth.

She stood there emotionless among the frenzied crowd, ghostlike, idly scratching at an old scar that encircled her waist at the belly button. Her eyes fell from the screaming mouth to the still, wet gore trailing several feet from its source; a broken head. She examined the lounging posture of its unknowing body and smiled sweetly. *My art, my beautiful love, my masterpiece.*

Her eyes clouded with a recollection that buzzed and swarmed like wasps. She thought of a boy she once knew; he died in an airplane before he could make good on his promise to marry her. She thought of an orange haired man who had found her lost soul, introduced himself as the devil, put her on stage, bathed her in pig's blood, gave her an adoring audience; so many, many years ago.

She refocused her wet eyes on the lounging man and felt a kind of love, burning and green. She heard the anguished cries of the parade onlookers, of *his audience*, and her love was peppered with envy. The thick scar around her waist seemed to tighten like a belt, sending prickly needles that beckoned dirty fingernails to scratch; tear if need be. She remembered the knife that had caused the wound at her torso as she lay uncomfortably arched over the dirty bathtub some ten years ago. Long and razor sharp it had gone straight through in one swipe, severing intestines, kidneys, spinal cord . . . That was when she was like the lounging man, when she had been a star. Her death had horrified the country. They had called her Black Dahlia. But now she had grown old. Her grandest death, one of many, had faded from the public's collective memory.

But she was still *his* instrument—the humble instrument of the orange haired man. Humble as a wrecking ball. And she still possessed a certain amount of strength.

The strength to commit beautiful, beautiful art.

BALTIMORE, 1943

CHAPTER ONE

PAL RAT

Her eyes were big green things, cool and sad, her nose thin and straight.

She was a pretty woman I guess you could say, but not the kind of woman that would necessarily come to mind when a guy got to thinking about pretty women.

Her mouth carried with it an eternal smirk, always turned up a little to the right, exposing slightly crooked teeth, canines maybe a bit long. Architecture-wise, the lady came with a swank floor plan from the ground up; slim ankles tapering perfectly to narrow hips, maybe a bit light in the keester for some, but more than ample and firm up top for any. A short, mousy brown mop of hair wagged around those emerald eyes, brushing against that pale, smooth skin in just the right way and I can remember times when I would look at her and shiver. What's the matter? she would say. Nothing, I'd answer.

I'm not sure when things started to go awry between me and Janice. The death of true love is as subtle and mysterious as the Big L itself; when it nixed for good I can't pinpoint exactly. I guess we stuck for so long because having each other was all we really knew then—and that was okay for a while. I mean we weren't really bugging each other or getting in each other's way, and just knowing that there was some other poor slob to turn to when things got to be a bit freaky and hard to face seemed like a pretty good reason not to make any changes in the routine. Pretty pathetic, I guess you could say.

But there comes a time in those relationships classified as "comfortable" when a guy just sort of snaps. Maybe sometimes it's the girl that comes out of it, but this time it was me. Restlessness hit like a poke in the ribs and suddenly I wasn't such a nice guy.

Maybe you've been in a similar spot. Lacking the kahunas to just lay things out and be done with it, you decide to make a big show of what a rat you are, hoping Miss Goo-Goo Eyes will wake the hell up, realize how much better she can do and tell you to take a hike. This scam is designed to make your partner feel righteous and victorious, leaving you with a sleek, streamlined, sparkling clear conscience. If you play it right (you imagine), you can actually come out smelling like the victim instead of your partner, who is, of course, the actual victim. Well, if you've been in this particular pair of loafers at one time or another you must damn well know that the ploy just doesn't pan out.

She thinks you're acting like such a shit because of something *she* did. Then she just gets nicer, developing irritating little habits like apologizing for no good reason and buying you thoughtful little presents all the time. Of course, in your state of bewildered frustration, you counter by just getting nastier, determined to get your point across. Then she gets nicer. Meaner. Nicer. Meaner. Nicer. Shit. Diamonds.

Then come the stories. Sweetly spoken tales meant to load on the guilt. Examples:

"Jackie, since you stopped walking me home from work at night a strange orange haired man's been following me . . ."

—or—

"Did you read in this morning's paper that another body turned up down by Penn Station? That's only a few blocks from here honey and you know sometimes I hear sounds when I'm alone. . . ."

Sure, baby. Whatever you say.

Things just get all out of whack and desperate-like for a dame when her fella's trying to shake her loose but he just can't come out with the skinny. It gets to the point where there's really no smooth way out for even the smoothest guy, which I ain't.

Of course, the most obvious solution was the one that didn't occur to me. The one that would have told me to run like hell.

Before I go on, though, I should probably tell you about the rat thing.

It happened right before everything turned to shit. I was hoofing across town to the Crockpit, the little hole in the wall seafood joint where I used to wash dishes. I was night shift.

Having to do that kind of work while the war was on was a real pisser. Things are booming all over—especially at the steel mills down in Sparrow's Point—and somehow I still can't get a decent job. Go figure. Every night I went in to work I was in a bad mood thinking about the mills and the good job I didn't have. Tonight I was burning about it extra hard.

It was about nine p.m. and the October air was stiff, clear and cold, the way I like it. Helps me think. I guess I must have looked a little whacked that night—even the panhandlers let me pass unviolated for a change. Then:

Crazy motion in the corner of my eye slowed my step. Crazy motion low to the ground.

A rat. A big orange, beady eyed, cat sized rat ran straight up to me and tagged me on the shoe. I froze—and hauled my foot back for a field goal. As I looked down at my squirmy little target, expecting either your basic mindless rodent attack or a scramble into the shadows, I hesitated, losing my balance and practically falling on the damn thing. It stayed put, see. Just stood there looking at me like it wanted to say something. I half expected it to ask if I would let it "hold some change". After I steadied myself and took a second to cool, I sort of stooped down staring at the fat, greasy shit, wondering if maybe it was rabid, nuts or some weird kind of smart. "OK, Bud, you got my attention", I said, hoping I guess, the sound of my voice would send it packing. But also sort of relishing the brief, strange communication that was going down. Me and Pal Rat hanging like a couple of swells on Franklin Street. Pretty suave. Fucking weird.

Then bam! it took off down the sidewalk towards the corner at Paca Street. I watched it bolt and let out a nervous laugh that must have sounded more like a cough. What a fucked up town Baltimore is, I thought. Even the rats are unglued in the head. I stood watching it skitter and weave down the cement and then it stopped dead.

Turned.

Looked, I swear, straight at me. Even from down the block I could tell it was looking at me. I stared like a stupe for a couple of minutes, then began walking slowly towards it, not knowing exactly (or even remotely) what I was thinking of doing, but feeling lowdown enough, I guess, that the idea of playing games with a rat made more sense than dragging myself in to scrape rich people's spit off of plain white dishes.

As I closed the gap between me and it, it began moving, slowly; deliberately. Stopping and starting, darting and pausing, as if waiting for me to catch up, sniffing like a dog then darting again.

I followed it cautiously, wondering if it knew it was being followed. Or if it meant for me to follow it. Who was the boss? Who was the brains? Who was in charge? Me or Pal Rat? I guess I figured if I kept on its trail I'd get some answers. He'd vanish up a drain pipe, leaving me washed and stranded in the worst part of the Southwest side, all by my lonesome without my rat buddy. More likely he'd just freak, let out a little rat kamikaze screech and take a hunk out of my ankle. But nothing logical ever happened.

Truth is, I still don't know who the stalker was that night. Or maybe I do know and can't bring myself to admit it.

Suddenly, Pal Rat just wasn't there. Gone.

A light drizzle began to fall and there I was standing in the dead middle of the shit side of town on a bleak stretch called South Carey Street. S.Carey Street, the sign said.

SCarey Street.

I thought about hailing a cab, but there weren't any to hail.

Across the street there was another sign. "Maryland House" this one said. Looked like a grease pit, but I was tired, hungry and starting to get wet. Like a rat, I crawled in for shelter. Like Pal Rat, I just sort of disappeared.

I wonder if I have haunted the dreams of Pal Rat as he has haunted mine. I wonder, do rats dream?

CHAPTER TWO

WEIGH YOUR FATE—FIVE CENTS

The steel front door of the Maryland House seemed rusted shut at
first, but after taking a second glance at the "open" sign for reas-
surance, I threw some weight on it and it gave with a short, sharp shriek.

The joint had that silver-grey chrome and pale-green tile decorum
that prisons are famous for; the crew of wrecks that occupied the stools
along the counter seemed right at home with the hellfire coziness.

Sitting shoulder to shoulder strictly in groups of one, the melancholy
bunch kept their eyes glued to the blue and green speckled counter top or
stared straight ahead. A heavy, tragic looking stiff stood behind the counter
working his way through an onion kind of slow and purposeful with a knife
about three sizes too big for the job. It was probably just the cut onion
messing with his eyes, but I swear for a second this look he had was just
exactly like one of Ma's old Jesus pictures. The one in the crapper, hanging

over the medicine box. The eyes in that picture just made you sure that this Jesus guy really did have the answers to all human suffering. And now here was this burger'n grease jockey with the same exact eyes. I had half a mind to ask him to fill me in on the human suffering shtick.

I parked myself on a stool and ordered a cup of coffee instead. Jesus the Cook nodded solemnly and poured me a black one.

I inhaled the thick, warm air deeply and heaved it slow, staring into my cup. Somehow grease is everywhere in joints like this. My mind began to drift a little, watching the little circles and ovals of grease floating on the surface of the steaming black liquid, seeing faces. The faces were contained within moving outlines, their features pushing against the boundaries with a quiet, twisted abstractness that made me think of the kind of twenty pound stillness that can sit in a guy's chest when he gets hit with a piece of prime bad news.

It's amazing what a fella can see in a cup of coffee if he's feeling a little blue and his mind's maybe a little blank.

The light in the Maryland House was flickering fluorescent, casting a bright chill on every naked, shivery detail of the room. It was tough not to squirm like a cockroach under its stinging eye and the thought occurred to me that this may be its very purpose: wig out the bugs. I mean, for the kind of hole it was, the place was weirdly devoid of any insect life. Cockroaches. Fucking cockroaches, I thought. The great survivors.

The thought of bugs and survival sent a sudden shiver of aloneness through my soul, and my thoughts skittered guiltily back to Janice. Always Janice. Janice; the only one whoever cared enough to try to understand a shit like me. Janice; my wife and best pal. Janice who I couldn't love right but couldn't live without. A tremor of rage shook my skeleton like an electrical current.

A finger of piping java jumped from my cup, biting my wrist with an inaudible splash. I craned my head around to see what had caused the reflex jerk of my arm. It was the oil starved shriek of the front door, this time yielding a damn good looking woman. On this side of town, you would normally assume a classy looking number like this could only have one kind of business in mind, but something told me a hooker she was not. Nope, this one had a story, I guessed. And guessed right.

Not quite shoulder length black hair framed a face of pissed on innocence. Her pouty red mouth sat delicately in creamy white skin beneath two scared, searching eyes, a little too close together maybe but sizing the place up with a cold, clean beauty that shone a brilliant grey in the harsh diner glare. She was all covered in a black cloaky thing with a fur collar and trim, the whole package hovering over purple stockinged legs and spiked heels.

"Hey mack—got a phone?" she said in a coarse whisper to Jesus the Cook. Then, after the slightest hesitation, "It's an emergency".

My body stiffened, somehow anticipating what was going to happen next. Maybe I subconsciously heard his footsteps, cutting cool and sharp along the sidewalk, or maybe I just got hit with a feeling. It was shaping into one of those listen-to-your-gut kinds of nights.

Just as Jesus started to offer a sad, all knowing, "Sorry, lady. There ain't no -" a kick, swing, slam of the front door triggered the sound of scraping chairs and scattered mutters of "What the.. " and "Wo Jeez ... " An unexpected and unwelcome intermission for the house orchestra.

A royally pissed looking bugger slammed his way in and stomped his way up to the black haired lady, hissing real edgy through clamped teeth, "C'mon. Now." Saying the word "now" just a little louder than "c'mon". His voice was kind of high pitched for a big guy. Unnatural sounding.

"Christ, Mike. Just cool down, wouldja? Got a cigarette?"

Mike blew a gasket. I know the feeling. Poor shit probably eating his heart out, his world maybe reduced to ashes by this cute broad, and she blows him off with a curt reprimand and a demand for a cig like that's more important than this poor sucker's grief. I felt for the guy. So would you, I bet.

"Fucking bitch," says poor ol' Mike, who I really felt bad for at this point, "I'll kill ya." He grabbed her by the arm, sort of twisting it sideways as she spat a poison threat or two his way. She dummied up pretty quick though, when she caught his other hand, balled in a fist, right in that pouting puss.

Now, although generally speaking, my gut sentiments were in this Mike fella's corner, I have another, deeper gut response to the sight of a guy smacking a girl. No matter how much a guy gets jerked around by a broad, he's a damn fool if he doesn't expect it at least a little, especially with a looker like this one. And taking a swing at a woman just doesn't wash with me, no matter what the circumstances. I got up.

Just as he was winding up for another pitch, I hooked my paw around his wrist, holding him steady, like a friend might, I thought, and said real gentle like, "Easy, Mike. It's not worth it".

If you pay attention here maybe you can learn something from my mistakes, because this, boys and girls, is where things got unfixable.

No matter how good a fella's intentions may be, it's probably never a good idea to try hero stuff on strangers. Especially when it looks like a guy might have just got himself dumped. When a fella feels jerked around by a woman, see, its like he thinks he's got to jerk around the whole rest of the world just to keep from getting laughed at. I really thought I was doing this guy a favor by stopping him so he could think things out. This dame could make it plenty tough on him with the cops if she had a mind to, sporting a black eye or a bloody lip. Anyway, I shoulda just layed back and enjoyed the show.

Mike thanked me for my concern with a mighty jab in the ribs with his free elbow and a hearty, "Fuck off, dirtball," which I didn't care for much. Gasping for air, I grabbed his mouthy little skull in both hands and heaved it full force onto the counter top. Jesus the Cook hustled his fat butt into the kitchen to use, I presumed, the phone whose existence he had earlier denied to a lady in need on the bad side of town.

Mike sort of slumped to the ground in a daze, staring at me with more hate than I can recall seeing in two eyes, and I guess I've seen maybe a truckload or so of glaring hate-filled eyes in my day. Mike's girl was muttering something hot and righteous, rubbing her cracked lip. Blood mingled with grease on the tiled floor. I heard a *shick* and looked down at Mike, who I no longer felt sorry for, as he shoved himself up from the ground, switchblade in hand. Grinning the grin of the doomed and stupid, he croaked, "Say goodnight, asshole."

He lunged, knife hand thrust forward, and I tangoed leftways to shame Xavier Cougat, feeling the threads of my shirt pull and tear against my side as the blade went past. Spinning, to shame Gene Kelly, I wove my body around and behind, connecting my fist to the back of his neck in a full arc. Mike fell forwards, grunting, all his spirit and rage gone, gone, gone.

But I was still pissed.

After all, the guy came at me with a blade, murder in his eye and all I did was try and do him a stinking favor. And I was unarmed even.

In a blind rage, I landed on his back and began pummeling the back of his head with my fists, the blood roaring like fire in my brain, drowning out the commotion around me. Just as the back of Mike's head was becoming noticeably more pliable, I felt myself being lifted up by the armpits. I stared at the blood on my throbbing, raw knuckles as I went up, up.

It was Jesus the Cook.

"Jeez mack, enough already". I steadied myself on the saviour's trembling, meaty shoulder and looked down at Mike, who was eating tile and not moving. I mean *really* not moving. Belatedly, I responded to the dead man's last request on this earth.

"Goodnight, asshole", I said. Jesus the Cook's calm, tired voice brought my rage to a simmer.

"You better ship off, pal. I think he's dead. Cops'll be here in a minute. Fucking crazy shit. Yeah, better clear outta here. Pretty quick if you got a brain."

A wave of guilt and panic paralyzed my movement and sent my brain dipping and tapping to shame Fred Astaire. As she got her senses together and made for the door, Mike's girl touched my shoulder and I heard her voice through my brain fog; without any respectable amount of emotion she said, "That probably wasn't necessary, but thanks, I guess." She was out the door.

Ship off, pal. Cops'll be here. Pretty quick. Better clear out. Crazy fucking shit.

I heard sirens. I bolted. The door did not stick.

Sometimes panicking makes perfect sense.

Sometimes simple things like the crushed skull of a dead jerk, bloodying up the pale green tiles of an inner city diner, cannot be satisfactorily explained to the stony sensibilities of folks like cops and judges. Panicking comes easy in the face of such plain rain.

But then maybe "panic" is a strong word. I was just a tough luck joe forced to think on his feet. And that's what I meant to do. But meant ain't is.

My legs throbbed and buckled as the soles of my second hand wingtips slapped fast and hard on the shiny, wet concrete of SCary Street. Sirens shouted, flipping my frantic brains like huge, hot flapjacks in the too small skillet of my skull. My fried egg eyes, jersey-side down, locked to the bouncing, sparkling reflection of the lamplights that laughed up from the glasphalt street.

My lower spine took the shock of the pounding street hard, and my arms began to shake wildly before me as the skin of my hands and wrists were overcome with an odd prickly sensation. The tingling quickly spread to my forearms, my shoulders, then my neck; I imagined a million nerve endings pushing like needles through my tensed hide, straining to listen, to hear, pleading with my brain; FOCUS, FOCUS.

The sound of running, guilty feet echoed loud and lonesome to me then. STOP RUNNING a voice panted, my own. Control and free thought struggled to regain possession of my physical movement.

I veered off into a concrete alley wall, hitting hard, stagger-bouncing. I stood wobbling for a second, slumped against the wall and sunk down between two trash cans, one eye on the flood of yellow light spilling into the alley's mouth from the street lights on SCarey Street. A passing black Lincoln caused the shadows to swoon and swallow light for a split second.

The smell of bad, stale hops and a nearby cardboard sign with rough painted letters warning, "STAY OUT OF TRASH—VIOLATORS PROSECUTED", told me I was in some wino-haven trash heap. I gasped the foul air as my body jerked and spasmed from exhaustion and fear, letting the tainted oxygen feed a tainted clarity into my brain. My face felt wet and warm and I realized I was sobbing.

As the sirens faded and my mind cleared, I settled calm and quiet as a babe in my womb of cold, damp cigarette butts, broken glass and rat shit. Crying makes me sleepy and I found myself starting to doze. A sliver of glass that found its way into the ball of my hand kept my eyes open though, and like a kid with a puzzle to solve I began to work out in my head what sort of success rate I may have if a dialogue with the cops should happen, which was way more than likely.

The thought struck me funny somehow, and I felt a sleepy grin stretch across my tear soaked face.

I decided that things probably looked much worse than they actually were. The only truth that could possibly have any weight with the cops was the worst kind; the fact that I had no good reason to be on this side of town on this particular night. Not good at all.

No, a confrontation with the cops, obviously, had to be avoided.

I stuck my head out of the garbage far enough to get an idea of how far this particular alley stretched away from SCarey Street. It was hard to tell, but it seemed to wind quite a ways out to the North East, moving deeply and surely into blackness. And the deeper it went, the blacker it got. Good. As any slippery joe prone to running situations can tell you, the darker the escape route, the cleaner the getaway.

With any luck, I could string together a side street here, an alley there and make my way home, safe and sound. I would have to do a little explaining to Janice, maybe make up some story about getting canned at the Crockpit and going for a walk to cool out. Yeah, that would work okay—I'd probably get canned anyway for not showing up. She'd be pissed, but plenty concerned and supportive as usual and things would be right as rain by morning. Suddenly, I felt grateful as hell to have such a swell reliable gal like Janice waiting for me at home and I vowed that I would start to show a little appreciation. No more games. No more crapola.

Shivering in slime and filth, dead man's blood and brains drying between my swollen, throbbing fingers, I thought of Janice then and felt a kind of sun. That impossible leap of reality was, to me, proof of the existence of true love. Or the closest I would ever get to it. I was right, too. Looking back now, I know I was right.

As I pushed myself up, muscles complaining, my eyes came across a junked scale, lying on its side in the garbage across the alley. It was one of those fortune telling kind that you see at the carny. A single sliver of moonlight stretched thin on its ruined sideways face. "Your Fortune—Weigh Your Fate-5 cents" it said. Without thinking, I reached down and touched the outside of my pants pocket, feeling the round shape of something smaller—a penny or a dime—but no nickel. Nickel-fates, nickel-fates, I thought, wanting to doze again but knowing better. Nickel-fates.

I stood up with surprisingly steady footing, and began, as quickly and quietly as possible, to make my way deep into the black end of the long alley, wincing at the sound of crushing glass beneath my feet, but feeling a little more together now that I had some sort of plan. I made it about thirty yards before I saw something that practically made my heart jump out of my throat.

My shadow.

I was in pitch blackness, see. So a shadow made no sense. Unless, of course, some kind of strong light was hitting me from behind. Like headlights, maybe. Maybe, nothing—the sound of an approaching engine and tires on wet cement confirmed my fears. I didn't bother to turn and look. All the sureness and calm left me and I was back where I started, scared and sprinting.

Wheels squealed as the car gunned, accelerating fast. I noticed absently that there was no sound of sirens accompanying it. Funny. The headlights behind me did not illuminate my path, but rather, gave the alley a sort of surreal chopping motion like a Charlie Chaplin picture. I couldn't see or judge my progress, my arms flailing ahead of me like a blind man's. I knew I was sunk, but I ran anyway.

I'm not sure how, I mean, I must have slipped or slid or something, but suddenly and briefly I was distinctly airborne, then sliding roughly on my right ear and shoulder across the alley cement, my neck bending painfully. Beneath the roar of the hot blood in my ears, I heard the car screeching and veering to keep from running me over. How nice.

I layed in a pool of the awful smelling liquid that always seems to puddle up downtown alleys, my head and face bloody and pounding. I began, lamely, to assume the position, spreading my limbs so's not to get roughed up too bad when the cops jumped out of the car, ready to play some tough-boy cop games. My whole body clenched, waiting. A car door opened. Footsteps. Strangely light footsteps. "Shit, Paul. Looks like he banged up his head doing that aerial stunt".

A woman's voice.

"Look pal, we didn't mean to scare you. I just finished having a pretty unpleasant chat back at the diner with the cops about our dead friend. They gave a real life-like description of you, so they know who they're looking for at least by sight. I thought you might appreciate a lift. They won't pull the same car over twice." A pause. "I owe you". It was Mike's girl.

I looked up, squinting in the headlamps. She was beautiful in the harsh light and shadow, eyes shining sincere but somehow mean.

"Fuck you", I croaked.

"Alright, look—get in or don't. I just wanted to pay you back for the favor you did me. Mike was a real psycho shit and I was in deep trouble when you stuck your neck out like that. So get in or don't, but you're bleeding pretty bad and even if you weren't you still don't look so good. Tell me where you live. We'll drop you there. No tricks".

I thought about Janice and a warm bed. Mike's girl guided me to the black Lincoln. I fell into the backseat, face forwards, head swimming. The rough texture of carpet pressed against my cheek and closed my left eye. My body angled upwards onto the upholstery as the car door pushed my feet the rest of the way in, bending my spine unnaturally but without resistance. Mike's girl, softly, "Where do you live?" My brain took a steep dive then, like a dream of falling. Janice's voice now, *"I love you, Jackie, don't hurt me. Please come home, baby. Where do you, live? Christ Paul, look at him. I don't think he can hear me. Just as well. Smooth as ice, in fact. Come home, Jackie run. Run away. I love you. Next stop The Big Punch, eh Maxa? Showtime."* Jumbled nonsense. The side of my head pulsed like a drum. I listened intently to it and to the black, cloudy voices. *"Showtime."* My awful reality slipped away then.

I dreamt.

In the dream I was five. In my father's house, running and weaving around the furniture, wailing like a little girl, "No, Daddy, stop it pleeeeaase!"

"C'mere you prissy shit. You sissy. Damn you, be a man."

"But he's not a man! Tom Dellus, you listen to me! He's just a boy. Leave him! This is wrong!" Mother's voice, typically, inconsequentially hysterical.

"No, dammit—we've been through this a thousand times. It's a business. Dead people are my fucking business. My father's fucking business. My grandfather's and his father's too. Do you want me to let this piss pant runt let the family history dribble down his leg because he's too scared to look at a damn corpse? I've got to straighten him out while he can still be hardened. Now if you won't help me then for God's sake at least be quiet and don't make this any harder."

"Mommmeeeeeee!!!!"

"He's just a baby, you monster!"

"Damn you. Damn him," Dad muttered in hot pursuit, turning over a table here, a chair there. My cries were clear, perfect and innocent. The angelic despair of a frightened child.

He cornered me in the triangle of space beneath the stairwell. I hesitated, eyes shooting to the right, to the left, then body darting to the . . . *right*. Pop was too quick, though. My feet left the ground, shoulder slightly dislocated, arm stretched, steel grip jerking upward on my wrist. His palm was hot and rough. My cries raised a half step in pitch, as if compensating for my new altitude. I looked up and was already half way to my destination.

The basement door.

"Gotchabastard", I think he said, though it might have been a grunt that just sounded like it. Poor, dumb Dad, I thought in the dream.

With one hand on the basement doorknob and one clamped around my tiny wrist, Pop cleared his throat to give me the same bewildered but firm speech that he always gave at this point.

"Jack," he said with a touching softness that was barely audible beneath my wails, "Jack," he said, "my boy, this is harder for me than for you, and believe me when I say that I feel for you 'cause my old man taught me the same terrible lesson. But the Dellus family deals with the dead, always has. The sooner you stop your bawling, the sooner this type of learning won't be necessary, and the sooner we can start learning a more productive end of the trade. I ain't asking you to love the dead, boy. Just deal with it." Then, just before the closing part of the little ritual where I'm shoved out of the warm living air of the house and into the stale, refrigerated air of the basement, he lost his preaching tone, "Chrissakes boy, at least try to fake me out by *acting* brave. I at least pulled that one on my old man. Use your noggin."

He opened the door just enough to push my small body through, then yanked his hand back in, slamming the door shut, damn near slamming his own fingers in it.

Like putting a noisy cat out for the night. The deadbolt clicked.

Now was the tricky part. Screaming at the top of my lungs and pounding frantically at the door while simultaneously listening intently, ear pressed against the door, monitoring Mommy and Daddy's movements on the other side; it took a tremendous separation of attention to pull off. Eventually, the bitter tones of deteriorating wedlock became distant as my parents ascended the steps to the second floor, seeking shelter from their consciences as their baby boy wailed terrified and alone in the room of the dead.

I gave them time to hide in their bedroom and lock the door against their demons before I shut up, throat aching, and softly padded down the steps.

The temperature in the viewing room was always very cold until about an hour before the guests arrived, and I could see my own breath. I walked slowly, trembling, to the table. To the open casket.

Mrs. Kelly had died of tuberculosis, which explained why she looked as if she'd been dead ten weeks instead of her actual ten hours—even with Dad's pseudo-resurrection make-up job in full swing. Beneath the forceful delicateness of the heavy pink undertaker's powder, her last moments of deathpain remained telling across her stretch-skinned, tight-featured face. In the dream, I saw past the sunken, thin tissue of sealed eyelids and was somehow with her at her final moment of truth; was able to feel the shock and agony of her death, could see her final memory of internal vision with unflinching clarity. And this thing that I somehow saw through her dead eyes should have unnerved me but didn't, should not have comforted me but did. The vision was of a blinding blackness. The image of approaching death.

I must have stood there staring at her through the clouds of my own breath for a good three or four minutes, the smell of the powdery stuff mingling sweetly with the scent of ripening dead skin and embalming fluid. I stepped closer, without thinking, and lifted my hand.

Five year old penises tend to have minds of their own, and mine decided that now was a good time to have an erection. My young mind had no preconception of what sexuality was, not a clue; all I knew was whatever my bodily urges and impulses threw at me. And right now my bodily impulses were pressing painfully against the zipper of my pants.

I reached towards her, touching the middle and forefinger of my right hand to her falsely blushing, stiff cheek. I rubbed, dragging my fingertips about an inch. Pulling my hand back now, I looked at the fine powder on my fingers, rubbing my thumb against them, feeling. Smooth.

My member stiffened to its humble limit, now, the raging hormones causing the space behind my eyes to buzz like a cheap blender. I placed my hand on the cold smoothness of Mrs. Kelly's left breast and leaned my face into the coffin towards hers. My lips touched soft to her cheek and my free hand slipped around behind her head, stroking her hair. I pressed her face to my mouth, hard. My tongue slipped out, tasting stale, sweet skin. I had to keep myself from using my teeth, heart pounding, wanting badly to bite. My tongue inched its way to her mouth, sliding between lips, brushing icy teeth. Shivering in moist fever, I pulled back, wiping the powder from my lips absently, looking down at the green-grey patch of skin I had left exposed. I knew I could not leave any permanent visible marks on the corpse, at least not on the face.

I began to unbutton the blouse.

What comes next I can never remember exactly; it's as if memory won't allow an event so scarring to pierce through the insulated mind-skin of bad dreams into the more sensitive, technicolor world of the conscious . But I remember the image of Mrs. Kelly's ruined body afterwards and I remember all that followed:

My knees wobbling violently beneath me and my eyes filling with tears, I: wanting my mother. *Mommy, help me please*, or something to that effect I always squeak in the dream. I was scared. But being scared and repulsed didn't keep me from swallowing the putrid thing—the thing that was once a piece of Mrs. Kelly—that had somehow found it's way into my mouth.

My left hand contained a crop of hair that I had pulled from Mrs. Kelly's head at some point during the missing part of the dream. I opened my hand and looked at the gray and brown locks, shivering, my face wet, my groin damp and limp.

The hair moved. And had become orange.

Suddenly, the hair was not hair. It was a fat, sleepy looking, smiling rat. Pal Rat. "I'm late, I'm late," he spoke in the voice of an Englishman, "for a very important date."

Pal Rat's stoned, happy eyes wandered up towards me, his pointy toes fastened to my palm tightening and relaxing like a kind of breathing. Pal Rat spoke with Janice's voice now, "Why can't you love me, Jackie? Can you feel love? Love me. Love me, baby." Pal Rat's whiskers twisted into a weird rat grin. I closed my hand and squeezed.

Pal Rat shrieked and bit hard into the meat at the base of my thumb. I screamed in harmony, shaking my hand in the air like a limp rag, but he hung on tight, jerking and swinging along with my arm, laughing his little rat laugh, shouting about a lot of crap I didn't understand, a lot of jabber in different voices; men, women, children. One of the voices was louder than the rest, it was the hysterical voice of a man with a deep southern drawl; "Listen to the prophet with four legs! Fear the angel! Hurry, hurry! FEEAAR! Listen to the prophet! Hurry!!"

I broke into a run—that's what five year old kids do when they're scared and hurt and don't understand. I ran in circles around Mrs. Kelly's coffin. But it was not a coffin, now. It was a coffee table. I was back in the living room, being chased by my father, "C'mere you prissy shit ... "

The dream had begun again, as it always did. As it would, over and over like a circle, a trap. I learned early in life that dreams are traps. And tough to wake from sometimes.

As the dream ran its course again and again through the night, I listened for the sound of rain, prayed for it. The dream always stopped, you see, when the rains came.

Thunder finally did crash and the sssshhhhhhing sound of water on the ground finally soothed and pulled and took my soul out of the loop of dreamcircles.

My eyes opened and I was in darkness, the sound of running water still present. I knew I was wetting myself, I always did, waking from the dream; it was the only way out. I made no effort to stop myself upon waking. What was the use? I was already soaked in piss. It was just a shame I was fully clothed.

Lying there in the dark, I became aware of the fact that I was on some seriously foreign turf and, as the events of the night began to resurface in my mind, I became aware also that I was probably not only knee deep in a steaming pile of bad luck but sinking fast. Let's say I went from dead asleep to wide awake real fucking quick.

One thing for sure: I was not warm in bed with my sweet, loyal, Saint Bernard of a wife. I missed Janice bad as I lay there shivering and I had a strong hunch that it might be a while before I'd get to resume my blessedly boring, normal life with her, if ever.

The floor was wooden and the room was small, the musty odor of dust thick and heavy, mingling with the pee smell. The base of my thumb throbbed where I had bitten it in my sleep. Without getting up, I groped around searching for a door or any sign of a way out. Really, any indication of just where in hell I had landed would have been a welcome, swinging groove. I'm an easy dancer; give me a beat, I'll samba.

The opportunity to samba never presented itself. I lay breathing and thinking for a couple of minutes, my tired eyes struggling to focus in the blackness, when I realized that what my brain had mistook for a phantom of shadow-glare left over from the dream was not a phantom. It was what it appeared to be—a sliver of light. A crack in the wall.

I guess there are folks who might find it comical, a grown man finding so much comfort in a thing as small as a crack of light. But I saw nothing in it and I saw everything in it and at that moment it was all there was. I watched that crazy little sliver, hell, I prayed to it, for a good five minutes or so before I got the bright idea that if I crawled a little closer and put my eye right up to it I might actually see something. Maybe get an answer or two.

Through the crack I saw a girl.

She was someone I vaguely recognized—but at the same time didn't at all. What I mean to say is I recognized her—but in the mixed up way that you recognize people in dreams. The way in dreams where sometimes a person doesn't look any different than they ever have, someone who you may know very well in waking life—but in the dream they're distinctly *un*familiar. They're a grey area, a memory hole, a nagging collection of features—nose, eyes, mouth—that somehow don't add up to a face quite right. A stranger unstrange.

Dreams are funny that way sometimes. And sometimes it's the opposite—sometimes you recognize a face you got no business recognizing. In dreams close friends can look nothing like how you remember, how you know they should look. But they are themselves anyway and there's no denying it, just accepting it. Because it's a dream—and when you're in a dream you have to play by the dream's rules.

Well, anyway, I recognized this girl in the strange way of dreams.

But I knew I was awake. So I had to be nuts. Or dreaming and very confused. Nuts. Dreaming.

I pinched myself until I bled.

So this is madness, I thought. Ain't so bad, really. I relaxed, crouched in my own piss, wondering if I could get the hang of the basket weaving racket. I never was much for crafts.

I kept my eye to the crack and noticed that the girl inside was pregnant.

The scene was like a play. She was walking briskly through the tall grass of what looked like a field of weeds. Every twenty seconds or so she would shut her eyes tightly, teeth bared and grinding. It was obvious she was in a lot of pain. I figured this probably meant the stork was heading down the home stretch—and onto a one way collision course with cold air and hard earth, no less.

I felt a relieved detachment in knowing that she could not be real, that she had to be some odd symptom of my particular brain fever, my madness. There was only one thing I could do, really.

I watched.

CHAPTER THREE

HELL'S FENCE

L ight was an orangy commodity, but I could make out that the pregnant girl was walking alongside a weathered white picket fence. A smothered chortling told me that the livestock on the other side of the fence was pigs, pigs, pigs.

In the back of my head I heard a sweet choral music in and around the pig sounds and I attributed it, with astounding calm, to the jim-jam jumpless orchestra of madness that swung low and ugly in there, taking the joint (my mind, that is) over slow like sly politics.

Through my crack of light I could make out that the girl was moving in my general direction or just past, towards what looked like a house in the blowing shadows of an overgrown field. The tall grass was oddly patterned in its random, patchy growth, somehow intentional and orderly in its chaos, somehow rascally and untrue. Even the stars in the sky held an ugly artificiality; stiffly painted to the black sky in dull blobs and flecks of white.

There was no moonlight to give the structure of the farmhouse any sense of shape or size, but a yellow glow shone around the cracks of the door frame and dimly illuminated a lone shuttered window near the door. As she got closer to it, the music got clearer somehow, its melody more recognizable; a Christmas carol. "God Rest Ye Merry Gentlemen" it was. In October? Yes, it was October . . .

As she reached the door, she raised a fist as if about to knock—then didn't. I let myself believe that she lowered her fist in an effort to preserve a final possession: self respect. In that instant the caking mud that crept from her boots up to her knees transformed from the melancholy mud of fallen bicycles and rainsoaked graves to the stronger, more saintly mud of battlefields and holy causes. She turned to walk away from the door, away from charity.

It took two seconds of proud walking—one *Mississippi* two *Mississippi*—before another painful contraction hit her, spinning the muddy-shinned girl on her heel and throwing her against the door, pounding and sobbing, mouth open, eyes wide with terror and pain.

Jeez, what tough spots we humans find ourselves in sometimes. All talk of bravery and blind inspiration aside, I gotta admit I was relieved to see what decision she'd made. I mean, what use is pride really, especially when you got the responsibility of looking after a kid who could wind up being born, well, dead, or damn close to it if she didn't get pretty damn resourceful in a hurry.

The door opened not a crack but wide, assaulting the young mother-to-be with warm yellow light. Getting a better look now, I could see she was in sadder shape even than I had originally thought. Her dress was no more than a bunch of filthy rags sewn together. In a reflex of dumb vanity, the girl threw her arms around the sad little dress, embarrassed by her exposure, squinting.

The man at the door was maybe forty with orange hair. His face was freckled and doughy, directing a cheap brand of kindness at the girl. Laughter and the singing of party guests, mostly female, rang out louder as the crack of the door widened. His eyes were trying "deep concern" on for size, "Dear girl, look at you." He seemed to be suppressing some sort of European accent.

"Merry Christmas, sir", she said, trying not to whimper, "I'm so sorry to bother you b-but m-m-my b-b-bay-b-baby . . ." She gave into her sobs, gasping uncontrollably.

His arms went out to her, into the night, "Of course, of course, come in quickly. You poor, poor . . ."

"What the hell!", a loud drunken female voice roared over the man's quiet tone. His body rocked sideways as the voice's owner, a huge blonde woman, staggered into him, trying to get a look at whatever was causing the disturbance. Now, when I say huge, I don't mean to say that she was obese or even, well.. she wasn't unpleasant looking at all. Most definitely an odd looking piece of work.

"Jesus H. Fucking Christ, what's that stink? Who in fuck are you talking to, George? Damn beggars are worse than rats in this white-trash-farm-fuck neighborhood you force me to live in." Her mouth was a hellish awful thing to hear but not too hard on the eyes at all. Her nose was classic and small, framed by full, smooth cheeks. Her lips were plump and red, the lower one protruding a bit in a natural pout, conforming with her wide, angular jaw.

Her teeth were small, white, straight, perfect.

She was a tall glass of water, measuring in, I estimated, at around six foot six and towering over that George guy by an arm's length or so. Tall as she was, she was proportionate as well, looking damn sharp in a long, black, silky night thing, four parts class, six parts tramp.

The gown's generously low cut neckline exposed quite a bit of the white curve of flesh that strained meanly against the black material before sliding down around a perfectly angled ribcage and swooning like a song to a waist slender and sleek. Wide hips swung luscious and large, rudely wrapping her lady giant's frame, while the sleeves of the gown tapered wide, ending in black fur lined cuffs, brushing soft against large hands that seemed oddly muscled for a woman. Her fingers ended in long, red nails, sharpened to a point.

As I watched poor old George shrink away from her, shaking like a jazzcat waiting on his evening fix, it became plain that I was about to watch a pussywhipping of epic proportions.

I crossed my legs. There is an ancient law of survival that forces men to do this when witnessing a brother being compromised of his manhood. (Fellas: The ancient laws of survival are there to protect us— we must never go against them or allow ourselves to feel stupid for obeying them. Remember that. *We the cats shall hep ya, so reap this righteous riff* . . .)

Something about the dialogue between the two was like the weeds in the yard and the stars in the sky. There was a distinct not—rightness to it—forced, awkward, stupid. Scripted. Like a play.

"Francie, dear", he whimpered, twisting absently at his bathrobe, "I think, uh, that is, this poor girl seems about to, uh,—a doctor, I mean, uh, the baby's about to .. we've got to phone an ambulance. Yes, yes . . . we'll keep her by the fire until . . ."

"WRONG. Wrong, wrong, wrong! This is my Christmas party and this *thing* came to ruin it. If you let this dirty, pig stinking bitch in the house I'll be very upset, George. *Very* upset."

scripted . . .

George knew he had to do the right thing no matter what the consequences. "Sorry, girl, I can't help you.."

He did not do the right thing. He began to close the door slowly.

The pregnant girl caught the door in her hand, "Please, sir—my baby! It's Christmas night—please have pity!"

George became suddenly bold, but the wrong kind: "Look, you, you.. *thing*, if you don't get off this property in a hurry you'll be having your swine brat in a jail cell."

scripted: badly, awkwardly . . .

"Tell her, dear", purred Francie, as her left nipple broke free from its oppressor, sliding halfway out of the black silk, breathing cold air, hardening. She made no attempt to fix it as she turned to the girl and spoke in a soft, mock-concerned motherly tone that could make the skin of a an alligator shoe crawl, "Listen sweetie, instead of a jail cell, why don't you have your swine baby in the pen with the other pigs. They'll make fine playmates, darling, I'm sure." Her voice trailed off to a fluttering angel's laugh as she closed the door. The door didn't slam—it simply closed.

Hate hung in the damp, cold Christmas air.

A light snow began to fall—a snow as unreal as the stars and the grass and the meanness of the giant woman—a snow fluttering to the ground slow and crazy like ashes.

The grunting, slobbering noise of the pigs was suddenly clear and profound—and very real. The girl stood quiet for a couple of seconds— *one Mississippi two Mississippi* . . .

then began to giggle.

"There is no God", she whispered. Giggled some more. "No God for Christmas". She started laughing; laughing as if she had suddenly gotten the punchline to a joke told to her by a dirty uncle years before she was old enough to understand, a dirty joke pondered for a lifetime, a good one, the funniest possible joke, the LAST joke. Then, singing it loud and merry, "No God for Christmas, no God for Christmas, no God, no God, no God for Christmas!" Watching the glassy death in her sparkling eyes hurt mine.

I guess seeing her sanity slip away so pitifully was what brought mine back, or rather, made me realize that I was unqualified for the very tough and complex job of being nuts. I found my voice—but it came out as phony and scripted sounding as anything else in this weird universe I'd stumbled into.

"Hey! Hold on! I can help! Hold on!" She did not hear. I crawled, feeling in the dark, searching for the way out that had to be there, knowing that I had to reach the girl. I had it in my mind to make like Tex Ritter in *Trouble In Texas*, to swoop down and save the girl, everything a movie. And once I'd placed her out of harm's way I'd deliver the grand message that movie heroes deliver: *Yes, the world is a cold and awful place, but there is always hope; there will always be some person or thing that gives a damn and maybe, yes, maybe even a God.*

I'm not sure if I believed those things myself, but for some reason it was important to me that I make *her* believe them. Maybe I figured that believing *something* was her last chance. Anyway, I knew I had to try to help her.

I searched thoroughly by sense of touch—very thoroughly, I thought. There was no door, no escape. Just where in fuck was I? I figured it must be some kind of storage area or shed—which would at least make some kind of sense with a farmhouse being so nearby. Would also explain the absence of an inside door latch. But who put me here? What happened to Mike's girl? Last thing I remembered I was passing out in the backseat of a black Lincoln on the lam. This farm scene just didn't fit in. Was it really Christmas? Not unless Christmas had swapped calendar spots with Halloween lately it wasn't. Maybe I was out cold for longer than I thought—some kind of Rip Van Winkle trick. I imagined Janice dressed in black and not knowing.

Maybe I'm over sentimental, but I gotta say that the idea of getting tossed in the slam sounded better to me at that moment than the idea of putting Janice through the wringer anymore than I had already done. I had to get out of there. But I had a more immediate concern. The girl.

Why couldn't she hear me shouting to her? Is madness a deafening thing? I shouted some more and, for an instant, imagined her eyes had cleared and found me through my crack of light. Her mouth stopped singing and my ears filled with a hissing. Then, as quickly as they seemed to find me, her eyes lost me, resuming their mad, dead dance, lips grinning, mouthing her song of the damned: *no god no god no god.* The hissing in my ears faded and ceased. Hissing? Later, even this small detail would make sense, but not now, not yet.

Suddenly, she shrieked in pain and fell backwards onto her haunches. She leaned backwards, arching her back, legs spread, screaming, "Jesus, Jesus, nooo!" She rolled half sideways away from me, legs separated in an impossible contortion, pushing with both hands on her stomach. I couldn't tell if she was trying to deliver the thing or kill it inside of her— maybe both. She gasped and sobbed in agonized rhythm and I stared helpless and quiet, hearty strains of "Joy to the World" drifting over from the farm house, mixing awfully but somehow correctly with the chortling of the pigs.

The girl gasped sharply inward—holding it—then shaking as if in convulsion. She let out the air in the form of a slow, deep pitched moan, starting quiet and growly, crawling gradually to a quivering soprano of pain, body rocking side to side. Her shaking screams were then joined by another, stronger, more healthful, hopeful cry. The cry of a newborn babe.

She yanked the screaming thing from between her legs, pulling it roughly out of her tattered skirt by the head, like a magician might pull a rabbit out of a hat. I heard the sickening wet sound of tearing meat.

She slammed its soft, screaming skull to her breast, "Shut up! Stop *SCREAMING!*" Then, pulling its head away firmly, holding it by the ears, she turned away from my vision and pushed the tiny, screaming mouth to the ground, straddling its small helpless body with strong legs; enraged and reasonless. She sat up straight then, looking down at her child, getting a grip on reality, I hoped. The mother was breathing hard but quiet, sitting.

Soft and easy, "Quiet, my darling boy". It was a boy. "Quiet now. You will have fine playmates. Fine playmates, darling, I'm sure."

scripted . . .

Her hand shot down to the ground before her, then jerked up, high above her head. I saw it was holding something.

A baby's arm.

She threw the arm casually over the fence to the pigs in rhythm to the carol that she had begun to mouth along with; *"Joy to the world, the Lord has come, let heaven and nature sing . . ."* The pigs played, hawing louder than before.

I watched, dry eyed and still, unbelieving as she tore the little tyke apart in merry rhythm, tossing red and dripping pieces over hell's fence. The pig sounds got deafening and I became aware of another sound, the sound of hundreds of human voices, screaming, shouting.

My crack of light went black.

The carolers stopped singing. Psycho-mom made not a sound. The pigs stopped hawing. But the hundreds of voices shouted and cried and screamed on. What the fuck, I thought.

As I stared into the blackness I began to put the whole strange, shitty scam together. Suddenly, I knew, and my sanity came rushing back full force, unwelcome.

SCRIPTED

Light poured onto the field. The girl, the blonde and George all stood together holding hands, smiling blankly, facing vaguely to the left of where I was. They bowed. Shouts of bravo, shouts of revulsion, shouts of laughter both wicked and relieved, polluted the cool, moist air of the theater. Lights went on, illuminating an audience.

A play. It was some sort of wacky fucking play I had been seeing.

I rolled over on my back, rolling onto a nail that was sticking out of the hard wood floor but not caring, breathing in deep through my nose. Beneath the smell of piss and dust I detected for the first time the heavy presence of dankness and mildew that I associated with my father's basement. I realized that wherever I was, it was underground. How far under, I wondered? "Pretty damn far, I bet", I answered aloud, beginning to laugh and wishing again that there was a functioning door in this dark, wooden prison, but not wishing so much that it made me want to keep looking for one.

I lay still on my back, feeling the nail, laughing and waiting.

The bluish white of the long tubular fluorescent bulbs in the hallway poured into my naked pupils without warning. My hands flew to my face, my body curled and turned on the floor.

"Phew-eeeee! Smells like sleeping beauty done peed hisself. C'mon fella, time to meet the boss. I think it might be smart to make a quick stop down at wardrobe first though, so's you can change up. Jeez, fella, if you hadda go you shoulda just hollered." I was being pulled to my feet by large gentle hands, my own still clamped to my eyes. "You sure did throw a monkey wrench into that last sketch, fella. Heh, heh. I guess Mr. Redd woulda been pissed about that if it weren't such a hoot. Reckon The Punch can be a right nutty thing for a fella to wake up to, especially being shut up in the dark and all. 'Course, if I thought you could see out, I woulda stuck ya someplace else, so don't blame me. Nope, ol' Henry didn't mean a lick of harm. I never do."

The voice instantly betrayed its owner's shortcomings in the brains department, but was also good hearted, deep and strong—I sensed I wasn't in any danger at the moment. Henry guided me slow and careful, like a boy scout might guide someone's grandma, through a long hall, its only outstanding quality other than its length being its brightness. As my pupils shrank and I began to allow light a little at a time through my cracked lids, I started to get a better feel for my surroundings.

It immediately struck me as odd that the walls and ceiling of the corridor were concrete and cinder, lined and X'ed with steel girders. Normally, this would've made sense for a cellar of an old building, but as I mentioned earlier, the floor was distinctly wooden, and as the hollow clomping of our feet stated plainly, not altogether solid. As we passed an old porthole-looking window situated about an inch above floor level, I deducted that we were not walking on what the building's designer had originally intended to be the floor of the cellar, but what had to be the top half of a later renovation, cutting the cellar into two levels. I wondered about the strange logic of architecture, figuring that there must be complex, technical reasons for things like this beyond the understanding of regular, dumb guys like me and Henry. The circle of the porthole was surrounded by heavy bolts, welded forever shut with thick, unforgiving steel. I wondered where it used to lead, or where it had led from, and why it had been decided that it should be made so utterly inaccessible. Henry's rambling patter broke my train of thought.

"I reckon a few folks in the audience musta thought you was part of the act, what with you hollerin' and shoutin' about coming to the rescue and all. That sort of thing ain't real popular at The Punch, though, mister. People don't like happy endings round here, no sir, don't want no heroes, so I sure hope you didn't take it personal when ya got hissed at a little by the crowd, no sir, nothing personal a'tall, just a big misunderstanding. A real hoot when you think about it, though, don'tcha think, mister?"

"Yeah, a real hoot", I said, not thinking it was a hoot at all, but starting to warm up to this Henry guy and wanting him to like me too. I figured I may be hurting for friends in the not so distant future. Wild hunch.

Henry's mouth ran like a faucet, annoying as hell but reassuring, as we made it to wardrobe as promised "so's I could get changed up". The room was huge, and not as brightly lit as the corridor, downright dim, in fact. The floor was littered with wooden crates and cardboard boxes, filled with all kinds of stage props and junk ranging from wigs, hats and scarves to what looked like severed human spare parts; feet, fingers and ears to name a few, presumably fake, but damn convincing. Along the same lines, there were racks filled with every imaginable type of clothing; from average grey business suits and denim farm duds to stuff more of the psycho variety: straightjackets, body harnesses, studded jackboots and bullwhips among them. Henry told me to change into anything I liked. I decided to pass on the exotic stuff and go with a nice pair of plain grey pants and a white shirt, dumping my pissed on duds in a heap in the corner.

As we cleared out of the wardrobe, Henry yammering and chatting all the while, I sized up my tour guide and decided he was straight up ok. A big old country lug, forty-five if he was a day, Henry was going slightly grey at the temples and dressed in a suave high-end Italian suit, minus the jacket. The pants were loose and suspendered up high, mafioso style. I got a strong feeling that he'd have been a lot more at home in a pair of overalls stooped down beside Ol' Bessie, milk bucket in hand, and I wondered what his story was. How do regular people get into irregular situations like this, anyway? But then, we all start out as regular people, don't we?

By the time we made it to our destination, a plain steel door, behind which, Henry's "boss" presumably waited, I had, for the most part, pieced together the puzzle of where I had landed, and even had a pretty good idea of how I had gotten here. I had also figured out who the girl in the play was and where I'd recognized her from. I expected she would be waiting behind that door, too.

CHAPTER FOUR

LONG AND WRONG, RIGHTEOUSLY GONE

Henry banged on the steel door three times quick and pushed it open without answer or invitation.

"Special delivery! Da jimmy-da-jam and I'm off onna lam! Anything else, there, boss?" Henry's offer of additional servitude was a monument to subtlety in false advertising; the point being made that he sure hoped there wasn't anything else needed doing. The boss didn't miss a beat.

"Why don't you hit the sack, Henry. You look spent."

"Thankee kindly, Mr. Redd. 'Night, sir. 'Night, Miss Maxa. 'Night," the last being directed at myself. Henry's bulky form bounced on out.

The boss was young in body and face but old in eyes, a deadly wise twinkle of grey framed by a crackle of crow's feet. Purplish freckles that could pass for liver spots dotted the smiling, self satisfied face. His hair was vaguely brownish but unconvincing, dyed most likely, and the freckles seemed to suggest a lurking redhead. His dress was a tasteful chorus of blacks, greys, more blacks; casual but neat. The desk he sat behind was large and oak, the thickly polished surface of which accommodated stacks of paper, neatly piled. A well stocked set of bookshelves supplied the backdrop. Mr. Redd, like everything else I'd encountered so far in this strange place, appeared posed, artificial, cheap.

Mike's girl sat in a chair next to the desk, legs crossed, chipping nervously at remnants of red nail polish on her left thumbnail. She was still wearing the peasant girl outfit from the play, smatterings of fake blood accentuating her cool, bored babydoll appearance. Man, this girl was bent; a real lost cause. Long and wrong, righteously gone.

I decided then that I found her more than just casually attractive. In fact, as I looked at her I got weaker by the millisecond. Although I realize now that this condition probably had more to do with the loss of blood I'd experienced from the previous night's alley acrobatics, at the very least, I found her distinctly distracting. And in light of everything, I figured any distraction I could get that might give my cranium a refreshing dose of trivia; a temporary sense of non-urgency, was more than welcome. I kept right on looking. She didn't look back, though; never glancing up. Chipping, chipping.

Mr. Redd broke the brief, awkward silence. He had a prissy showfolk way of talking:

"You must think we're barbarians here. Maxa, dear, why didn't you tell me our guest was injured?" His speech was perfectly deliberate, like a man trying to hide an accent. "We'll have to dress those wounds immediately to stave off infection, if it's not already too late, that is. Dear, dear."

I guess the pain that racked my hands from bashing Mike's skull, not to mention the throbbing in my ear and noggin from my little spill in the alley, had been with me the whole time—but in the tangle of hysteria and panic, the physical sensation of it had, until that moment, miraculously slipped past my conscious thought process. Suddenly, the siren song of pain traveled fast to the forefront of my mind—and I instantly didn't like this prim bastard who had awakened it. Deliberately awakened it, it seemed—as irrational as the thought may have been. And I didn't want to be his guest, sure as hell didn't want his charity.

"I'm fine," I said, a little sharply. Then, after an instant of consideration, of not wanting to offend; "Thanks, though." I wasn't out of the woods yet, and being rude to people who hang in underground gore theaters probably isn't a safe thing to do in general.

"As you wish, Mr. Dellus," he said with genuine concern, making me feel like a jerk, "but it's no trouble at all should you change your mind.

"I'm sorry that our meeting has been under such, shall we say, strained circumstances. Indeed, sir, I'm afraid that I have some more bad news for you regarding the aftermath of the other night's, mmmm . . . *unfortunate* chain of events."

I sensed a steam roller coming my way.

Then, suddenly something clicked about what he had just said and I decided to call him on it. I'm the kinda fella who says what's on his mind, especially when I got a feeling maybe I'm about to get duped, which I was strongly anticipating right about then.

"I don't mean to interrupt you or anything, mister, I mean you've been decent to a stranger and you all seem like a nice enough bunch of folks here, although I have to admit I'm not so sure about your particular brand of entertainment. But hey, to each his own, I always say. It takes all kinds of people to make up a world, ain't that right? I'll tell you I am a little confused about a point or two that maybe you can set me straight on." I figured I'd soften up the ground a little before digging.

"I thought, at first," I said slowly, trying to sound dazed and confused, which I wasn't, "that the lady and her friend brought me here when I blacked out because she didn't know where else to put me. But the fact that you know my name tells me that someone must've snagged my wallet while I was in dreamland, maybe to find out who I was, which is okay, I mean, no hard feelings about that. None at all." I reached down to feel for the *absence* of a bulge in my hip pocket, expecting to confirm that these sickos had snatched my wallet while I was unconscious. The dumbness of the move dawned on me as I felt the smooth empty pocket—if the wallet *hadn't* been snatched, it'd be in the piss soaked pair I'd left in wardrobe—I had no way of knowing whether it had been taken or not. Trying to appear unfazed, I clung to my pet theory and held my course; "But if you got my wallet then that would also mean that you got my address. So how is it that I ain't home?

I mean, wouldn't it have made more sense to just drop me off like the lady said she would?" I was trying real hard not to sound like I was challenging the guy, and I guessed I'd done okay, because he was smiling when he answered me. Kind of a smug, playful smile that made me plain edgy.

"Right you are, sir. No other course of action would have made any sense. And that's exactly what Maxa and Paul did, in fact." I must've changed colors or something when he said that because he suddenly tossed an exaggerated look of concern my way. Maxa finally acknowledged my presence by picking up his story for him. She still didn't look up, though. My pulse quickened as she spoke, her voice was detached and monotone; pure inert sexuality.

"The police were at your apartment—waiting for *you*, I guess. I mean, it had to be that, right? I don't know who tipped them off or how they got there so fast, but there they were." At last she looked up, staring at me hard, steel grey eyes numbing the throbbing in my hands momentarily, "Can you think of any other reason they might have been at your place? The cops, I mean." Her slightly suspicious tone made me want to have a good logical answer for her.

"No," I said. Nothing else to say. I'd kept my nose clean with the law for a good three years now. Her attention again focused on her thumbnail. Chipping.

"Well, it would have been a rotten thing to do, just handing you over, so we kept driving. Even if we had decided to be rats, how could I explain to the cops how you came to be all huddled in the backseat when I had just gotten through telling them that I had never seen you before in my life. We had to come back here. No choice."

Redd took a turn picking up the strange little ball: "Which brings me to the bad news that I'm afraid I must burden our guest with." I thought that I had already heard the bad news. I braced myself.

"It seems, Jack—may I call you Jack?—that in the last twenty-four hours you have become quite famous. Notorious, I should say." He handed me a morning paper with a real attractive picture of yours truly right on top. It was a mugshot from an old B&E rap. Hey, things are tough all over, buddy.

The headline shouted its accusations at me like some demented padre of the Inquisition:

BOLTON HILL BUTCHER'S RAMPAGE OF DEATH NEARS END!!
4 Dead in Last Night's Bloodbath,
Total Body Count Now 18
Police Declare Prime Suspect At Last

Late last night, 4 more names were added to the growing list of victims attributed to the psychopathic killer who, by terrorizing a local Baltimore community, has established a dark notoriety on a national level. Although last night's murders were the first of the grisly series not to occur within the Bolton Hill neighborhood, police are confidant that they were perpetrated by the same man, and, in fact, now claim to have recovered incontrovertible evidence as to the killer's identity. This evidence, say police, points to one man; John Matthew Dellus, a 30 year old white male resident of the 1200 block of Bolton Street, located in the heart of the Bolton Hill area. Dellus is currently still at large and considered extremely dangerous.

Dellus' alleged "rampage of death" began in May of last year when Susan Dunn, a resident of Linden Street in Bolton Hill, was abducted on her way home from Juicy Lucy's, a showbar on the corner of Mount Royale Avenue and Saint Paul Street, where she worked as a dancer. Police are now investigating the extent of familiarity between the victim and her assailant before the crime, as well as any possible motives.

Miss Dunn's body was found discarded on railroad tracks beneath an underpass adjoining the Mount Royale Train Station one block from the Maryland Institute Art College. Police say she was a victim of not only rape and torture during her approximated three days in captivity, but also physical mutilation,

Continued on Page 11A, Column 3, Bloodbath

I flipped numbly to 11A.

When I found the page, I was welcomed by a photo of a priestly looking cop in a trench coat, standing in an alley littered with squad cars and garbage. The caption read, "Baltimore Homicide's Detective Robert Black traces the steps of the Butcher's latest murder spree." In the lower left hand corner of the picture, I was able to make out words that I recognized peeking up sideways from a pile of trash; "Weigh Your Fate—Five Cents".

I read on, my eyes feeling dry and pocked as golf balls:

Bloodbath, Continued from Page 1A Column 1;
her left breast having been cut off neatly, as if by some meticulous, demonic surgeon. This last gruesome detail was to mark the beginning of the butcher's trend of trademark "souvenir collecting". When Dellus is apprehended, police expect to uncover remnants of this grisly collection, linking him to many, possibly all, of the known murders. The police have also begun investigating the possibility of Dellus' involvement in several other unsolved missing person and homicide cases still on the books that were formerly considered unrelated to the Bolton Hill crimes.

The trail of "torture-mutilation" murders similar to Miss Dunn's that had left the police baffled and clueless and the Bolton Hill community in a paralysis of fear for longer than a year, finally saw some light of revelation in the aftermath of last night's horrors when, as Baltimore homicide detective Robert Black says, "Dellus just got sloppy".

Several eyewitness accounts have placed Dellus at the Maryland House diner on the 1400 block of South Carey Street last night at approximately 11:20 PM, when police were called in to investigate a disturbance. A young couple, whose identity is as yet unknown, were said to have begun a lover's spat in the diner when Dellus got up from his counter stool in a rage and began beating the man relentlessly about the head and face with his fists. The frightened woman fled the diner before police arrived. Dellus also fled the scene, in too much of a hurry to take one of his trademark souvenirs for the first time in his blood soaked career.

The suspect immediately attempted to escape detection by hiding in a trash heap in a nearby alley, adjacent to Carey Street and directly behind Norman's Bar and Grill on Arlington Avenue. Dellus was apparently discovered by an unfortunate homeless man, also unidentified, who may have been searching the alley garbage for food. Dellus stabbed the man 19 times and removed both of his eyes with the murder weapon, taking the time on this occasion to return to his goulish habit. Baltimore Homicide's forensic department is currently analyzing a patch of bloodied hair and skin found in the dead man's hand; it is believed that the grisly remnant was pulled from the murderer's head in the violent struggle.

Dellus managed to illude police once more, hailing a cab and heading not home, but to The Crockpit Restaurant on North Avenue, where Dellus has worked for the last few months as a dishwasher. The cab was found two blocks from the restaurant, its driver, Max Steiner of Parkville, dead inside. Mr. Steiner's throat had been cut and both of his ears removed. The backseat of the cab yielded what Detective Black calls "the case's clearest breakthrough"; a Maryland State driver's license with Dellus' picture on it.

This bit about the license especially didn't ring true. Remember, I'd already figured on my wallet having been snatched by Maxa for purposes of IDing me—but that wasn't conclusive either. She could have dropped it or tossed it—or even committed the murders with her pal, Paul, and planted it in the victim's car herself. I rubbed my eyes, a hammering migraine just kicking in, and continued reading . . .

From the scene of Mr. Steiner's murder, Dellus walked to the Crockpit Restaurant, where he slipped in through the kitchen entrance unnoticed, gaining access to the office of Neal Turner, the restaurant's owner. Dellus then threw a pan of scalding grease, taken from the kitchen, into Mr. Turner's face, silencing his screams by removing his tongue and lips with a knife. Mr. Turner was found alive, but died three hours later in Mercy Hospital's intensive care unit from complications arising from burns, loss of blood and shock. Again, Dellus was able to leave the scene undetected.

Although police efforts to locate Dellus have been so far unsuccessful, Detective Black is optimistic that he will turn up soon; "The psychological profile that he is exhibiting is pretty standard stuff. At first he was real careful about not leaving clues, taking his time about every move he made. Now he's not as calculated, not as controlled. He's killing out in the open, leaving major clues, maybe on purpose. I think he knows he's a sick individual and wants to be stopped. We'll stop him, alright."

John Dellus is married to Janice Garvey Dellus, the daughter of Charles Garvey, renowned doctor of anesthesiology at the Johns Hopkins Medical Center, downtown. The Garvey family saw its share of tragedy in the past decade when, in the fall of '33, Mr. and Mrs. Garvey's five year old son, Ronald Scott, was abducted and brutally murdered in a still unsolved case. Mr. Garvey's wife, Madeline, committed suicide shortly thereafter.

After an intensive interview with police, Mrs. Dellus declined formal comment to the press, her only response to the relentless onslaught of reporters being a tearful, "My husband did not do those things!"

Dellus, the son of local funeral home director, Thomas Dellus, spent much time in and out of youth correctional institutions until reaching the legal adult age of 18. Since that time, Dellus has been in and out of jail on assorted petty charges including breaking and entering and public drunkenness.

CHAPTER FIVE

BENEATH JESUS

"Maybe you should sit."
I couldn't tell if Redd was genuinely concerned or just a little nervous that I may puke on his nice oriental rug. My mind just wasn't in any shape to decipher such things.

"I'll stand." I did lean forward, though, both hands planted against the oak desk, head bowed towards the twitchy little man, eyes fixed on the paper, hoping, like a child might hope, that the words would just go away. Go away and leave me alone.

The words blurred together and moved like ants.

"As I mentioned before," Redd began softly, "this has become quite a puzzle. I've given the predicament quite a bit of thought and have decided that there are several possibilities as to where the truth may lie."

"Funny you should say that," I said thinly, feeling pretty beaten, which always brings out my flip side. "Sounds like a pretty airtight case to me. I say hang the bastard, which is saying a lot considering who the bastard is."

Redd continued as if I hadn't spoken, deducting and presuming; a warped vision of Sherlock Holmes brought on by a dinner of bad oysters: "The most striking element of concern is that the police seem to have given up on catching the real Bolton Hill Butcher altogether, opting instead to take the easy route and pin the whole bloody mess on an innocent, or at least largely innocent, man. From the tone of the article, it would seem that they're prepared to hang every unsolved murder in the books on you, Jack. They'd probably stick you with the national debt if they could work the angle." He chuckled at this last cutsie remark and I tossed him a look that must have chilled his jolly liver because he pulled the plug on it quick. The national debt. Very fucking funny.

"No need to get worked up, friend. If you're not the killer, which I'm fairly certain you're not, the Real McCoy will more than likely resume work before long, business as usual, proving your innocence." Redd's smugness hung in the air like a rich man's fart. "Only problem is, as long as you're our guest here, the killer can kill all he wants, and it will still look like you're the perpetrator. As long as you're unaccounted for, so are your actions. You may be safe here but your sparkling virtue is not."

As I worked out the logic of what he was saying, I could feel my face turn a nasty shade of red.

"I don't mean to sound ungrateful, pal, but what exactly is *your* angle?" I no longer felt the need to treat this character with kid gloves, or to keep my cool *period*, for that matter. Keeping me here just made everything look as bad as it could, made me look seriously on the lam. And this Redd bum knew it. I had to get some answers from the jerk. Extract them, if need be.

"Okay," I went on, "so if you have your reasons for wanting to avoid the cops, I can dig that. But you were never really in that situation, could have just dumped me in an alley somewheres; not your problem. I could never have fingered you for this little freak show operation before today and you know it."

"So what accusation exactly is it that you are working up to, Jack?"

He was suppressing a grin. The smug fuck. My blood felt hot. Maxa sat silent; chipping, chipping.

"Something big. I don't know what just yet, but there's something pretty damn big that you're not letting me in on. Come clean, you shit. I got nothing to lose. You don't know I ain't the butcher."

My empty threat was a limp dick and I knew it. It was obvious that we both had a pretty good idea who *wasn't* the killer. He seemed a little more sure than me, to tell you the truth.

"Quite true, Jack. Also true that I haven't told you everything. But I haven't really had the chance, we've only just met." The laughter in his eyes was momentarily eclipsed by a shadow of deadly stillness that passed through them, something akin to the dense blackness of the eye of a shark. Not human. Not nice. It was just a flicker, but I caught it.

"I haven't completely established your innocence in my mind, Jack," he spoke slow and even, with a professional sort of seriousness that held his good humor delicately intact, "but I have good reason to believe that you've done nothing wrong, other than pulverize a good for nothing scumball named Michael Merle in self defense. I have very good reason to believe in your innocence. Unfortunately for you, I may very well be the only man in the city that has any such reason." He paused, his gaze searching my eyes, then searching the floor, my eyes, the floor, my eyes. Then finally:

"Have you ever heard the term, *Grand Guignol?*" He couldn't be serious, I thought.

"Yeah, sure. You mean those little pancakes made out of tissue paper they make over in Europe? Yum."

His expression soured a bit.

"Let me educate you on a few things, Jack. I'll do my best to keep things in simple terms." Gee, thanks.

"Let's be honest," he continued, "when the evening paper spills the details on the latest atrocity committed by, say, The Grace Budd Killer or the Bolton Hill Butcher or whichever homicidal freak is the hot copy of the day, the next door neighbor's first reaction always seems to be something along the lines of 'but he seemed like such a nice, quiet fellow' or 'how can something so evil have happened so close to home?'—you know, the usual response of sleepy-eyed, dumb shock.

"But isn't there another, deeper response that bubbles under the surface of even the most responsible and meek of those same appalled 'concerned citizens'? A response that we refuse to acknowledge consciously, one that recognizes an act of pure, stinking, cruel force for what it really is and says, 'could *I* have done that?' or 'I wonder what sound the knife made when it tore open his throat?' Power of any kind eludes most average folks. As hard as it is to admit, isn't there a kind of power in acts of plain, dumb brutality that we are secretly jealous of? *Achievable* power? A power for the common man?

"Hell, isn't the real truth that if most regular folks were to wake up one morning in the shoes of the powerful, evil oppressors that they hate and fear so much that they'd probably do the same damn things? Isn't it true that the question of right and wrong is pathetically eclipsed by the question of who has the upper hand? Isn't it true?"

"Who in hell knows," I replied, not knowing exactly where this little speech was going. "Not me."

"The *Grand Guignol* is the name of a controversial theatrical project in France that explores these unpopular truths, frankly, in a very . . . shall we say—*brash* manner. For the sake of the audience's conscience, the theater's excesses of blood and perversions are thinly veiled with artsy-fartsy underlying themes dealing in 'the oppression of the masses', etcetera, etcetera.. But any casual theater patron can see this for the front that it is: a spoonful of medicine to help the sugar go down. It makes people feel better, you see, to think they're taking part in something wise and profound, something with an ultimate ground in morality and truth. Something with a damn point.

"Naturally, these higher notions just cover up the lower, darker face of it, the real truth. It's the horror perpetrated by the *bad guys* in the plays of the *Grand Guignol* that people really want to live out, to experience. And don't be feeling so superior, by the way—this sort of truth applies to all of us. Yourself and the saints included." I wasn't feeling particularly superior, to tell you the truth, but I didn't feel much like arguing either.

"It is also true that the *Grand Guignol,* and theaters like it—this one is no exception I might add—are for the most part, harmless, perverted fun. But even so, it's a good idea to be aware of just how the party got started; and it isn't a pretty tale. There used to be a bit more to it than strict play acting, you see."

Redd apparently didn't have any pressing appointments to keep and of course neither did I, so he took a deep breath and proceeded to tell, in great detail, the story of the French Revolution and how it related to his little local copycat version of the Grand Guignol perv theater. You'd think I'd have nodded off, but to be truthful, he told a good tale and my normally short attention span made an exception. I don't have the patience to repeat it all here, so let me just fill you in on the jist:

After the French Revolution, there was a big cleanup campaign known as The Reign of Terror, headed up by this real whacked fella by the name of Robespierre. The idea was to cruise France, collecting up any chump who might've so much as passed gas in a counter revolutionary way, and teach 'em a little respect by trimming about ten inches off the top via guillotine. Old Robespierre wouldn't just settle for the top brass either, he wanted to pull in anybody who even smelled counter revolutionary, and the sentence was always the same. So business was brisk, to say the least, at the guillotines. They lined 'em up like they was waiting to see the latest Broadway smash, and, well, it was a hit show in a sense, but the people in line were the stars, not the spectators; chop, next, chop, next, chop, move it along, fella, next, chop . . . well, you get the picture. There were hundreds of human heads piling up and about the same number of bodies without heads. Some folks idea of justice just plain ain't sanitary.

Well, at about this time, a group of crafty out of work directors and actors who were looking for a good gimmick to make their ticket the hottest in town, thought it might be a cute idea to borrow a few of these headless bodies and manipulate them with ropes and poles to create a fresh, new approach to the world of puppeteering. Now, this might have been a tough thing to pass off as a morality play with some sort of golden lesson to be learned, but it was a real heavy draw among the teeming lowlifes of the community, nonetheless. Of course, the authorities eventually squelched the fun, as authorities have been known to do, publicly beheading the folks responsible just to show how much they disapproved of such vulgar, violent entertainment. But the seed was sewn and the point was made.

Blood sells.

And poor folks would give up their last nickel of bread money for a peek at something tragic, forbidden and smelling of death.

I can see the truth in that, I suppose.

In fact, I think it would be fair to say that most folks are more likely to blow a week's wages at the freak show to see Jello Jack the Amazing Boneless Boy than they are to spend an hour in church for free. People are funny that way.

After wrapping up this little spiel on the seedier side of French history, Redd studied my expression—as if he wasn't sure whether I'd been paying attention or not. If he'd a quizzed me I'd have aced it, though. But class wasn't out yet—he was just taking a breather, and after a self conscience glance or two at his shoes, he went on:

"Now, most folks passing through town might think of Baltimore as kind of a square, wholesome, not too big, not too dirty, semi-tolerable city. In fact, I bet there are folks who have lived here all their lives who share the same naive way of looking at the old girl.

"In some towns, like New York or Chicago, it seems like the slime is proud and uncontrolled, like insects with wings that fly right in your face while you're awake and bite you in the ass while you're asleep. Bugs like that can be hard as hell to spray down or nail with a rolled up newspaper, but at least you can see what you're up against. It's that real apparent, obvious kind of slime that makes the papers, gives a town a bad rep, puts fear in the hearts of strangers.

"But the slime in this town doesn't have wings. The slime in this town lives under the ground, in the sewers of the city and in the foundations of the big old mansions of the suburbs. The slime in this town feels shame and is not proud. If you don't want to see it, you don't have to, because the truth is it doesn't really want you to see it, it likes its privacy. But if you have two good eyes and aren't afraid to look around and maybe dig a little, well, there it is. Slithering and shaking and sucking and fucking and rolling around in

God knows who's cum and blood and sweat like a cheap, fat, lipstick smeared whore-escapee of the state psycho ward.

"With some towns you have to look real close before you see what's really at the heart of it, what keeps it breathing and moving, what makes it big and dirty and growing all the time. And in case you haven't read the Bible, the most powerful type of evil is the kind that's not so obvious.

"Ah, hell, who am I fooling?" he interrupted himself with a grin, "I haven't read the Bible."

He didn't have to explain; I haven't either. But I've looked at the pictures and I've read the captions.

And God knows this city's an old girl with a secret or two.

Now, guys like me, we can retain a truckload of information and some damn minuscule details if we figure it'll lead from point A to point B, or hell, even if it just leads to the next hot meal. Guys like me, see, we're bright boys and real attentive to detail if it's somehow useful or necessary to be bright and attentive.

But this guy was blowing wind plain and simple, and sucking wind is never useful to guys like me.

So naturally, my moody little attention span shrunk to nada lickety split and likewise, my patience took a steep dip just as fast. Even my basic desire to get some kind of understanding of my most unusual sitch just sort of shriveled up all to hell at that point. And all the good manners that my Ma taught me? Well, let's just say Miss Manners dumped me cold on the roadside with no way home on what was supposed to be a hot, hot date. So Miss Manners could just drop dead for all I cared. I cleared my throat:

"Whoa, big fella. That was a touching speech, I have to tell you, yes siree. Got me right here; deep down inside. Way, way, *way* down. In fact, here's a little back atcha." I spat on his nice oak desk. The spit was bright red. "I'll be honest with you, pal. I don't like you. I don't like a lot of people, but most people I don't like I get paid to spend any amount of time listening to. You wanna know what the truth is to me, pal? Truth is that right about now the idea of a nice cold jail cell sounds like a better deal than sitting here listening to you spout off about your damn nuthouse theater, your damn make believe morals, your twisted fucking way of looking at the world.

Fucking gallows sounds like a sweeter deal. I know dishwashers with deeper visions than you, buddy. Hell, I am one. You get me, jack? I'm outta here. I don't need your help or your pity. Thanks but no thanks."

Letting out all that steam felt pretty ace, but I knew that nothing had changed in the upper hand department. I still didn't know where in hell I was, let alone the way "outta here". I figured I'd still have to do some world class weaseling, when old wacky boy Redd pulled another wild card.

"Show him out, Maxa."

"Right. C'mon, Butcher." She got up, nail polish crumbs fluttering from her lap to the floor.

Something wasn't right.

All I had to do was flap a little lip and spit a little blood and bam! I'm calling the shots? No way. Things come that easy to hard luck jerks like me in the movies only. The only thing that seemed certain was that leaving old Wacky Boy's office had to be a step in the right direction. And letting Maxa lead the way at least provided a view I couldn't complain about.

Of course, it wasn't strictly the view that had me going on this Maxa broad. Sure she was a looker, but there was something else; something that you couldn't see. There was mystery in her eyes and in the way she walked, mystery in spades. The pairing of beauty and mystery has always spelled trouble in my book of experience, and I made a point to keep this fact in mind as I got up and followed her out the door, trying to think of a good way to break the ice just as soon as we were out of earshot of Chief Crazy Horse. I didn't have to, though. Twenty feet down the hall and she was talking all on her own.

"Things aren't as simple as you probably think they are, Butcher." The hard quality in her voice that I was just getting used to was gone and I realized that the tough girl act was a scam meant for Redd. "Things aren't simple at all."

The absurdity of her statement threw me for a loop; things were *obviously* not simple at all. Which meant that there was more trouble in the pot than I knew about—or more likely, she just wanted me to think there was. She wanted to rattle me, to suck me into some grander, deeper hole. Or maybe she really wanted to help. Maybe *she* needed help. I decided the safest course of action was to play dumb. My specialty.

"Things are simple for me. I'm a simple guy. Cops don't scare me. I'm a breeze; gone. Just show me the door and let me worry about the disappearing act. And don't call me that." *Butcher.* "I'm clean and you know it."

"I meant it in the nicest possible way, dear." She smiled. It was the first time I'd seen her crack one, a real one, I mean. Not that other smile, the one that I had seen through my crack in the wall. The smile of a mad mother killing her child.

"Nice smile," I said, meaning it.

"Redd isn't finished with you. He's scared." Interesting.

"Yeah, well, me too. I got a reason. What's his?"

She half turned and looked behind us, as if she expected someone may have followed us. No one had. She pushed open a door on the right, seemingly at random, took me by the hand and squeezed tight.

"Follow me," a whisper. A warning shot rang off in my head, issued instructions, told me what to say: Fuck off, missy, I ain't following you *in* no place. Get me *outta* this nuthouse. *Now.*

But I did follow her, her hand closed tightly around mine. It felt that good.

As she shut the door, I instinctively groped around for something to hold onto; that has always struck me as the natural thing to do when you're in a strange, dark place—and I'm sorry to report that I was starting to feel strangely at home in strange, dark places. My hand found a cold stone wall, and I pressed my back against it, waiting for her to switch on a light.

The room remained dark.

Another thing she didn't do was speak. I sensed her leaning against the wall beside me, but I could not hear her breathing in the dead quiet; I imagined her holding her breath. I also got the feeling—no basis for this—that she held her eyes closed tightly, very tightly; like a frightened little girl might. I wanted to speak—no, dammit, I wanted to shout. I wanted to grab her by the shoulders and shake the Jesus out of her, tell her she'd better quit with the games, that she was messing with the wrong jerk. Start making sense, babe; or else.

I said nothing.

And then I heard a sound. It was distant, faint in the way that you can make out the sound of a car backfiring from miles away on a clear, smoldering summer day; faint, but clear and recognizable. It was the scream of a child. I absently wondered if this building may have apartments in it where children might be holed up, screaming in the mirth of play or in the throngs of hunger or for any one of a million reasons that a child might scream.

In a neighborhood, there's something undeniably comforting in the sound of screaming children; it signals that all is healthy and right in the world. Usually accompanied by the sound of barking dogs, it is the creator of that strange mixture of emotions within a parent's heart that falls somewhere between annoyance and indescribable joy. Oddly, it is actually quite rare that a person may hear this sound where its cause is actually terror or pain.

A moment later and this sound, this unlikely link to normalcy and the outside world, was gone. Numbly, I recognized the absence of sunshine and barking dogs and the smell of freshly cut grass and wondered if terror and pain were, on this day, as innocent as usual.

They say that the blind have a better sense for their surroundings than sighted folks, and I guess that's probably true because I know that sometimes a fella can feel things out better in the dark, sometimes just from closing his eyes. And this may sound kooky to you, but right about then I felt a jolt of fear shoot across at me from nowhere, hit me square in the gut. Not my fear, mind you. Sure I was feeling quite a bit of my own, but this feeling, the one that was broadsiding me now, was hers.

"Those murders from the other night," she said, letting out a chestful of sweet smelling air, "those awful killings. It was a play."

"How's that? You mean they weren't real? You lost me, lady." I started to get the feeling that she was a little confused about what had happened the other night. It gave me a good feeling that maybe we weren't on different sides of the fence altogether. Or maybe she was thinking about losing me down another side street. I pushed the fear and emotion out of my skull, knowing that now was the time to pay attention; to the tone of her voice, the sound of her heartbeat, to the shifting of her soul. I listened hard, as hard as a guy can, I guess.

"You're scared. I know you are but I don't know why. Talk to me, Maxa. Let's work this thing out. I need you to say something that makes sense. I need it bad."

"Not actually a play, I mean. . . . I mean the murders really did happen it's just that . . . *oh shit!*" She broke into short, rhythmic sobs. I pretended to be patient and understanding while she pulled herself together.

"The way those people were killed in the newspaper," she began again, "the first with his eyes gouged out, the next with ears cut off and the third with his mouth, his mouth . . ." She trailed off, then recovered: "We have regular attractions here, Jack. The most popular skits run every week, sometimes every night if its a hot one."

I listened hard. I listened so hard that, in the blackness, I imagined I could see her mouth moving, forming the words, just from my listening so hard.

"For the last four weeks or so, the skit that's gone chic is a longer piece called 'See No Evil'. We've been closing the house with it every night. In that play, three men are killed. They die exactly as those men died last night. Every detail. It's not a coincidence. It can't be."

"You're saying someone in the theater company is the real killer."

"Yes. Or a regular. But they would have to know you."

It made sense. How else could the killer pin this mess on me so effectively? My driver's license. The Crockpit. And my exact whereabouts that night. Someone had followed me. But why?

The picture of *two* grown men chasing a rat through the inner city jumped into my head and I couldn't help letting out a snicker.

"I'm glad you're taking this so well, laughing boy." She was getting annoyed; it's a shame the room was black—I bet being annoyed looked pretty good on her. "Now it's your turn to do some talking. Who's your sick pal? The one who doesn't like you too much. We can narrow it to someone who has been to the Punch in the last month or so. Who do you know that knows about this place?"

"I don't know. What kind of freak hangs out in joints like this, anyway?" I was genuinely stumped by this point. "I never knew about this place. I gotta assume most people I know don't know about it either. Look, lady; you gotta know how this looks to me. I'm a simple guy. I got set up; I know that, you know that. And the realm of possibilities of who might have done it is getting pretty damn narrow if you ask me. And yes, I bet Redd is scared. I would be if I was him."

It took her about two seconds to figure out what I was implying.

"You're saying it was me. You fuck."

"Or the guy that was driving. Maybe you had him do it. Maybe it was Redd's idea. It had to be one of you. Before today, I had no connection here. Now I'm a fucking legend. If it wasn't you, then it was a coincidence, and I don't believe in coincidences. Especially the kind where you gotta be a rocket scientist to figure the odds."

"No, it wasn't a coincidence. And you're right about one thing; you are a simple guy. Simple Simon. No, you're not the killer; you don't know enough about The Big Punch to have done it. And Redd knows it. It can't be Redd or me, dipshit, for the same reason in reverse. We don't know enough about you. There's someone in between, someone who knows us both. Whoever it is, he's implicating both, and by doing that he's implicating neither. It's a game to him."

Twisted logic, but it worked.

"Okay, let's say you're right. I need a list of your regulars. Is there such a list?"

"Yeah. Redd keeps close tabs on everyone who even knows about this place. He has to. Too much of what goes on here is illegal. There's more to it than you know."

I assumed that she meant Redd was doing some drug running or pimping on the side. Probably both.

"Well, that figures. I need those names. If I recognize someone on it then we can figure this mess out. Otherwise we got nothing to work with."

"Can't do it," she said. "Redd keeps it under lock and key. It's his insurance policy. Most of his clientele are affluent people. If anyone sings on Redd then the party's over for the whole lot of them. If Redd leaks any names then the party's over for him. And he's a dead man. Trust is a delicate and terrible thing in the criminal world. But there's an associate of Redd's who has a copy. Redd trusts him—but I have a feeling about him. I think he wants out."

"This associate—Redd trusts him with the privacy of his affluent sicko clientele, with this whole ugly house of cards? Sounds farfetched. Who is this guy, the Pope?"

"Not quite. Redd trusts him because he *is* the security of The Big Punch. He's a cop—"

"Get it," I said, losing my patience again. "Just get it. Be slick. No one has to know. You're a cute broad; snuggle up to your cop with a conscience. Find out where he keeps it. "

A pause. "I'll try. But whoever has those names . . ."

Another pause. I hate it when broads take a long time saying something short.

". . . whoever has those names isn't safe."

Jesus Fucking Christ, I thought. You'd think the President of the United States was on that list the way she was carrying on. It had to be no-names, freaks, perverts, I thought—what's the big deal? As it turned out, I was right about the freaks and perverts. And I wasn't far off base with the President either. But I had no way of knowing that then, see . . .

"Listen, honey," I reached in the dark towards the sound of her voice and found her shoulder. I thought, suddenly, irrationally, of slapping her. Instead, I pulled her close to me. "We might not like each other too much, but right now we're stuck with each other. We need each other. I'm real sorry about that."

"I'm not, Jack. And I do like you." The smell of her breath was warm and rich, smooth and sweet as chocolate. "Are you sure you don't like me?"

I liked her plenty and she knew it. I kissed her.

Her small, gentle hands cupped the back of my neck and pulled me in; her soft, sweet tongue searching, caressing. Yes, chocolate . . . Her right knee rose slowly, brushing maddeningly against the outside of my thigh.

My hands found her waist. I felt a sharp pain, like an insect bite, at the back of my neck. Her fingernails

chipping, chipping . . .

scraped lightly around to the front of my neck and down the length of my throat; scraping and then pushing inwards. Her long right leg now wrapped itself around from behind and pulled me closer to her, the gentlest rhythm begun. She fumbled with the top button of my shirt collar and became all at once impatient and tender, tearing and pulling it open. She bit my lower lip, first slowly, seductively; then hard, too hard. Instinctively, I pulled my mouth from hers. "Hey," I whispered, tasting the blood of my lip, "go easy ... "

"Okay," she said, pushing me away roughly. Her footsteps echoed emptily as she walked towards the end of the room that was in the opposite direction from where we had come in. She was laughing, no; giggling. Giggling like a mean first-grader making fun of the fat kid: the sound of it mixed metallically with the taste of the blood in my mouth.

A feeling of subtle not-rightness gently washed over me.

The mosquito bite on my neck throbbed and stung like a pinprick, I imagined the hole widening slowly; tearing, burning. My senses took a sudden dip and the sensation of blood-rush in my brain sent me reeling; my arms shooting out for balance, touching nothing.

(Not-rightness . . .)

My heart didn't pound but, rather, seemed to flutter in my tightening chest while my head swam slowly in its own boiling blood for long rubbery seconds that stretched like hours. Suddenly the black floor became depthless; and I had this crazy feeling like I was suspended above it, spinning weightless in the dark, her laughter circling in and around my head, tiny and mocking like a toy clown in a jack in the box. I reached out for the wall that I'd been leaning against just moments before, needing desperately to touch something solid; somehow, inexplicably, gone. I attempted to dash for the door, assuming foolishly it would be where I had left it, but my legs would not carry me, flailing and kicking in the darkness, striking black, hateful air.

As my pulse seemed to double my breathing seemed to slow, and, in horror, I realized that something was choking off my access to the stale, dusty air; something warm and wet, wrapped around my throat, squeez-ing. My bulging eyes seemed ready to burst, my ears threw up mysteries of ill defined shouting, warnings I couldn't make out, instructions I could not follow or understand. I felt a warm surge like a thousand angry whispers flood my brain, deafening, like an ocean of angry, unanswered prayers. Slowly, agonizingly, my body began to bend backwards impos-sibly, my spine cracking loudly with the effort, arching until my ankles reached up from behind my back and pressed together against the sides of my neck. My lungs strained to the point of rupture for the air that was so near, dancing on my tongue, but unable to pass the closed tunnel of my throat. As my eyes exploded out of my red, unscreaming face, I thought of happy times, of spring rain, the smell of pollen and the taste of a sweet, cold peach on a hot, gorgeous day.

And I remembered, in those blood-soaked moments, the astonish-ingly delicious softness that a young boy experiences when touching a pretty girl's hand for the first time . . .

I sat in the center of the room, on the floor, cross-legged and naked.

The room was as white and clean as a hospital, the lighting bright and sourceless. There were no windows, no furniture. I was staring down between my legs, arms wrapped around myself, feeling a fear that crawled over my shoulders like ants.

I was gently jarred from my daze by the sensation of two tiny fingers stroking my temples; soothing. Then a voice, from behind me:

"You mustn't tell. You must never tell any one about me. About what I did. Promise you won't." It was the voice of a child. A boy child. I reached up to touch the hands. They were cold and soft.

Gently, I pulled him around to face me.

I recognized him at once. It was the face of a boy I had seen many times in my childhood. A child I had known as a playmate; the only friend that I had trusted blindly, that I could tell my touchy boy-secrets to. But this boy, I knew, had a few boy-secrets as well. He had done some horrible things. Evil things. And he had trusted me.

He looked at me now, with innocence and expectancy, awaiting a response, smelling of urine and death. When I was a kid—a kid his age—his sweet, terrible face was something I prayed to avoid but could not, never able to escape his piercing yet tender glance. It was a face that I was forced to look upon every day. Everyday in my father's house, in the upstairs bathroom, beneath the hanging, knowing head of Jesus.

In the mirror nailed to the medicine chest cabinet.

"Promise you won't tell."

"I promise," I whispered.

"You were the only one. The only one who understood. I love you."

"But I don't understand. I never understood. I only did what you told me. You made me." I was whimpering now, I was behaving as *he* should have behaved; as a runny nosed brat. "It wasn't my fault. You made me," I offered lamely.

"No. You made me. And you must never, never tell."

He curled into my lap then, like an infant, and buried his head against my sobbing, heaving chest. I rocked him until I stopped crying.

Without warning, he slowly sank his small, sharp teeth into my chest. There was pain—but I was unimpressed in the dream and didn't pull away. I closed my eyes tightly. The blood tickled me as it ran down past my stomach, dripping warm onto my crotch, and I shuddered as I heard the sound of soft gulping.

When I opened my eyes again, he was no longer there. But the dirtiness of his soul lingered in the air like a thick smell. Of course it did.

(Not-rightness):

Against the plain white wall before me had appeared a cross. On this cross, an old woman was nailed, her body grey and withered, the skin of her arms hanging in loose sacks as skin sometimes does on old people. Her face was frozen terrible and stretched in agony but covered in pink powder and lipstick, eyes done up with blue shadow and long fake lashes; whorish and awful. Upon her head was a bright yellow wig and from its untucked and unwashed lining fell tiny beads of blood, falling like droplets of dew onto her sallow cheeks. She looked at me, and through her eyes I was able to peek past her tormented exterior and

into her soul, and in that soul lurked none of the anguish that the agonized expression on her face spoke all too clearly of. Only a smooth
silence; peace, sympathy. An impenetrable heart born of profound, ultimate understanding. An understanding not human. No pain.

"Take this bread and eat it for it is my body." Her voice was monotone, defying the emotion of her eyes and the gravity of her horrific
circumstance. "Take this wine and drink it for it is my blood ... "

A voice in my head spoke then. A voice from a bathroom mirror.
Beneath Jesus.

"Do it," the voice said.

I walked to the cross.

I stood beneath the woman and looked up at the soles of her feet. I
threw my naked body at the rotten wood, wrapping my arms and legs
around it, pulling myself up. Splinters from the aged wood made residence in my stomach and groin. The bottoms of the woman's feet touched
my head as I reached her and, as I pulled my way past, I could see the nail
that had been driven through them and into the flaky hardness of the
cross. Her blood had dried on it, dried the color of rust. Orange rust.

But something was not as it should be; the skin of the old woman's
feet was no longer old; suddenly smooth, young, the toenails polished
and the polish chipped.

My blood raged and burned in my body, whipping inexplicable sensa-
tions of violence and lust through my terrified heart like bad Mexican
whiskey. With my legs squeezing ever tightly around the base of the cross,
I flung my hands upward, grabbing onto the no-longer-old woman's firm,
muscular hips, pulling murderously at any piece of her that I could grab
onto. As I jerked my body upwards, I felt the head of the large nail that
pierced her feet catch and tear at my groin and I screamed, my face now just
below her belly, smelling sweet, wet chocolate. My ruined, bleeding privates roared in agony and yet the terrible wave of violent lust only intensified. I clawed my way across her body, gnawing and scratching at her
perfect skin along the way. As my face finally became level with hers, I
wrapped my arms tightly around her, crushing her to the cross, struggling
frantically for penetration,

do it.

my desperate attempt to rape the woman on the cross was foiled though; strong, defiant legs closed tight, forbidding. I looked into her eyes then—*Maxa's* eyes; her laughing, mocking eyes, and continued to hug her with my trembling limbs, blood running down my thighs. She laughed, eyes sparkling.

In a frenzy of frustration, I grabbed at her throat, pushing my hands together with all my strength, then slamming my forehead into that giggling schoolgirl mouth. Her laughter stopped, but she did not seem angry or hurt; rather, the violent jolt only brought another wave of sweet calm to her face. Maddeningly, she looked at me with what appeared to be love and pity.

"I thirst," she said.

And she was no longer on the cross. In fact she was nowhere.

And then it was me on the cross. But somehow I was outside of my body, looking down upon myself—and the cross was a smaller cross, for I was a child.

in the dream I was five. . . .

At my feet were a dozen or so other children, several of whom suffered grotesque physical deformities; the kind that spelled bucks for a good traveling carny. The others appeared normal—under the circumstances, that is. The most striking of the deformed children was a young black girl of about ten years who seemed to have four legs.

All but two of the children were crying.

Although I did not know Janice when she was a child, I recognized one of the uncrying children to be her *(I recognized the girl in the way of dreams)*. She was holding the other uncrying child in her arms; it was the body of a small naked boy covered in blood, bruised and cut up, its tiny skull smashed in. She walked to the foot of my cross and layed the delicate, battered creature at my feet.

"Why hast thou forsaken us?" she said.

I screamed and screamed.

CHAPTER SIX

DREAMBOAT TO NOWHERE

"Iss okay, Mista. Wakey, wakey, now. Iss jussa bad ol' dream izzall. Wakey, Mista."

My screams burst into waking air.

After a moment of labored breathing and a rush of relief as the image of the dream mercifully vacated itself from memory, my eyes anxiously focused through a murky soup of half-sleep to find a strange angel. A young black girl of nine or ten years hovered above me, wiping gently at my hot forehead with a ball of cool, damp toilet paper. The sound of her voice was instantly calming.

"Thass right Mista, everything's always a little diffint when iss not a dream, lot betta sometimes but sometimes a lot worse.

"A dream iss like a boat that driffs out to sea when dey ain't no captain, no tellin where iss gone end up, no sir. Could go to tha place of true pair-dice, with love and comfort and purdy ladies an' hansum menfolk or could go some place hurtful and fearsome where devils is friendly and treat you sweet like a momma and angels is monsters that skin you alive and fry your soul in pigfat fo a mean ol' angel suppa; a place so bad and backwards that you cain't even imagine it awake cain't even understand such badness and sometimes the dreamship don't go no place a'tall juss goes straight past where yo' heart and mind can see an feel proper and slip right smack into the black secret back part of the soul that only God hisself know about an when dat happens then iss mo' likely than it ain't that the dreamship won't come back never a'tall no more cuz dreams like that God don't let a soul wake from—bein' that God has his secrets an secrets need to be kept, specially when iss God's bad ol' dirty secrets. ... "

Her words were disturbing but oddly comforting; I watched the gentle, rhythmic motion of her brown-pink lips and let their tender sermon soothe me into consciousness. Any remnants of the nightmare that might have lingered were now pushed away with a merciful abruptness by the sweetly sickening aroma of grease-cooked food—and with it the sudden acute awareness of the fact that I hadn't had a square since the day before yesterday. Unless you count nic and joe.

I pushed myself into a sitting position and found myself pressing against the squeaky springs of a small but comfy folding cot. Two disturbing realities hit me. One; that my already shaky ability to separate what was real and what was not was becoming shakier by the second, and two; that the act of pushing myself into a sitting position had caused a great deal of pain in the muscles on the upper right side of my chest. I pulled up on the fabric of my borrowed shirt and glanced downward at the pain's source. A small ring of blood was there, about the size of a half dollar. Parts of the dream began to fall back together at the sight, something about a boy I knew when I was small . . .

"Thass right Mista, I done gotcha nice big breakfiss already. Dokka Chollee sez he juss knew you'd be hungry fit ta eat a elephan', an' by tha way y'eyes be swellin' up at the sight I giss Dokka Chollee wuzz dead right, but Dokka Chollee ain't hardly wrong 'bout nothing, no-thing a'tall, no-sir."

A small metal serving tray was positioned between me and the girl, and at the center of it sat a large white plate. Southern-fried biscuits smothered in gravy sat alongside a large portion of gray, greasy grits and scrambled eggs with double helpings of burnt sausage links and bacon. I gorged myself, washing it down with a full pot of steaming black joe, letting the hot liquid singe my throat. The food and java put a hell of a queasy feeling in my gut, but the discomfort at least attested to a belly that has been fed. I didn't really mind the sick feeling. No, not much.

While I sucked grub like a farm animal, the girl went on and on, saying nothing that directly concerned planet earth as far as I could tell, saying nothing at all really, just slapping out a sweet and harmless rhythm of words. But the sound of her voice was so strange and pretty, filling me with an emotion that I could not acccount for, affecting my sense of logic in the tiniest way, changing everything for good. Her quaint yammerings of doomed dreamships and God's dirty secrets had a ring of truth that resounded with hopefulness and light somehow. And though this may sound whacked, her gentle rant seemed to fill my comfortably purposeless heart, however fleetingly, with a sort of purpose, a feeling that I was not in this crummy city, living this crummy life strictly on account of my own miserable luck. Not strictly.

I was here on some sort of dark mission.

A mission born of darkness that was lined with wasted life and perversions, sure, but through some divine purpose and my own inner strength, the mission could only lead to a conclusion inspired by innocence, washed by some inevitable and redeeming truth.

I could not be so lost, so tired, so frightened just because I was unlucky. It was not possible that life could be so meaningless, God so cruel. Was it?

I listened to her voice absently as I wolfed the food, absorbing the strange underlying meaning of her words, their pattern of weird salvation. I listened for the details of my divine mission between hurried gulps.

"Don' eat so fass, Mista, o' you go blin'. Dass what momma sez. An' momma know plenty 'bout God's awful ways. Momma sez God punish her fo' doin' less'n that by thrustin' upon her the monstah angel of me n' Becky. Say we a curse o' God, she say. She keep us locked up; locked up real good, too. We locked up so good an' so long that when she open the cupboard door so's she can dump out our li'l bucket o' doody 'n' pee the light o' the kitchen hurt my eyes real bad, so bad I gotsta holler out loud, make me wish ta be Becky sometime; with my head all nice and buried deep, sleepin' and thinkin' and knowin' things that ain't happened yet an' never havin' ta get her poor eyes burnt out from tha kitchen light ... "

Sitting beside my cot on a collapsible wooden lawn chair, her dress looked homemade and practical; a red and white checkered tablecloth sewn into a frumpy, oversized dress. Beneath the baggy outfit was a distinct largeness; odd bulges pressing outward from her scrawny child's frame. Bulges inappropriate for a child.

With child.

It has always struck me as cruel that nature has deemed it possible for a kid to get knocked up at such a young age. It's not right or fair, I don't care if it's the way of nature, sometimes nature is wrong. I wondered what chances this bony little kid would have in the face of the brutal, violent bully in her underdeveloped womb. She'd get her scrawny ass kicked is what. I looked at the body of this happy-tragic creature, trying not to stare at what seemed to lie beneath the tablecloth dress, and the realization dawned on me that she was not pregnant at all.

With child maybe—but not pregnant.

"Don' feel bad starin', Mista. Most folks do—an' I cain't says I blame 'em, no sir. Ol' Ida Mae 'n' Becky been stared at by plenny good folks an' some awful nasty ones; sometimes dokkas an' sometimes people juss curious dat ain't seen no monstah angel befoh. Sometimes Mommah made me 'n' Becky take off diss pretty dress cause a man with a lotta money wants to take a good hard look. Sometime da man, he wants to lay his cold hand on us an' sometimes if da man gotta a whole, WHOLE lotta money, Mommah let's dat terrible, cold touchin' man make us feel awful dirty an' sometimes he hurts us real bad an' I can feel Becky crying inside of me an' da tears from her poor crying head sting my heart an' feel like our insides all burnin' up.

"But now dat nice Dokka Chollie take us away from Mommah. He promise the nasty, rich white men ain't gone dirty us no more, an' maybe we can get some of em back foh what dey did, too. Dokka Chollie take good care o' Ida Mae an' Rebecca fo now on, thass what he say ... "

My eyes saw and my mind put together the pieces that did not fit but *were* just the same. I was not seeing double. The girl did have two sets of arms.

". . . . he say dat me n' Becky gone be famous like Molleen Deetrick, we gone be famous, yes sir. We ain't been ta Hollywood fo what Dokka Chollie calls Screen Tessin' yet, but we ain't quite ready say Dokka Chollie, we gosta get our akkin' skills primed up firss, dass why he bring us here. We learnin' how ta be movie stars here at da Big Punch. Juss like Miss Jean Hollow, say Dokka Chollie ... "

On the floor, beneath the shape of the dress, the girl's two feet touched the ground in the normal way. But on the child's lap, under the checkerboard cloth of red and white, two thin legs were folded tight in a crouching position, the knees pressing tightly to the child's waist. What I had mistaken for a pregnant belly was actually a second backside, the spine of which seemed to lead up to the girl's chest, ending about three inches below her throat. There was a second body, a body apparently dependent upon—and facing—the first.

A second body without a second head.

Momma say we a curse o' God . . . a monstah angel.

"I's sorry, Mista; I feel dat I bein' rude—you's a guest an' here I be ramblin' on wiffout even a proper inta-dukk-shunn. My name is Ida Mae an' diss here is my sista Rebecca. She ain't rude, she juss cain't talk. You can call her Becky."

Ida Mae gently undid the top four buttons of her dress, exposing the area of chest where her sister's spine smoothly disappeared. There, between two tiny dark nipples, was a crudely drawn picture of a smiling girl's face. It had been scribbled on with bright red lipstick and black eye liner, the eyes accentuated with a light green eye shadow—the same kind my mother used to wear to church when I was a kid.

"Pleased to meet you, Ida Mae," I said sincerely, "nice to know you too, Becky."

My brain flushed with the hot blood of fear that so commonly wells up in a man's mind when he is confronted with something so far beyond his ability to comprehend, so absolutely and positively unknown to his measure of experience, that he instinctively reads it as horror.

Becky. Evidence of the cruelest possible God.

Of course, my initial assumption that the two sisters shared one head between them was way off base. Becky certainly did possess an individual mind, just as sure as she had her own name. And there was no horror in this child, Ida Mae. She was simple and sweet and full of love and trust and all the things that had no place in this hellish underground world. And the love that she felt for her sister was equally natural and true, in defiance of these awful surroundings, the surroundings created by men and women born with normal bodies.

Had Becky been born normally, with her head outside of her body— and then one day found it plunged into its current state, then, yes, that would be plain old fashioned horror indeed.

But Becky knew no other way.

To her, true horror might very well be the thought of taking a breath, of seeing and hearing her surroundings, of smelling and tasting and seeing the awful men that touched her body for money. Horror, for Becky, may very well be the simple idea of experiencing the world in the unbuffered, firsthand way that her sister was forced to know.

OUTSIDE.

To Becky, life was "all nice and buried deep, sleepin' an' thinkin' an' knowin' things that ain't happened yet". The only true sadness of the twins lie in Ida Mae's melancholy jealousy of her sister's sheltered existence.

I wondered about Becky; I still do. I wondered about the tender cheeks of her face; how the endless caress of her sister's life-giving lungs, breathing for two, might feel against them. I wondered about the skin of her face and neck, having never touched the air or felt the sun's warmth, but most assuredly having felt what none of us, in normal human adulthood, can claim to have felt; the warm and constant nurturing of womb-life, and the odd sense of serenity that must lie in the knowledge that to continue living she must never, never leave it. And I wondered about her eyes, if they were fixed on some red and pulsing darkness or if they could see with a strange and natural clarity the beating heart before them, signaling the continued life of her protector, her sister. I wondered what sort of strange and wonderful communication these two sisters shared, and if it was really all that different than the communication between any set of sisters.

"I thank you lovely ladies for your kind hospitality. I honestly can't remember a time that I've shared better company." I meant everything I'd said; and it wasn't just because I wasn't particularly accustomed to being treated kindly by strangers. There was something strangely comforting about the twins. It was like the weird comfort that a kid feels from a parent or a favorite teacher or even a priest—the comfort that a child instinctively recognizes in a protector. "Now I'm the rude one,—my name is Jack—Jack Dellus".

With that irrational feeling of safety, I looked deep into my new friend, Ida Mae's, peaceful, trusting eyes, and began to remember.

I remembered the diner. I remembered the play. I remembered Henry and Redd. And Maxa. I remembered the madness of kissing her in the dark and the strange stinging sensation at the back of my neck and the sudden absence of reality and I remembered the dream of the cross.

"Ida Mae," I spoke to her evenly, "listen to me, doll; this is very important. I need your help."

"Okay, Mista Jack; I listen. I listen real good."

"There's some bad people in this place. People who are up to no good. They'd like to keep me here—keep me against my will. I need to get out of here so I can make things right. If I can't get out, then people will be hurt, killed maybe. And the bad people here want it to look like I'm the one doing the killing. And I swear to you, I never killed no one. Can you help me, Ida Mae? I need a friend, bad." Except for the part about never having killed anyone, truer words were never said.

"Sho' I can hep you Mista Jack!" She sounded downright ecstatic about the prospect of furthering our friendship. "I kin take ya double quick inny ol' place you want in diss big ol' house; I knows it through n' through. I give you da gran' guided tour of da house o' Big Punch! And I knows ya ain't kilt nobody cuzz Becky tol' me so. I take you all aroun' dis big house!"

The notion of a tour through this funhouse frankly made my skin crawl, but it also sounded potentially damn educational. I wasn't interested in learning just then, though—wasn't even interested in getting my gracious host in dutch with the cops. I was only interested in two things; *her soft, sweet tongue searching, probing. . . . yes, chocolate, somehow. . . .*

first off, I needed to get the hell out of this place and second, *I felt a sharp pain, like an insect bite, at the back of my neck.* I needed to find a way to prove *chipping, chipping . . .* that I hadn't committed those murders.

"No, baby. Just show me the way out. I don't have time for a tour right now. Maybe some other time."

She nodded sweetly, understanding, and took my hands in hers. Becky's hands pushed forward and up, lifting the sisters' awkward form out of the wooden lawn chair. "Whatever you say, Mista Jack. Po, Mista Jack. I know what iss like ta be scared. I know what iss like ta juss wanna go home. I git ya home, Mista Jack. I promise."

promise you won't tell . . .

She pulled up on my bandaged hands. Bandaged? Yes, so was the side of my head—someone had dressed my wounds while I slept, the wounds I had sustained the night of the Maryland House. But not the bite mark on my chest—the injury that I had gotten, somehow, in the dream. The dream of the cross and the crying, disfigured children.

a young girl of about ten who seemed to have four legs . . .

In the standing position, the sisters appeared surprisingly normal. Becky, of course, stooped forward towards her sister, her arms draping lovingly around Ida Mae's waist, fingertips lightly touching in a saintly not-quite-perfect forty-five degree angle, while Ida Mae leaned forwards only slightly accommodating her sister's awkwardness. She held her hands together on her sister's back as if her form were a table top, folded in front of her in the proper fashion that good girls and boys are taught in school. Behind Ida Mae, I noticed a small hump just below the shoulder blades caused by, I guessed, the constant pressure of Becky's head pushing inward against her spine. They moved towards the door—

with Ida Mae facing forwards. Their bodies moved with the surreal grace of a large spider, their feet scuttled and shifted against the floor with a precise and terrible rhythm.

Wondering if this strange creature would actually turn out to be my ticket out of this hell and into, well, into the next hell, anyway, I fixed my eyes on the small round bump below Ida Mae's shoulders and followed the girls through the door.

The hallway looked familiar; wooden floors and iron walls leading endlessly and randomly like the halls of the great pyramids, patterns whose meanings were very likely buried with the architect, and maybe better off for it. The towering ceiling followed the hallway's mysterious lead, obedient and unchanging; laced and lined with steel piping like the veins and arteries of some huge, mechanical carcass.

The echo of our six feet plodding and shuffling through the grey maze made me blue a little, and a feeling of melancholy paranoia crept up on me that said she was not leading me out, but deeper, deeper into the heart of it. The suspended fluorescent bulbs flickered and buzzed with sleepy menace.

The sisters finally stopped at the end of a long hallway, a hallway that didn't end with an option but a single steel door. They had to face the door sideways so that Ida Mae could reach her hand to the knob; she twisted and pushed it open gently. The door opened on a stairwell.

To climb the stairs, the sisters turned around, Ida Mae facing backwards, going first. Once the sisters had actually mounted the steps in this fashion, Becky's appearance became closer to normal; jarringly so, in fact. Ida Mae's slight elevation above her sister allowed Becky the unusual opportunity to walk almost upright. I guess I must have stood at the landing watching them climb for a bit long; standing and staring like a damn idiot who hadn't a care in the world.

"C'mon Mista Jack. Y'all bess hurry. We down near the bottom as it is an' day's a long way to the street up top. It'd be bess if no one sees us, too. Da house mostly asleep about now—we lucky fo' dat." I climbed up after them. They were surprisingly quick and agile on the stairs; I had to take two steps at a time to keep up.

When we made it to the next level, we trotted our way through a maze seemingly identical to the one on the first level with one exception; the hallway of the second level was lined with dozens of steel doors. The doors reminded me of some of the nastier prisons I've had the displeasure being a guest in; entrances to hundreds of tiny cells all crammed together. Had this freaky joint housed some sort of secret prison at one time? I tinkered with a few of the latches as I followed the twins, wondering if any enlightenment lurked inside. No luck. The doors were all locked.

Then another stairwell.

I tried to make mental notes of the hallway patterns, figuring that I may need to know my way around this joint in a pinch sometime soon. We repeated a real similar maze pattern four more times— six levels total- before the air became noticeably more breathable. I figured it meant that we were nearing street level. The last long hallway led to a door different from the others we had passed along the way; it was smaller and made of solid oak—not steel. Four heavy deadbolt locks kept it very closed.

"Well, I said I git ya home an' I guess that was only half true—I mean ya ain't home but leastways ya got a way out of dat ol' Punch an' dass a start true as ever. But all dat exa-size o' climbin' stairsteps tends to get da blood coursin' through ol' Becky's brain an' dat starts her thinkin' real hard an' when she thinks real hard then she sees real clear an' when she sees real clear, well, she jus' cain't help but ta tell ol' Ida Mae all about it. Not talkin' in da way dat maybe make sense to regular folk but talkin' juss da same. Becky likes you, Mista Jack—likes you a whole lot. An' she likes you cause she know you."

It's always nice to hear that someone likes you, of course, but there was something about that second part that sent me a quick shiver. *She know you.* It made no sense at all—it was damn impossible—but somehow I knew it was true.

"Tell your sister I like her, too," I said, "I better get going now. Thanks for everything, Ida Mae, I—"

As my right hand reached up to undo the dead bolts of the door, a thin brown hand shot up and locked around my wrist—Becky's hand.

There was something urgent, no—more like desperate, in the tightness of its grip. Ida Mae spoke:

"Do you understand, sir? Becky *know* you. She know *about* you. She know your troubles an' she knows you lookin' fo' some answers—an' in some o' doze answers lies a death-stinkin' black danger cause you don't know it yet but doze answers you be lookin' fo' be lookin' fo' you too. An' dey'll findja real plum easy cause dey know where ya live an' whatcha look like and what you likely to do, where you like to hide when you scared. Becky knows whatcha thinkin' bout doin' an' she's scared fo' ya'.

"You a nice man, Mista Jack, but you unlucky. It sounds like a mean thing ta say, sir, but Becky wants me ta ask ya ta please remember how unlucky you is. She sez it'll hep ya ta keep things in proper perspective."

Unlucky. What a fucking understatement. Ida Mae looked into my eyes hard then, her features scrunching up into a not so cute, kiddie—deadly seriousness. The small pink mouth opened then and spoke with the unsettling rhythm of a southern backwoods preacher, Becky's tiny hand held onto my wrist ever tightly:

"Put everything dass in your mind backwards from how it normally is. If ya thinkin' iss loose den iss probably tight if ya think dat iss wrong, well, it oughta be right if ya know iss black den iss sho' nuff white if ya bettin' iss left, son, ya betta be right. Backwards every time. Dass yo' best an' only protection. Don't follow yo' heart today, sir, don't trust in no intuition. Iss a matter of faith, sir, you bess know it, you bess understand it. Up is down.

"Five days. Dass how much time. Go against yo' common sense when you look on things. See things as different as you can, as many different ways as you can. Trust yo' enemies an' suspect yo' friends. Walk with the devil, turn your back on God. Diss is da hardest of all God's tests of faith.

"Your first revelation will smack you right in da eyes pretty fast on leaving here. You will be back because of it. Come back soon, Jack."

It was the first time she didn't call me 'sir' or 'Mista'. I noticed a small tear run down her cheek.

"Me 'n Becky we ain't got much time. Five days. You cain't save us but you can make things right."

The double torso of the sisters twisted slightly sideways as four hands shot simultaneously to the door's four locks and twisted the heavy bolts to the open position with a heavy clickclickclickclick. The four hands fell and I reached for the knob, turning it and opening the door on a beautiful spring day in the dead of fall. I now stood at the bottom of a concrete stairwell, a pile of crunchy orange and brown leaves blowing gently inward from a warm breeze. The stairwell led up to the back yard of a big house. Ground level at last. There were large, ancient trees turning colors in the yard and the sky was blue and cloudless; something about this yard was naggingly familiar, something about the feel of it, the smell of it. My thoughts were interrupted by a familiar scuttling, shuffling sound. I turned my attention back to the hallway I had just walked up from. The twins had left me.

Standing here strangely free, my brain sat uneasily in my skull, full of weird images and fears created by Ida Mae's weird talk. Her prophecy of salvation through seeing the world only for exactly what I knew it not to be. Her assurance that love and trust and God himself was the surest route to some hellish backwards universe of death and betrayal.

I walked to the top of the steps and stretched my arms luxuriously in the breeze, breathing the false-spring air deeply. My lungs filled with the unmistakable sweetness of fruit so ripe and perfect that it had no way to go but bad. I looked up to discover that the tree towering above me dangled hundreds of oversized peaches from its limbs. The tree cut even deeper into my memory, familiarity edging farther into the back of my noggin bringing me closer to total recall of this place—the whens, whos and whys of it. A large, ripe, perfect peach lay on the ground at my feet. My stomach growled at the smell of pollen and fruit.

Somehow I knew the peach was rotten inside, but I trusted that it was not. Faith, she said. I bit deeply and swallowed quickly, eyes closed tight.

Faith.

CHAPTER SEVEN

DEATH'S BLACK TRAIN IS COMING

The Yard of The House of The Big Punch was not fenced so I strolled out of it and into the cool, dumb breeze of the city's breath nonchalant as you please, like any happy, henpecked squarejohn sent out into traffic by the missus for a quart of milk and a dozen eggs.

It seems logical, I know, that whatever blurry recollections I may have had of this place would be most easily cleared up with a simple stroll around to the front and a quick glance at the name on the mailbox. But there are some things that a fellow feels obliged to keep in the form of a theory for as long as possible—a theory being a thing that remains technically untrue until it is scientifically proved otherwise. I decided that I'd do better to direct my strolling elsewhere first; clear my head, stretch my legs.

I was on a section of Saint Paul Street that I knew—not far from the fourth floor attic apartment where me and Janice lived. A comic image ran through my head like a moving picture:

Myself (played by Charlie Chaplin) runs home twitching and stumbling all helter skelter like, darting down the sidewalk and through the front door, zipping up the spiral stairs like a cyclone. Upon reaching my destination, I (Charlie) jump past the loving arms of my wife and into bed, hiding under the covers with feet sticking out, afflicted with a violent case of the shivers. The mind-movie played itself in my head for a sec and then played itself right back out; I knew I couldn't go home. Dicks would be there, natch. Plus, Janice was probably staying at her father's house by now, looking for some kind of shelter from the raging shitstorm I'd sent pouring down on her.

I thought of Janice cowering like a kitten under the protective supervision of her self important pop, a real pillar of the community he liked to think, and I thought about what that probably actually meant should my theory about the big house be correct. It wasn't damn funny, not one bit, but it just wasn't in me not to grin a little.

It is one of fate's humorless ironies, I guess, that the only sure shelter from life's roughest storms is always a place deep within the smooth, churning belly of the ocean's currents; *within* the consuming and indifferent flesh of the storm itself. The water's tickling, suffocating fingers are soft and silky beneath the surface; a blanket of warm death that protects us from the pounding tides and bruising unsympathetic skies. Or as Cab Calloway puts it with such eloquence; *It's a killer\ A honey driller\ Hoy, poy, joy, hoy, floy, joy, hoy, hoy . . .*

Janice was far from safe, I knew, but to try and help her now would be a reckless gesture. I had to calm my head, plan things out. Get structured.

The wind off the waves can usually help clear my head and get my brain circuitry connecting pretty good, so I thought a walk out to the harbor might be a good way of pushing the old noggin into a plan of some sort. It dawned on me that to go southbound on Saint Paul would take me too near the courthouse—as well as the police station—and would most likely land me into the deepest shit possible. I headed northbound, away from the water, walking and thinking.

The city's outer skin hadn't changed any during my night and day in its stinking gut. Panhandlers crouched in filth and casually harassed the passing droves of businessmen that pushed past; suits scrambling out of the sunlight like immaculate insects into the tall, hard structures that held their tidy wombs of employment. Young women carted heaps of dirty laundry to the Preston Street Laundromat like urban zombies, expressions of defeat and acceptance painted across their faces in broad strokes. Their tiny, shouting kiddies zig-zagged down the street unsupervised like an ever scattering litter of mongrel pups. The kids donned the same defeated expressions ingrained on the faces of their mothers—but a more joyful version and in even broader strokes. Motorists bumped and glided past the darting children, cautious and irritable, but un-honking. Blessed, hopeless, comfortable city rhythm.

I walked over the long metal and concrete bridge that ushered the harbor traffic past or into Penn Station and enjoyed the oddly burnt smelling air that train stations always seem to emanate. It made me want to cry, this dingy reality, this dank and complacent world of mediocrity and acceptance. It was a place where things made sense, where people may have a rough time of it but the odds weren't heaped against a fellow for no good reason and crazy, dangerous people were kept locked away someplace dark and secluded, in the city's back, secret side. On the side of the train tracks that regular folks don't go near or even talk about much.

As I neared the station, a sound tickled mosquito-like at my ears through the surging bustle of commuters and honking cabs that hunted down fares with casual desperation. My eyes needled and shoved a line of vision through the crowded thoroughfare to the source of the sound, an easy sound out of place in this world of the frightened wealthy who squirmed under the swelling, dead weight of the clock to be someplace on time, on time, on time.

It was the voice of an old black fellow. Strumming a guitar.

> *Oh that little black train is coming*
> *Get all your business right*
> *You better get your house in order*
> *For that train gonna be here tonight.*

I usually walk right past homeless fellows with guitars, but this old timer drew me in somehow, his voice weathered and cracked as old shoe leather but reaching into my tired heart like a pushy saviour demanding unquestioning faith and twenty-five cents.

He stood there with a plucky righteousness as he beat a choppy rhythm from the out of tune instrument, leaning against the station wall and hovering over a box marked "DONATIONS". I walked right up to where he stood so I could hear better and he looked right at me, or rather, right through me, as if I weren't there.

Blind.

His eyes looked fine, though—clear and brown—free of the telltale clouds that meant cataracts.

Oh that train has just on engine
And one little baggage car
Has all your deeds and darkest fears
Gonna meet you at the Judgment Ball.

I usually don't jibe too well with religious folks, but there was something about the blind preacher's simplicity that moved me.

It makes me laugh when I think of the misinformed folks who think they got God's ways locked, think they have any real answers on the subject. Everybody's got their own customized, self serving interpretation of the Bible that they say you have to follow if you don't want your soul slam dunked into hell after the inner city and the IRS get through with it. All wild interpretations aside, though, no one contests the fact that God didn't write the thing in the first place. I think if God were to sit down and write a book *himself* it would be pretty damn clear what he meant to say, that is to say I don't imagine there would be *any* room for interpretation. I doubt if God would waste time overestimating the intelligence of the human race with some big, fat book full of puzzles and riddles and stories about one thing meaning to represent another, with a different meaning if you read it sideways and still another if you look at it standing on your head. Mean what you say, say what you mean I always say. Learned that much in kindergarten.

When the colored fellow finished his song he looked at me—or through me—about two feet past the spot where I stood, I guess. He smiled. Like he had just located something that had been eluding him, like a lost child in a crowded market spotting mom. He began to strum his guitar again, looking out to the train tracks. He sang smiling, but with a mournfulness in his voice.

And I don't know
What I should have learned
I cannot find a lesson in this story
And I don't care
If it goes nowhere
God only knows this train is bound for glory.

The little hairs on the back of my neck started to stand on end a little when it hit me that this man, whom I'd never met, seemed to be looking into me somehow, the same way Becky had. I can't explain how I knew this or why it seemed to be a comforting thing instead of a threatening one.

As tears began to irritate and well up in my eyes, I decided that I wanted to help this old guy somehow. I reached into the pockets of the grey slacks that Henry had lent me the previous night, looking for change, expecting to find nothing. I felt folded paper deep in the right pocket, recognizing, with surprise, the grainy texture of currency. Whaddaya know, I thought, someone left a buck in there. I pulled it out and unfolded it to find that it was not a buck at all.

It was a hundred. On the back of it, some one had marked the shape of a heart in heavy black fountain ink.

Not entirely able to believe such luck possible, my mind exploded with plans of how I would exploit this random gift from the soulless, indifferent God of men; buy a train ticket to someplace far, lay low for a month then send for Janice, start over again. Bam, wham, bingo. The plan seemed simple and good.

Something was wrong, though.

Something that nagged at me. Some sort of fatal flaw overlooked. Or denied.

Well, I have loved the wrong
At times misplaced the truth
And I have held convictions that were hopeless
And I have beaten down
What innocence I've found
And I have learned that suffering means nothing.

I crunched the bill into a ball and took the three steps between me and the old man's cardboard money box on shaking legs. I dropped it in, turned and began walking quickly back to the place that I had left too soon. "Bless you, son", I'd heard him call out, as if the blind man could have known what I had just done. And then something odd happened.

As I pushed my way through the crowd, I heard his voice again, this time a whisper; "Be careful, Jack". It was impossible that he could have known my name—and equally impossible that I could have heard a whisper at the twenty feet or so that I'd shoved between us through the noisy crowd. I turned to face him, but the growing number of passing bodies between me and the preacher didn't allow it. When the flow of rushing people did momentarily ebb low, I began to understand a thing that cannot be understood. For where the man had stood, he stood no longer.

And he had not ever.

The weather in Baltimore changes quick, and it went from May to August (October being the actual month, of course) in the forty minutes or so since I had left the big house. The breeze had died, the temperature had risen and the air quality had thickened uncomfortably. Along with the weather, my attitude had altered greatly, a tranquillity having claimed me, my desire to formulate a plan of action having evaporated in the dry air. My feet carried me to my destination guided not by thoughts and intention but by logic and instinct. The return of the dull throbbing pain at the back of my neck was the only distraction that I was conscious of.

When I reached the place from which I had come, as Ida Mae had assured me I would, I walked past the front gate this time—although I no longer needed to check the name on the mailbox to know what it said. Charles Henry Garvey, M.D.

Dokka Chollie.

I had such a strong recollection of the place because I had been here so many times before. It was, after all, my wife's father's house.

Remembering the four locks on the inside of the basement door, I scoped the joint's exterior for an alternate route of entry. I wasn't yet sure why I was going back in there, or what I hoped to find, but I did know that Ida Mae and Becky, however nuts, were still just a couple of kids caught up in a very bad and dangerous web of grown-up criminal behavior. And Janice, well, she was probably in there too; warm and cozy as can be in her bedroom on the third floor. Yeah, that's my girl. Probably boo hooing into her treasured heap of romance novels in her typical immature, do-nothing approach to a crisis. Knowing nothing about the twins or the theater or Daddy's bad habits and strange friends or the fact that her beloved pop was almost certainly the master mind of a weird plot to frame her husband of an unspeakable string of horrors that Daddy himself, if logic prevailed, had to have some kind of hand in. My beloved missus: not knowing and not wishing to know. Wake me when it's over.

That's ok, baby.

I returned to this place not because of some self destructive character flaw (although I guess I got a couple of those, too) but because I had to. Yes, all my problems were centered and festering within the walls of this place, and if there were any answers, then those would be here too. And I still loved my wife—I had to wake her the hell up and take her away from this place.

I walked around to the back of the house, spying a window on the third floor that was reasonably close to a thick branch of the peach tree, maybe three or four feet away from it. The window was open.

After looking around for any potential snooping neighbors, I jumped up several times trying to latch onto the lowest branch that might support me. On the third try I caught it, swinging my feet to the center and pulling myself up and around into the tree's tangled but sweet smelling network of branches. I gradually made my way to a thicker hunk of wood that I hoped would bring me close enough to get in through the window with minimal risk and not too much noise, trying all the while not to look down. I was now at eye level with the window.

The throbbing at the back of my neck worsened as I looked in and I felt a swell of dizziness pass through me. I held onto my branch ever tighter, my grip seeming to weaken even so.

Their was no furniture in the room.

A grey and white cat was its only inhabitant, pacing the floor with the deliberate idleness that seems to rule the movements of all cats. My eyes bopped around the small pacing figure—there was something strange about the door, something strange about the walls, the ceiling, the floor. The doorknob was not metal or chrome or of any type that I was familiar. It was ugly and irregular. It took me about ten seconds before I realized what the doorknob was and another twenty before I was able to talk my senses into believing my eyes.

It was a human fist, sewn shut.

The throb at the back of my neck elevated its pressure into a pounding, my legs wrapping ever tightly against the tree branch.

My eyes fell away from the knob and skirted across a pattern of awful blemishes that ornamented the walls and ceiling. Every inch of the place was covered with a beige leathery material held in place with tiny carpet nails. In and around the helter-skelter patterns of nails were faces, not drawings or photographs, but actual human faces, stretched out flat and sewn onto the walls in the fashion of a patchwork quilt. There were dozens of them—faces of men, women, children—features stretched and blankly disinterested, betraying the hell of their circumstances. Their mouths were sewn shut but their glass-filled eyes sockets were round and open, seeming to acknowledge my presence, staring back at me curiously.

On the left wall was a face that I knew. It was a girl that I had known in grade school, a girl that was supposedly the first of the Bolton Hill killings. With a sense of dread, I realized that I had begun rocking back and forth against the tree branch that I was straddling. Dear God, I thought, what's wrong with me? The hole in my neck seemed to widen an tear itself open. Only the fear of being discovered kept me from crying out. An image from a dream shot into my head:

A child on a cross.

The cat stopped pacing, looked up. Hissed.

I made eye contact with the thing for a brief second before I lost my grip on the tree, falling the three floors worth to the ground of dry leaves, ripe peaches and hard earth. I began vomiting on impact.

The lingering image of Sue Dunn's bewildered, flattened expression on that hellish wall and the shock of my fall, caused me once again to struggle with consciousness.

As I lay dazed and shivering on the ground beneath the sweet smelling tree, a violent buzzing swarmed through the tiny hole in my neck and into my soul like sweet, thick honey pushing through the narrow passage of a hypodermic needle. The sensation was as intense and menacing as an army of angry bees—bees driven from their hive by a baseball bat.

I felt the feathery touch of tiny, invisible hands rolling me onto my back, invisible because my eyes had glued shut from the vomit and the wincing pain of my fall. I felt an odd breeze and realized that someone—or something—had rendered my right foot shoeless and sockless. A small wet mouth wrapped itself around the two smallest toes. A tongue rolled, sucked and then bit down hard at the pinkie toe, the pain unbearable.

I felt small fingers trying to push my lips apart, create an opening. . . . I opened my mouth to protest: bad fucking idea.

The small fingers took this opportunity to drop an object into my mouth; something small and salty, a sort of soft, irregular marble. I sucked lightly at the thing with a sort of curious horror, brushing my molars against it but refraining from a weird urge to chew. The invisible demon giggled then—a small boy's giggle—and I felt my skin crawl as I realized that the sound was coming from my own lips. There was cruelty in the laugh—not the subtle kind but the mean, unashamed kind.

A whisper then: "*you must never tell*".

The voice did not have the soft echo of dreams. The stinging brashness of reality mingled with its light, rose petal tone.

I licked at the ball of my hand and rubbed it frantically at my right eye , managed to open a single eye, winked my way into a curious focus. The culprit: a small boy, the same one I had encountered in the dream of the night before. He was standing above me now, dressed in clothes that I had worn as a child, looking down upon me with the contempt of a schoolyard bully who has just pushed a weaker child into the mud. His face was sweet beneath the cruelty, but it had been painted with the garish shades of undertaker's makeup; bright red lipstick, pinkish foundation, green eye shadow. Painted like Ida Mae's chest; like Becky's drawn on makeshift face. There was blood on the boy's cheeks blending messily with the lipstick.

The giggling boy-face drew closer to mine then, obviously relishing the fear in my eyes as it parted it's lips and spoke now with an adult woman's voice, a voice unreal coming from the lips of a boy—but one that I knew—*Janice's* voice. Breathing hard, licking bloody lips, the demon child spoke a strangely fearful word: *"gumdrop".*

With thumb and forefinger, I reached into my mouth to pull the soft object, the salty *gumdrop,* out. I held it before my spit-clean eye. It was a pinky toe. My toe.

Bawling like a babe, I doubled over on the grass, grabbing at my bleeding foot, trying idiotically to re-attach the ruined digit.

My toe stuck momentarily to my foot, glued by sticky drying blood, and then fell limply onto the grass—the show drew peels of delighted laughter from the demon child.

A new voice:

this one deep, breathy, adult and female commanded "Shoo!" and the midget villain scampered off in terror.

The woman that hovered over me now was unusually tall and primly dressed. She bent down to me and, to my foggy—headed surprise, instead of asking me what happened or who I was or if I was all right—the usual concerned stranger stuff—she hooked her hands under my armpits and lifted me to my feet, my weight teetering unevenly between the stinging four toed foot and the blessedly oblivious whole one. The creak of my aching bones, the tickly smell of pollen in my nose and the moist gum of vomit cementing my shirt to my chest reconfirmed that this was not a dream.

As I steadied myself against her shoulder, her hand reached behind me and I felt something being shoved into my back pocket. A piece of paper or an envelope. She turned me to face her, but didn't make eye contact—instead throwing a concerned glance *over* my shoulder; something or someone was approaching. The thrown glance was nervous; forced casual.

Who she was didn't sink in until her clear green eyes finally dropped down to meet mine. It was Francie—the amazon villainess from the play. Without a cruel role to play, she was beautiful and soft looking in spite of her size and obvious strength. I was no heavy-weight, but at a lean, mean 165 pounds, I wasn't a package that you would think a lady could pick up like a ragdoll, which she had just done with no fucking problem. No wonder the demon—brat, my little baby doppleganger, had am-scrayed like a bullet.

She gave me the once over, her shining eyes glowing like shimmering sea water above the smooth glossy pink of her lips. I looked at her unsteadily for a moment and suddenly broke the silence with a violent air sucking, convulsive sob, producing a snot bubble the size of a golf ball and wheezing out pitifully, like a child who'd mislaid a favorite toy, "M-m-m-my toe . . . " Great opening line.

I can be a real lady killer, you know.

AIS

CHAPTER EIGHT

BIG FACE

As she let go of me, I fell backwards from her arms and into a differ-ent, more powerful set of arms, the owner of which reeked of a particularly bad brand of cheap men's cologne. It was a smell that I knew; the stink of mean-spirited, small-time authority. The mouth that belonged to the new, strange arms and offensive odor grunted noisily in response to my shivering dead weight.

"Get his shoe, Kevin," spoke the arms, smell and mouth that kept me from cruel gravity and blunt, grassy ground. "Friend of yours, Miss?" This last bit was directed at Francie the Amazon.

"No, officer. I was just walking past and saw him lying there. I'm sort of in a hurry, would it be all right if I—"

"Any idea what happened?" Officer Arms wasn't ready to let it go like Francie was hoping. Cops obviously gave her the jitters.

"No. Like I said, I was just —"

"Did you see any suspicious person or persons, some one who might have been the attacker?" Impatient but cordial.

"No." A lie.

"All right." I couldn't see his face, but I felt the chill of his searching stare graze my ear as it filled the dead air of his pause. "Sorry for the trouble. If you can think of anything at all call Central District and ask for Detective Black. Grab his feet, Kevin, we're taking him down for questioning."

What—no ambulance? No emergency room? No fucking "you ok, buddy?" Of course with the steady loss of blood, the shock, etcetera, etcetera.. my mouth wasn't in shape for forming words of protest or of any other sort. Francie walked away quickly, correctly fearing that the slightest hesitation would give the detective time for more questions.

As the two men hoisted me into an unmarked blue Sedan, I cracked my wincing eyelids long enough to get a good look at the cop called Kevin who, with his arms looped under my knees, looked at me like a kid beholding the amazing-but-true three headed goat at a circus sideshow.

"Jeez, Detective Black. . . ain't this the guy — that fella who done all those—"

"Shut up, Kirkwood. Just get him in." Detective Black spoke with the self-righteous edginess of a person in power who had just been caught breaking his own rules and didn't much care for it being brought to his attention. As I quietly considered the recent sentence that Kirkwood had not been allowed to finish, it occurred to me, with a little amusement, that since Black's arrival there hadn't been a sentence started that wasn't cut off in its prime by this razor tongued bull. Undaunted by this fact, Officer Kevin Kirkwood attempted to continue:

"Shouldn't we take him to E.R.? Doesn't look like the bleeding's slowed up any and . . ."

I bounced gently on the springy cushion of the backseat, my shoe thoughtfully tossed in after me. The slamming of the car door kept me from knowing for sure whether Black had let Kirkwood finish that last sentence, but I'd bet a bundle that he hadn't. I gingerly placed two hands;

eight fingers and two thumbs over the place on my foot that used to have a small, round toe on it. The action seemed to stifle the flow of blood, but my pinching fingers also succeeded in embellishing the not-so-groovy rhythm of pain there. My eyes filled up with wet salt and the skin of my face turned to concrete. My gritting teeth grinded slowly as if meaning to chip and flake enamel.

The ride to the station was short and bumpy.

A beefy lady cop xknelt before me in the holding cell, dressing my poor tootsie with the tender loving care of a scout up for a merit badge in noose tying.

"Do you know who I am?" Black asked the question casually as he breezed in the door of the holding room; so casually that I wasn't sure if the question was directed at myself or Florence Nighting-mare.

The lady cop added a final rope burning yank to her work, very pleased with herself and twittered in a high, musical, elfish vibrato, "That should hold you!"

She stood up and glided behind me on tiny feet that handled her bulky form admirably. Black's eyes remained fixed and impatient in my direction, waiting for an answer.

What he really wanted to know was had I read a fucking newspaper lately—he had made himself a big name and a big face for being the bloodhound on the trail of the Bolton Hill Butcher. As you know, I had recently been updated on that very case. In fact, I had joined the cast in a starring role.

"Sure I know who you are, chief. You're Clark Gable. And I'm Lana Turner. How's about a smooch?"

The rubber hose that smacked the side of my head had a small metal nozzle on the end of it that reverberated against my skull with a *thwack:* like the sound of two heavy, damp chunks of wood slamming together in a freight yard.

"Show some respect to the Detective, Mr. So-and-So, or you'll get another. And I've got better things to do than sitting around bandaging up your boo-boos on a count of your big-"

"Thank you, Martha," interrupted the Detective in a kind of good natured annoyance, "but I'll let you know if I feel that sort of er.. rough handling is warranted. It may be that Mr. Dellus' flippant attitude is the product of the unusually bad day that he's been having."

"But this is the guy that's been-"

"*Thank* you, Martha," his stern glance shut her up righteous quick, "but I'm fully aware of who and what Mr. Dellus is. Now if you'll please stand right outside the door so we can have a few words in private. I'll call out if I need you."

"But—"

Another cold glance from Black and she was out the door.

He grinned at me, amused it seemed, by Officer Martha's school marmish brutality. "I hope you'll pardon Officer McLearnon's enthusiasm for her job. I'm afraid she's been personally touched by your case—the mother of the Dunn girl was an old school chum of her's—they had glee club together or some such crapola."

He stood for a moment, propping up his elbow with his right hand so he could rub his chin contemplatively in just the right way.

"May I be frank, Dellus?"

"No. You may be Clark. And I may be Lana. And if you don't kiss me this very minute I'll just die." Yeah, I was just making matters worse by being a snot, but I guess I figured I was a done duck on his way to the chair and how could it get worse really? Plus, he was right—I was having a hell of a day and I was starting to get cranky.

"Pardon my coyness," he said as he bent down to face me, grabbing my head in two heavy hands that felt like sandpaper against my ears, pushing his mouth against mine. I began to call out in shock and revulsion as his tongue pushed through between my teeth, a huge, dry sticky worm that twisted muscularly in my mouth, sopping up spit. I felt a wiggle of nausea in my gut as nose hairs tickled the side of my left nostril, my arms and legs squirmed and flailed spastically until finally my body managed to twist itself out of the chair, pulling myself away, forcing the awful tongue out. Before releasing my head though, Black latched onto my lower lip momentarily, biting hard.

I tasted salt. I tasted pretzels and beer. I tasted a ham sandwich with mustard.

I lay on the ground retching so hard that I thought I would puke through my huge stinging eyeballs. Outside I could here the sound of soulless giggling and looking up I saw Fat Martha peeking in through the small square window located at the top of the grey cell door.

"Get cute with me? I can get cute, too." Black paused as I got out the last of my dry heaves. He stood like a statue in judgment licking blood off its concrete chin. "So tell me Dellus. How does a five year old kid get it in his head to fuck an old lady's corpse?"

I only half heard this last comment as I made a comic grab for the back of the steel chair in an attempt to get to my feet, raising myself only two inches before thumping solidly back to the hard floor. My grip on the heavy chair failed to loosen in the fall, twisting my wrist around backwards for the split second or so before pain signaled me to let it fall—its metal clanging inspiring renewed hilarity from the one woman peanut gallery in the small square window. Black yanked me up by the wrist in one brutal motion, dislocating my shoulder. I steadied myself on the table with my good arm, trying not to breathe too hard, trying not to appear as weak as I felt. I nonchalantly pushed my shoulder back into joint with an inaudible pop. Black's question sat on the outskirts of my brain, triggering a defense mechanism that sent my thoughts in a circle like a line of covered wagons getting ready to fend off injuns.

An old lady's corpse.

Oh yeah. Right. So the good detective wanted to help me work out my childhood traumas. Or rub my face in them. I couldn't think of a smart ass reply and even if I had a zinger I probably wouldn't have had the guts to let it fly just then. I just looked at him, waiting to see where he was going with it all.

"Kids can do some weird shit I guess, given the wrong circum-stances, the wrong surroundings," he spoke to me now in an even, patronly tone that seemed designed to sooth my recently frayed trust in the justice system. "I've seen some terrible things done by small kids because of the wrong surroundings that they were brought up in. Terrible things.

"Once investigated a murder case where a nine year old girl took a hammer to her baby brother's skull—she was brought up by folks who ran a slaughter house, you understand. Said she was just playing. Playing 'Mommy and Baby Veal' or some such wacko shit. Most little girls who want to pretend to be like their mothers play with lipstick and high heels. But that wasn't the example that this particular little girl had put before her, see. Pretty little girl too. Green eyes. Yellow hair. Sweetest face you ever saw. Never did understand that what she did was wrong. Damn shame."

He paused as if waiting for me to respond. "Damn shame," I echoed.

"Yeah, you bet," he continued. "Now, growing up in a morgue like you did . . ."

"Funeral home", I corrected.

"Right, right—funeral home. That's a situation that I can easily imagine twisting the mind—uh—let's say *affecting* the behavior—of a young adolescent male. I mean there you are—a young buck starting to get that nagging feeling in your balls for the first time, maybe with no access to girls your own age or, hey, maybe you just can't get anywhere with the ones you do have access to. Who's to say that any other young awkward kid with hormones jumping around in his pants might not feel a little temptation what with all those dolled up lady corpses lying around not protesting or seeming to mind a little sexual curiosity on your part. I guess I can see how something like that could happen, how it might even be considered explainable—especially if the kid in question lacks a certain amount of parental guidance, of moral understanding. Yeah, for a teenage boy with a hard-on, cooped up in a human meat locker—"

"Funeral home."

"Uh, that's right, funeral home—stuck in a place like that since he was a baby—I guess I can see how that sort of behavior can be interpreted as, well, tragic really. Not evil or malicious at all. Just a reaction to a warped view of the world that he had no control over. A little sick, sure, but curable, right?"

He leaned down enough so that he could talk lightly into my ear, a hand on my shoulder. "But we're not talking about a teenage boy here are we? No. We're talking about a fucking five year old. We're talking about a child without hair one on his dick, a kid with no business thinking thoughts about women in that way at all. And we're talking about cannibalism, too. That's what I don't get, Casanova. That's what makes me sick to my Goddamn stomach."

I sensed that this dramatic little oratorio would be building into a climax peppered with a little police brutality about now; maybe a coldcock to the chin or a broken finger to punctuate his disapproval of my childhood exploits. I tensed for the fireworks but caught a gust of salty air instead as Black heaved a troubled sigh.

"But I've seen it. Can't explain it. No, no, don't get me wrong, I can not explain these things. But I've seen it before. Seen it and seen it.

"Little children. Little children who feel things and do things that they should be incapable of, that they should have no knowledge of. Something terrible must have happened to them, to the little children. Something that triggers a part of the brain that should be left alone. Left alone or taken out completely. Like I said, I can not explain these things but I do wonder. But explaining and wondering is not part of my job. I'm a cop. Cops are garbage men. We get paid to collect the garbage and bring it into the dump. We clean the streets, make them sanitary. We aren't paid to ponder and judge—no, that's the job of other, more qualified minds. And sometimes these men that sit in judgment tell the garbage men to put the garbage back out on the street where they found it, as if doing so might change the garbage into something else—a pot of gold or, hell, maybe just a rock or a stick or something that's not so damn offensive. I don't pretend to understand why these decisions are made, but I do what I'm told and many's the time that I've put the garbage back on the street. And many's the time that that same garbage has gone on to cause more grief and suffering. And I'll tell you, Dellus, there have been plenty of times that the garbage starts out as little children who never should have felt the things that made them do the terrible things that they did. And the garbage that they become infects other little children who grow into garbage that is taken off the street, put back on the street, taken off—it's a cycle, you see, it goes around and around.."

Black was getting a might melancholy in his rambling, sure, but I was starting to like where all this talk of putting the garbage back on the street seemed to be going. Was he implying that he had been ordered to let me go? Had the real killer been found? Just as things began to get interesting, though, he changed course entirely.

"Tell me, Dellus, have you ever heard of a narcotic called POP?"

"Nope".

"Stands for Pseudoeuphoric Opiotic Phenylalanine. Took me a week to learn how to say that. Not surprised you haven't heard of it, though—it's kind of new on the market, hasn't even made the market actually, real exclusive stuff it is . . ."

"So what's it got to do with me? I mean—"

". . . it's funny to think now of how it came to be." As if I hadn't spoken. "What it was supposed to be. Something entirely different from what it is now. Funny thing.

"See, there was this doctor, a famous doctor, and something awful happened to this doctor's family. He had a son who was only five—the boy was kidnapped. Missing. I was in charge of that case—the chief assigned me twenty of his best men—an unusual number for a simple missing persons case. But simple it wasn't; the doctor was high profile and pals with the mayor to boot so the case was a real red ball; and the media latched its slimy teeth into it accordingly. Cases like that get special treatment. Was hell on the family, the way the media played it up. Twenty detectives. And we never found a clue. Nada.

"Inside a week the boy's body was found. His arms and legs had been carefully cut off then sewn back on with fishing line. His torso was cut neatly in two, also sewn back together. His mouth had been carved into a huge grin, eye to eye, and his genitals had been scraped off with a device that might have been a steel bristled scrub brush. The techs who examined the body decided that the killer had kept the boy alive for most of the mutilation—they decided this because of the bruises. Corpses don't bruise, you understand.

"Garvey", I said, recognizing the details of the case. The details of how Janice's little brother, Ronnie, had been killed. The murder, unsolved, had happened twenty-one years ago.

"Garvey. Yes." Black's eyes had reddened. He continued:

"So, Dr. Garvey became suddenly very distracted from his work as an anesthesiologist hotshot at Hopkins, switched his focus on the field of psychiatric medicine. To be more specific, he had begun researching the behavior patterns of psychotics, sexual psychotics in particular. Strange how a scientific mind works, don't you think? Most guys would be tearing themselves apart from the inside out, blaming themselves, wanting revenge, hating God Almighty Himself. Not Garvey. Nope. Garvey wanted to understand why. How it could have happened, what could have prevented it, what might keep it from happening again. Mrs. Garvey was a bit more conventional in how she dealt with her grief, more conventional but less practical, I should say. She hung herself. Little girl found her. Your wife was only nine at the time. I'm sorry." His sympathies were strictly insincere; and I responded with appropriate cold silence. He went on without a blink:

"After about a year's studies, searching for extreme examples of sexually oriented murder in nature, Garvey found nothing, save for old faithful; the black widow spider. But the black widow doesn't really fit the bill—sure it fucked and killed all at once—but it was hardly conscious of the act, there was no pleasure in it, no excitement. No, to the black widow, its mating practice is about as evil as taking a leak, strictly motor functions, you understand. Then Garvey came across an obscure article in a zoological journal. An article about a little dog who lived half way across the world—Australia, no less.

"Garvey didn't waste time arranging to have a pack of the things shipped to his university lab,—which the Aussies gladly did since this particular critter, it turns out, was a damn nuisance to the local farmers, a leading cause of lost livestock revenue. Hurting profits and making a damn mess in the process.

"Spotted hyena." Black stopped to clear his throat noisily and rub his left eye with the ball of his palm. He looked tired, repeated himself; "Spotted hyena. They're everywhere down there. Come down out of the mountains in droves. Wander into the villages sometimes, although they don't seem to have a taste for humans. Nope, mainly just livestock; cows and whatnot. Damn nuisance, they are." I wondered absently about how what should have been an interrogation had turned into a lecture on Australian wildlife. Neither option was much pleasant, but I appreciated not being the subject of conversation. I didn't interrupt.

"Garvey became interested in the animal because of its unusual mating practices. Like the black widow, the female kills the male during mating. Unlike the black widow, it is not the death of the male that is essential to the ritual, but the *act* of killing.

"The ritual begins calmly, the female circling the male slowly, seducing him with her scent. She circles him—waiting for him to make the first move." He paused, snickered, said: "Guess some things are universal in the animal kingdom.

"Finally, when he can resist her no longer, he mounts her; she is still just long enough to receive him, to become impregnated. When he is finished, she shakes him off. This is where it gets interesting." A thoughtful pause and then: "—I mean, for Garvey's scientific purposes.

"The female engages in something that resembles what we humans recognize as foreplay, only in reverse. Happening after the fact instead of before, that is.

"She wraps herself around him with all four paws, and proceeds to lick at his genitals. Most dogs I know are happy to lick their own, but I'm not qualified to have an opinion in these matters. A zoologist I am not. The male squirms to get away, sensing, the way guys can sense such things, what's about to happen. He can not get away. She eats his balls.

"The male is now still, in shock from loss of blood—among other things—and the female can move freely about her business. She gnaws at the joints of his legs, dismembering him gradually, seeming to know just how much damage she must do to get the job done and yet keep him alive. She chews away the paws first, then sections of the leg, a tail, an ear. She rubs her privates against his gushing wounds all the while; it is not pretty. The ritual can last for hours depending on the strength of the male. It always ends with more cannibalism, the female consuming as much of the carcass as she can stomach.

"Garvey observed the ritual many times under a controlled environment in his lab at the university until he understood how. Then he got to work on why. He went into the female's brain.

"He found a chemical in there that seemed to stimulate violent behavior when a surge in hormonal activity—sexual arousal in the female, that is—occurs. By isolating this chemical of the brain and mixing it manually with the female's hormonal fluids, Garvey was able to come up with a working model of the catalyst for sexual violence in the spotted hyena. He studied it, knowing that if he were to understand what caused such behavior, that he was much more likely to find a way to control it, to prevent it, possibly reverse it. I think he hoped to come up with some sort of vaccine for sexual deviants. Maybe that's what was intended. I think it was . . ." The last two sentences trailed off into mumble—land. He scratched his chin for a moment and continued:

"This infant version of POP was first used in test studies on rats, then cats; dogs, then monkeys—the usual food chain of science. The result was the frenzied behavior typical of the spotted hyena with one significant variable; the more intelligent the test subject, the more cruel its methods of violence seemed to be—and the more clever it was in finding ways to keep its victim alive and conscious longer. The chimps were the worst. They could keep there hapless counterparts alive, bleeding and screaming for days sometimes. I've seen things, I can tell you. Terrible, terrible things.

"But that's not the worst of it," he said, perspiring visibly now in the cool cell. He rubbed gingerly at the back of his neck as he spoke, "the worst of it was the dependency factor. All of the test animals suffered from acute withdrawal symptoms only twelve hours or so after the completion of their psychotic episode." He grinned at his shoes.

The grin vanished: "You've had about six hours sleep. You spent about an hour and a half chatting with that freak and then strolling around town." I didn't get it.

Then I did.

Maxa and the kiss in the dark. Her hand brushing the back of my neck and the stinging sensation there. My loss of consciousness and the dream. Maxa had injected me with this POP crap.

The dream. It had been a waking dream, a dream of psychosis. But what had my body done while the dream played in my head. How had I satisfied the mating ritual of the spotted hyena?

"You have about four and a half hours before you begin to feel it. Headaches. It always starts with headaches." He spoke the last sentence through gritted teeth, watery eyes.

I can be a little slow sometimes.

It dawned on me that I hadn't been brought into the station house to face charges at all. I was brought here because I had unwittingly become a part of something big and ugly.

Something that stank to high heaven.

"Someone doesn't want you touched," he went on. "I didn't pick you up to beat a confession out of you. Hell, anyone that knows this case from the inside knows you ain't it. Doesn't fit. You're the victim of a prank." Officer McLearnon giggled oafishly through the glass. When I looked up she ducked down and out of view like a bad child hiding just outside the kitchen with a stolen cookie.

"I picked you up because you didn't have the sense to stay down. It's better for everyone if you stay out of sight right now. It's better if it is believed that you are the killer and that you have eluded custody."

"Whoa, big fella. You mean to tell me—"

"Do you visit your mother, Dellus?" His eyes turned black and drilled through a space in the middle of my forehead. "Do you? Didn't think so. Don't suppose you'd have much to say. You put her in that place, you know."

He was talking about Spring Grove, the state asylum. My mom got real sick a while back. Mental troubles.

"She doesn't know me anymore," I offered weakly. "She doesn't recognize me. There's no use—"

"She never knew you. Never knew that her son was capable of the things that you did, that you were committing those crimes right under her nose. I remember your case—got a snicker out of it at the time.

"Your father admitted to the police that he knew about the desecrated corpses but he thought that there were rats in the cellar, that the rats had done those very strange, umm . . . *things* to the bodies. How could he have known the truth. The awful truth about his own five year old son. How could anyone imagine such a thing, let alone suspect it.

"The strange part—or should I say the strangest part—was how the authorities found out. How was that Dellus? How'd they find out?"

"I told them."

"You told them. You came forward. You confessed. When no one even suspected that such a thing was going on. You could have gone undetected forever—how could it get out? But you just came right out and—"

"I needed help! I thought if I went to the police—"

"Needed help? Why didn't you go to your parents for help? Why the police?" I was shaking, couldn't respond. "Answer, damn you!"

"Because . . . because. . . ." I began weeping uncontrollably. "I hated them. I wanted to hurt them. They were killing me.. it was killing me. My father, he.. he.."

"He caught you. Isn't that right? He caught you by surprise one night when you thought you were alone, when you thought they were safely upstairs. He saw you with a body. And you were naked, weren't you? Naked with the corpse of a woman, isn't that right?"

". . . . yes."

"And what did he do to you? Did he beat you?"

"No . . ."

"Did he threaten you, did he shout?"

"No . . ."

"Well, Jesus, man, he musta done or said something.. what was it?"

He would never have bought the truth:

My father looked at me. He looked at me not with anger or disgust, but with sadness. Sadness and guilt and love. And then he spoke: "Dear God, forgive me. I have done this. I have done this to my boy." Then he hugged me and held me and cleaned me and clothed me. Then he told me that it wasn't my fault and that he was sorry and that he would shut down the funeral home and take us far away from there, some place where a boy can grow up normal. Then he told me that he loved me, loved me more than life itself, and as he held me in his arms and rocked me, he prayed out loud to God. And as he prayed, he cried.

"He did nothing," I said.

"He tried to protect you, to hide what you did, what any parent would have done. And you double crossed him. You went to the cops knowing that it would be hardest on your folks. Your mother had no clue about your shenanigans until the cops came to pick her and your father up for questioning. At first she didn't believe it, but after the truth finally set in she became catatonic. She hasn't spoken a word since then. Your father had to take the blunt of the publicity on his own. His business was burnt to the ground by the family members of your victims.

"After the court's decision to lock you away in a ward for criminally disturbed children until your eighteenth birthday, your father moved to another city, another state. There was no future for him here. You left him with nothing."

That was true. As far as I know, my father is to this day a janitor for a low income housing development in some place called Liverpool, Ohio. I know this because he had written to me. Once.

I never wrote back.

CHAPTER NINE

THE MATING RITUAL OF THE SPOTTED HYENA

Maxa picked me up from the station in the black Lincoln and no words passed between us on the ride back to The Big Punch.

Black had informed me that I would be staying at a room in the theater house where I was to remain discretely "at large" in the custody of Redd and Garvey until things were straightened out. I wasn't exactly sure what straightened out meant in Black's twisted world, but I was pretty sure that the influential person who didn't want me touched had to be Garvey himself. He wanted me cleared, in due time, of course, for the sake of his daughter, my wife.

Maxa pulled the car noisily onto a gravel alley peppered with reddish brown leaves that ran alongside the big house and got out, leading me in through the front door. Her heels clicked loud on the hard wood floors of the house's roomy, circular entrance area—not the way I'd remembered the place at all. Everything about it seemed so foreign to me now, foreign from the times not so long ago when Janice's dad would have us over for dinner and a game of cards. The man struck me as so passive and gentle then, and the big house always seemed so quiet. It was strange to think of the freak parade that had no doubt surrounded us from above and below while we chatted and flicked the little peanuckle deck in the thoroughly modern kitchen at ground level. Stranger still to think that Janice had lived there so many years and had not known. Had she known? How much had she known?

Maxa glided through the room and up the circular staircase, motioning for me to follow. On the third floor landing, she made her way down the hallway with a brisk pace that my weary sack of bones didn't feel particularly obligated to keep up with. She looked mighty annoyed when I stopped momentarily to eyeball an antique suit of armor perched about halfway through the hall; all yellow brass plating and silver chain mail. Museum stuff; fancy and expensive. Janice's dad seemed to have no problem spending cash by the bucketful on useless junk. Held sternly to the left side of the thing was a beautifully preserved gold and silver sword, a wolf's head molded intricately into the handle. It was sure some piece of work, but something about it gave me a sinking feeling.

After I'd soaked up about twenty seconds taking in the metal gorilla suit, Maxa cleared her throat noisily and I parted company with the thing to follow her once more, only vaguely curious about where we were going. We walked four doors past the sword side of the armor before she stopped to twist a knob.

The decor of the room was tame in comparison to the opulent knick-knacks of the living room and hallway. The hardwood floor had a large, round, Chinese rug tossed crookedly in the center of it. The wallpaper was equally modest; yellowing white with a modern deco pattern of green bars and triangles striping it vertically. The walls held no paintings or decoration of any kind; only a single electric light fixture protruded from its surface above a small writing desk and chair. The light made me very aware of, though not surprised by, the absence of a window. Windows seemed to be a commodity in this joint, at least from the inside. The only other bit of furniture present was a comfy looking single bed, topped with fresh white sheets and a soft, worn red blanket. My aching back shook at the sight of the thing, and I plopped into it without invitation, elbow first.

"It's not much but it'll have to do," she said with the same irritating blankness that she had displayed in Redd's office. It was as if we had never had that conversation in the dark, as if we had never kissed, as if she didn't owe me some kind of explanation for sticking my neck with that poison. "Am I gonna have to lock this or are you gonna stay put?"

"Whatever, lady," I deadpanned back, letting my bones settle into the mattress and my eyes settle into the simple patterns conjured by the rug's thick, plain thread.

"Look, " she said softly, "I'm sorry that things are the way they are. I can't change them any more than you can. You don't know the half of it so don't go judging me." A pained pause. Then: "Try to get some rest." She didn't say see ya later as she moved for the door, but she did say: "I'm stuck. You're stuck. We're all just stuck with it. Maybe things'll change. Maybe things'll get better. I'm sorry you got mixed up in it. I didn't mean for that to happen, although I guess somebody else might have."

I should have been moved by the sudden return of Maxa's tender side and I admit that the idea of grabbing her by the shoulders and kissing her hard took a stroll through my libido. But this trollop had infected me and I knew that she couldn't be trusted. I dropped the ice-face, though; it's an odd instinct of mine to always respond to an apology with a counter—apology, even when none is warranted. I don't know why, it's just a sort of irrational sense of courtesy that my mother drilled into me when I was a sprout, I guess. I fumbled, unprepared, into that direction:

"Well, gee, I'm sorry too I guess.. I mean I'm real sorry that, uh—". I pondered the rug like an idiot for several long seconds.

"Yes?" she said grinning, enjoying my awkward stab at making friends in the infuriating way that women seem to enjoy awkwardness in men. I admit that I can be a little over sensitive if I think I'm being made sport of, and when that happens, I can get pretty ugly with my mouth:

"I'm sorry I caved your boyfriend's head in," I said coolly, wanting to wipe her grin out of my eyes. Instead, it only stretched wider.

"Boyfriend? Man, you really are confused! Boyfriend? Imagine that!"

She closed the door and I could hear her laughter fading as she moved down the hallway, back to the stairway where we had come from. She left the door unlocked, figuring, correctly, that it wouldn't make much difference—the door was light and if I wanted out I would just break the damn thing down.

I didn't want out just then though. I wanted to lie down, rest my eyes and listen to the quiet of the small cozy room. I wanted to try to conjure a little quiet in my wrecked soul if I could—even if just for a short while. I had no intention of sleeping, but as soon as my eyes closed, I began to dream.

But not dream, really.

I mean I was wide awake with my eyes closed and suddenly I was staring into the face of the singing preacher man that I had seen at Penn Station that day. His eyes were clear, gentle, sad, righteous. Blind, blind, blind:

don't dream now, boy. there's no time for it. those girls of mine got troubles—they need you. five days, boy. thass it. five to make it right, five to fall or fly, sink or swim, do or die, shine or dim, feast or fry, read or skim. open 'em boy, open dem baby browns. gotta piss out that evil in ya an' do some good . . .

My eyes slammed open. My head was throbbing.

You might not be able to relate, but there's nothing more annoying than a damn ghost sticking his face into your closed, tired eyeballs, talking in riddles. If you got something to say, make it plain, I always say. Being from a Goddamn spirit world doesn't make it right.

The ghost had made me restless, anyway.

I sat up, stood up, made my way to the door, turned the knob. The door opened and I heard a sound. It was a gasping, sucking sound—low in pitch but female. Couldn't tell if it was pleasure or pain that I was hearing, but I was feeling a little bit lonesome and at least it was a human sound. I had no particular place in mind destination-wise, so I wandered out and after it.

The sound took me deeper into the hallway, getting louder as my feet carried me. I must've been pretty close to its source when I came across another little decoration that interrupted my progress in the same way that the suit of armor had. This was not a museum piece, though.

It was a small table, pushed up against the wall beneath a large oval, bronze framed mirror, holding a flower arrangement and a small, ornately framed photograph. The photograph was of Janice. The flowers were orange and yellow. She was more beautiful in the picture than she was in life, her features having been smoothed out and tinted with birthday cake pink and violet, a sparkle of perfect green in her pretty if somewhat dumb-looking eyes. Her expression was radiant and sad and I had a hard time deciphering how much of it had been the creation of the touch up artist. I decided that there was a part of it that was real, a part that I recognized. The sucking sound intensified then and my eyes fell away from the picture.

And landed on a door that was painted black.

And on the black door an image had been painted in white. Two faces had been melted together in the image, one above the other. The bottom face was the face of a woman, passive and seductive, her eyes clear and thoughtful, thin lips closed in a straight unsmiling line. The top face was the face of a monster. Its cold dead eyes sat without emotion, surrounded by cracked, wrinkling flesh, hovering over a fleshy lump of a nose. A sinister, toothy smile sported too many teeth directly above the woman's placid eyes and each tooth was sharpened to a point. The monster's chin and the woman's forehead were of the same flesh in the painting, which sat in the center of the door like some kind of unholy seal, a warning against trespassers. As if to make the impression of foreboding just a bit clearer, the door was knobless on the hall side. Without thinking, I placed my hand on the jaw of the monster and applied a little weight. To my surprise, the door swung inward without a squeak. I wasn't surprised to see what room the door opened into; the room of flesh and faces and nails that I had spied from the peach tree. But I was surprised to see it inhabited by a creature other than the grey cat, surprised also to realize that I recognized the kneeling woman instantly—even though she had her back to me. Since my voyeuristic experience on the peach tree, someone had shuttered the lone window with heavy, black-painted wood and the kind of nails that Chinese immigrants use to fasten a piece of railroad to the earth. Peeping tom prevention to the extreme.

A naked bulb swung subtly above the equally naked figure of Francie the Amazon, causing her shadow to circle her body slightly on the weird texture of the flesh covered floor. Her yellow, shining hair lay loose around her shoulders, matting stickily to her sweat slicked back as her left hand pinched her heavy breasts together, kneading in rhythm with her hips and the pained sound of sucking air through perfect teeth that had guided me through the hall. Her right hand held something between her legs, something that she held still as her hips rode back and forth over it, plunging and pulling. She had not noticed my entrance.

The image triggered something in me, something deep and ugly; beyond primitive. Something that was awakened by the POP coursing through my veins . . .

Without warning, my brain screamed and swam in my skull and I felt my knees go wobbly—it was the exact sensation I'd experienced on the night Maxa injected me with my initial dose of the stuff. The pain in my head sizzled and sung in ugly harmony with my rocking legs. As my temperature rose swiftly, a perverse symphony of urges fired in me, urges that surprised and revolted my quickly scramming senses. Images of spotted hyenas danced dimly through my consciousness as the drug's strange effects caught up with me—as Black had promised they would. The need that the drug imposed—or drew out—the need of the spotted hyena, was one that I could neither comprehend nor fight nor stomach. The desire that it flushed through my gut and groin was not of the garden variety man lusts over woman kind, you see—it was a desire to destroy, to tear with my nails and teeth, to devour.

It must have been God Almighty Himself, I thought, who forced a momentary light into my rapidly blackening soul, sweet Jesus who caused me to turn on my heel and reach for the fist—knob. Francie was still too preoccupied to notice my presence; if I could pull my body away, I could just leave.

I saw the grey cat in the corner of the room as I turned to leave. The grey cat with white feet.

My uninvited presence in the room, its home, had apparently broken the intense concentration that a cat needs to accomplish a good tongue bath. The cat glared at me, throwing a hearty hiss my way to display its annoyance.

The sound of the angry pussycat turned Francie the Amazon's attention to me—her right leg lifting just enough to spin her weight around on her left knee. Facing me now, her reddened, dilated eyes locked onto mine as her lungs sucked a terrible gasp that held hard to her lungs for an unbreakable, rubbery moment. The tiny silence between gasps amplified the stifling heat of the room, the heat welling in my own body, sloshing like an oil fire through my veins.

The cat returned to its bath, oblivious and cool.

I stared in shivery wonder as Francie pulled the thing from between her legs slowly, a long dagger of polished wood, carved jaggedly on the sides from tip to base and rounded at both ends. It looked like the kind of ancient ritual knife that might turn up in one of those "weird tales" detective comics; "Incredible Tales of Torture by Ungodly Black Magic Instruments in Darkest Africa! WARNING: Not for the Squeamish!". The thing shook in her trembling hands, droplets of red fluid falling lightly onto the skinfloor. The smell of blood reawakened the overwhelming suggestions posed by the narcotic in my system—and I took a step forward . . .

A flash of humanity crossed her face then, and with it, eyes heavy with tears. Of terror? Pain? Remorse? I'll never be able to answer that, I guess. Just as suddenly, though, the red eyed animal created by the drug returned to her face, seeming to sizzle the tears into salty steam.

Her hard gaze paralyzed my movement, making me unaware of anything but the red and grey intensity of her eyes. A thick pink tongue lolled out of the formerly lovely mouth—with the slightest trace of foam—and licked at dry lips in one sweeping, slow circle.

As she dropped the wooden dagger, her hands lifted up to her waist, placing long, sharpened nails lightly onto smoothly muscled hips. The tips of her index fingers dragged up and along the curve of her waist and ribcage, following the swell of her breasts with a thin red line that did not quite draw blood. The pointed nails then circled her nipples once—lightly—as her wet tongue completed its circle, slowly painting her upper lip with moisture. With sudden pressure, the finger tips pushed hard into the round pattern that had been drawn there, and circles of fresh blood appeared. She closed her eyes tight and pulled her hands away from her body quickly, as if the wound had been inflicted by some other force, a force that the core of her soul, however dope—blurred, intended to fight. Eyes again open; a thick smile of cruelty regaining control of the battlefield that her face had become. Tiny droplets of blood trickled from her breasts. Her palms slapped with bruising force onto her injured chest and pushed up hard, causing blood to well between her fingers as she once again pulled in the heavy hot air of the room between clenched teeth with a hiss. The hiss trailed off into a word that, for me, severed her soul from humanity with a snip:

gumdrop.

I realized then, at that moment, that this girl—a girl who had probably wanted to be an actress or a model or something glamorous but who took a wrong turn somewhere, a girl who was, in any case, extremely beautiful however extremely lost—had become something that was not human.

My brain hollered for me to bolt, but my nine toes yielded to the madness of the POP that wrecked reason and threw me forward into the center of the hellish room towards *it*.

The Francie Thing rose to its feet like a flash and side stepped me with the surefootedness of a bullfighter, giggling its amusement as I fell like a sack of rocks to the floor.

The Francie Thing began to move around me slow then, a big cat on the stalk, smeared blood and sweat marking its tensed body like some kind of grim tribal war paint. As its feet padded out their silent circle around me, I locked its eyes to mine, trying to estimate how quick and devastating the monster's reflexes might be, knowing that any sudden movement might cause it to spring.

I fought hard with the narcotic driven desire that shoved its way through me, the desire to make the first move, to lunge.

The snarling animal inside me barked hoarsely at the weakening threads of reason lingering in my soul, demanding surrender.

I can't remember how long I held out before I caved in to the voice of the drug in my veins, but I only got so far as a twitch before The Francie Thing responded to my sudden movement, taking one long step back, then leaping forwards into the space between me and it with a dive, its long, lean form sailing onto the floor in a forward somersault, landing several feet before me in a hand stand with a light thump. Balancing topsy turvy on its hands for a moment, the creature bent elbows slowly and dipped, head just touching the floor—then pushed hard at the ground, catapulting its straightened legs feet first in my direction. Before making contact, the legs swung open and around my midsection, holding tight. Somehow I kept my balance, avoiding the inevitable fall backwards into the wall of dead, stitched faces. I felt its powerful thighs shut swiftly and tightly, winding me bad while the monster's arms repositioned on the floor below to support the weight of its upper body. The Francie Thing's ankles locked behind me in an instant, giving it the leverage needed to exert full pressure, and I heard a crackling sound come from my spine as I squirmed in its grip, struggling to pull unwilling air into my lungs. Maintaining the crushing force of its scissor hold, The Francie Thing methodically arched its spine backwards into a sharp curve, rolling its head beneath its body. Before the head of The Thing disappeared completely from view, I watched the milky grey irises of its eyes roll up and out of sight, exposing hard, tense yellow-white. Foam bubbled and hissed from between its teeth.

Just as the already tingling feeling in my legs was beginning to dissolve into numbness, The Thing's iron leg-lock loosened. Desperately, I sucked at the air. Before I could get a chestful, the scissor hold resumed at full force, pushing the air out and filling my head again with hot blood. The room swerved and dipped as my body gave up its struggle and went limp, falling sideways. The Thing released me before I hit the floor.

As I lay curled on my back, holding onto my gut with my knees pulled up to my chin, I gulped wildly at the hot air of the skinroom. I heard a heavy *thudthud* and my wincing eyes pulled open enough to find two bare feet planted firmly at either side of my head. Panting slightly,

The Thing squatted down to face me and whispered once again, half-grinning: *"gumdrop"*. Still squatting, it threw its hands above its head, causing its long spine again to arch unnaturally and the air to fill with a hellish hiss. With whiplike motion, The Thing threw its arms in the direction of the floor but missed, palms slapping, instead, hard and loud onto my ears. I felt a warm wetness as its nails pushed into the sides of my scalp. My own warm blood trickled gently into my ears.

Then, and with surprisingly little pain, a popping sensation exploded at the base of my neck as my head was yanked upwards, my body following limply through the air until my face stopped the sudden rush of movement by smacking hard into the cartilage of another face—a face that was sewn into the wall's patch quilt of death.

Before I could bounce back down to the floor, The Francie Thing was on me again, twisting my left arm behind me hard, bringing me from a crouch to a full stand. I felt its tongue and teeth pressing against the back of my skull, breaking skin and shoving my face into the wall harder still, the sound of its tongue lapping the blood from my hair and ears all I could hear, turning my stomach, deafening. The cool leathery softness of its lips shoved their way up to mine then, forcing tiny nail heads to scrape at my cheeks. My wincing eyes struggled to open, to focus.

Sue Dunn's glassy stare surveyed my terror disinterestedly.

Forgetting to scream, a shot of energy erupted within me, pushing my body away from the wall hard, falling to the floor in a tangle with The Thing. On top of me in no time, the monster held one hand to my throat, the other landing a heavy fisted blow to my temple, knocking me dizzy.

I heard a tearing sound and felt a rush of warm air where there should have been a zipper.

I looked down at myself to find my privates standing at attention like a good soldier. The Francie Thing lifted its pelvis over me then and everything slid into place, wet and hot.

With a yelp and a shriek, the monster threw its elbows forward to the floor, its forehead slamming into mine with a sickening crack. I felt its hot, slick tongue push stiffly against my closed eye and, as its mouth yawned wide, I was stifled by stale breath and sharp, hard teeth dragging roughly from the bridge of my nose to my chin. Lifting itself to a sitting position, The Thing worked me with its hips, rocking back and forth, up and down, and I watched as its eyes once again rolled up and around, exposing orangy white instead of yellow now, a trickle of foam bubbling from its lips. The scalding juices of the Francie Thing melted me inside of it and as I came its body shook with a long, loud, wheezing gasp.

A heavy sigh blew a dry wind in my face as the monster recovered from its near climax; shoulders now slumped, arms dangling at its side from exhaustion. The eyes that now looked down at me at once agin regained their humanness. *Its* face had become *her* face once more.

Still breathing hard, my member still inside her, Francie looked at me with an expression of fear and confusion. Gingerly, she pulled my right hand up between her heavy breasts, frightened questions pouring from her eyes as she held my hand tightly in both of hers. Still rocking back and forth slightly, but with a gentleness now, she caressed my hand into the shape of a fist and smoothed both of her palms around it. No words. As if waiting for a cue.

Without warning, the monster returned.

A look of rage washed its face bright red, twisting Francie's pretty mouth into a roar, lacing her fingers into a vise that pushed in on my closed fist like a nutcracker. It was not the pain but the horrible sound of snapping, popping bones that forced the scream from my throat. The Thing trembled violently at the sound and I felt it come at last, watching its eyes glaze over.

I remembered what Black had said about the ritual of the spotted hyena—about what happened after . . .

With horrifying tenderness, The Thing opened my crushed hand, putting my index finger into its mouth, sucking at it softly, carefully. It slid the finger out just long enough to say sweetly again, *gumdrop*. Small, sharp teeth latched firmly to the first joint of my finger then, pushing together slowly and evenly. The more I tried to pull my hand away the more pain was inflicted; I kicked and flailed about—to no avail. The Thing ignoring my clamor coolly, licking and sucking at the blood that trickled from the broken skin of my hand like dog might patiently gnaw at a porkchop bone. I cried and begged. According to Black, this was to be the beginning of a long, painful journey into hell.

Suddenly, the eyes of The Thing opened wide and its head snapped sideways, the smooth, hard jaw slacking and letting go. Its eyes became clear of its orangy glaze and washed human again, full of shock and fear—and falling rapidly towards mine. Instead of connecting forehead to forehead though, as the laws of physics would have certainly demanded, the head spun, the back of it impacting impossibly to my closed lips, rolling off of my face and bouncing lightly past. I tasted sweat as her hair brushed past my mouth. Sweat and something else.

Francine's head padded softly on the floor beside me, her long yellow locks strewn across my neck, tickling. Long yellow locks specked with red.

I focused above me and saw a fountain of blood gush upwards, hitting the high ceiling from a stump—a stump that used to be a neck—used to hold a beautiful head, an awful head. Francine's arms raised and waved about frantically in the stream of blood where the head used to be, their movements short, quick, panicked. I turned my line of vision from the overwhelming sight—but if being overwhelmed was what I was avoiding I should have turned right instead of left. Wasn't thinking.

The head:

Francine's eyes looked directly into mine; blinking and rolling, mouth trying to form words. There was a terrible look of fluttering innocence in the lines of her face and in and around the lines there lay a grim acknowledgment of the disaster of her situation. The acknowledgment carried with it a mixture; two parts horror, three parts relief.

Her body fell to the right due to the pressure of the blood that shot to the left, and I heard the sucking sound of a man and woman separating after making love. But the drug still had me in its grip and I was not sickened by the sound as I should have been. It had the opposite effect, in fact, and I found my body being overtaken by a hellish wave of renewed lustful vigor. I looked at Francine's still, warm, headless corpse and thought unwholesome thoughts.

"Mista Jack? You okay?" It was Ida Mae. Over the hunched body of her sister, she held a long sharp sword in her tiny brown hands. The sword was gold and silver and the head of a wolf squirmed beneath her fingers. The blade had an area of bright red about six inches long; dead middle.

"You okay, Mista Jack?"

My eyes looked at the sisters and my arms pushed my body upwards and into the direction of the little girl's voice. My mind lost its connection to my actions, then. My conscience became an uninvolved bystander, a coward with the *power* to intervene, to stop the madness, to protect the innocent—but not the *balls*.

I looked at the girls and felt a smooth moist foam on my chin.

"Mista Jack?"

"*Gumdrop*," I said.

The worn soles of Becky's two tiny black shoes rushing towards my head were the last image I remembered before plunging, once again, into oblivion.

CHAPTER TEN

INSTRUMENT OF GOD

M y eyelids cracked slow from long, dreamless sleep.

I recognized Ida Mae's calm brown features before I recognized the little bedroom I was in—the same one that Maxa had lead me to upon my return from the precinct. I was fully clothed, shoes and all, beneath the red blanket.

"Welcome back," said the girl, "you been gone too long, two days asleep plus one from before is three dat leaves two and two is not a-nuff."

There was no big breakfast waiting, no dancing gladness to see me in her eyes, no sympathy beneath her serious calm. She spoke:

"Can you drive a car?"

"Yes."

She tossed keys on the blanket.

"Can you shoot a gun?"

"What?"

She responded slow and with long pauses, a question now geared for an idiot: "Caaan . . . yooouuu . . . shoooot. . . . aaaaa . . . guhhhhn?"

"Well, sure but—"

She threw a gun on the bed. Snubnose .38.

"We goin' to Missouri. Jackson County."

"Missouri? What the hell is in—"

"Dokka Chollee be mad if he knew, but time is short and day ain't no other way. We gonna shoot the devil hisself. *You* gonna. Now, get up slow—day's gonna be pain between yo legs."

She wasn't lying.

I tried to swing my legs around to the floor but a wave of tearing agony shocked my groin and inner thighs at the attempt. "Jesus God, what happened to me.." I didn't have to look between my legs to know the answer to that, to know that something was missing.

"Surgery happened," she spoke tenderly, "Dokka Chollee saved you from da POP, saved you from yo'self. Iss da only way, day ain't no cure.."

"Sweet Jesus.."

"When da seizure izzat peak, the poison empties outta yo blood stream and inta yo balls. Dass when time is right fo cuttin'. Dokka Chollee took em right out, snip, snip. You healin fast, too."

"Dear God, no.."

"Doan be so sad, Mista Jack. Dem little jewels of yo's on ice. Dokka Chollee sez he close to figgerin' an' an-T-dote an' when he do sez he kin sew 'em back in."

"Like hell," I said choking on sobs. On ice, she says. Ida Mae might've been snowed by the old quack but I knew that this type of "surgery" was pretty much permanent. Maybe castration was the only way to get the POP out of a person's system (hell, maybe not, too) but I had a hunch that Garvey knew about my little marital breach with Maxa and probably didn't shed any tears over my loss.

"Anyway," she went on, "you'll get no more headaches, no more bad feelings, no more wanting to hurt people, no more crazy talk 'bout gum-drops. Now pick up dem keys and let's git gone."

"I won't. Fuck you and fuck Missouri. Leave me alone."

She picked up the gun and pressed its short barrel against my left eye. I didn't flinch.

"Go ahead and shoot you little freak."

"Now, goin' round feelin' sorry for yo' self won't help no one. If you hadn't a been with that bad Maxa lady, kissin' in the dark an' all, then you wouldn't a got infected in da first place, wouldn't be in diss fix. An' you a married man an' all—shame, fo' shame. Plus you ain't got no binness calling me a freak, Mr. Nine Toes an' No Balls—now pick up dem keys an' let's get moving or sumpin bad'll happen an' I doan mean no little thing like brains an' blood splattered all over dat wall behindja from diss here gun. Day's a whole lot at stake here, Mista. Now, come along an' I'll ex-plain in da car."

It wasn't her threats that made me give in but something in her eyes: terror, the Real McCoy. The kind that can beat the hell out of hope even in the heart of a sweet kid like Ida Mae, the kind of terror that could make a little girl point guns and talk about killing.

I had to take baby steps to the car, each movement of my feet bringing me about two inches, shooting sickly crunches of pain through my legs and spine. The car was a white pre-war Packard with Missouri plates.

After opening the door on the passenger side, Becky's thin arms wrapped around her sister's behind and pulled up, lifting Ida Mae about a foot and a half in the air. The airborne sister leaned forwards over Becky's form to keep their mutual body in balance while Becky's legs trembled with the weight of her sister above, whose legs wrapped around Becky's torso as she was lowered sideways onto the car seat. Once Ida Mae was situated, she reached down to Becky, who was now kneeling on the gravel and dirt beside the car, and hooked her hands around Becky's waist, pulling her little bottom into the air just enough to swing her folded legs onto the space of floor beneath the glove box. The complex ritual of getting into the car was completed with the motion of Becky's left hand reaching out from below, tugging at the little piece of dress that was hanging outside the car, pulling it in. Ida Mae shut the door.

I was feeling pretty crummy for calling her a freak right about then. Becky, predictably, snatched my thoughts and passed them on to her sister.

"Dass okay, Mista Jack. Lossa times people say mean stuff day doan mean. I'm sorry 'bout what I called you, too."

Mista Nine Toes an' No Balls. Good one.

She opened up the glove box, shoved the pistol in and pulled out a map. I started up the car as she unfolded the thing, which turned out to be a ridiculously large piece of paper. When she got it open I saw that a route had been marked on it in crayon, from Baltimore to Jackson. Jackson County was circled and decorated with crudely drawn red and orange flames. Directly above it, smiley faces with upside down smiles surrounded big red letters: POCKALIPPS START HEER.

As I began to back out of the driveway, I turned my head and noticed for the first time that there was a man curled up on the backseat, laying sideways. The man looked somehow smaller and weaker than I remembered him, but I recognized him anyway. Guess getting killed will do that to a fellow.

It was Michael Merle, the man that I had beaten to death at the Maryland House three nights ago.

The loss of my pinky toe was a bit of a shock, sure, but the family jewels getting snatched—now that was a real lollapalooza. I mean, how does a guy explain something like that to his wife? How does a guy with no balls face the world, how does the world face him? Big thoughts like these plagued my mind on the way to Jackson and distracted me plenty. Distracted me so bad, in fact, that it didn't phase me when, after about an hour of driving, the dead man in the back seat sat straight up and stretched, yawning loudly.

"Betcha thought you killed mah daddy, dintcha?" said Ida Mae with a smile. I didn't answer, only half listening, wondering if my jewels on ice were sitting next to a pork chop, wondering if they were wrapped in plastic.

"Nah, he ain't dead, Mista Jack. No sir. Juss hurt real bad. Dokka Chollee sez he got watcha call a subdermal heba toba—thass when someone gets day skull cracked so bad dat blood an' brain water rush to the spot thinking it can fix the crack. Instead of fixin it though, it only make it worse; swelling and filling that spot next to the skull crack so bad that it makes a little water balloon. But day ain't no room fo da little water balloon, so it shoves itself against the skull wall, shoves itself inta da brain, trying to make room. My daddy coulda died from dat water balloon of blood an' brain water if Dokka Chollee hadn't a poked a hole in his head to take away the pressure. Subdermal heba toba day calls it."

Wait a minute, wait a minute. *Daddy?*

"Did you just say—"

"Dass right, Mista Jack—subdermal heba toba. Dokka Chollee teaches ol' Ida Mae lossa big words. Teaches me what day mean, too."

I looked up into the rear view mirror. Merle was staring out the window with a goofy grin, watching the trees along the interstate go by.

"My Daddy feelin' lots better, now. He cain't think so fast and he can only talk one or two words at a time but he don't worry so much. He ain't scared all the time like he used to be."

Thoughts of pork chops and freezers no longer occupied my mind.

"Ida Mae, are you telling me he's your father, are you saying—"

"Yessuh, I sho am. Bess Daddy in da whole world, too. I luzz mah Daddy."

It dawned on me that maybe I'd beaten the hell out of the wrong person that night at the diner.

"But don't you feel bad Mista Jack. My Daddy is a sweet kind man but he done a terrible sin that brought all his problems and tragedies upon him. It wasn't you who beat my daddy's head so bad, it was God doing his awful work through you—you just a regular instamant a God.

"You see, Mista Jack, my Daddy is a white man and my Mama a negro. An' Mama says dat mixin' white folks with colored izza crime against nature, da worst sin against God day is, worss dan murder, she sez."

As the white Packard rolled down a long, straight, empty stretch of Interstate 70, Ida Mae spoke calmly, rhythmically. Her story came out

JACKSON COUNTY, 1963

The big black and white television, crucified up high and out of reach by thick steel bolts in the corner of the rec room, doled out the usual barrage of soul numbing game shows and soaps to its blank-faced audience at the State Facility for the Mentally Handicapped Of Jackson County. It was a Tuesday—TV day.

We interrupt the regularly scheduled programming for the following special report . . .

Not five minutes later a nurse had to leave for the powder room, her face in her hands as if trying to push the tears of shock back *in*; shaken. Regularly scheduled programming never did resume that day as all channels dedicated full attention to the BIG NEWS, to the massacred president. Shot dead by a crazy commie-or-other.

Some of the faces at the facility showed traces of emotion—a few cried. Several complained about the afternoon soaps they were missing . Most just stared at the screen deep in private thoughts, like always.

An old black woman watched the instant replay of the motorcade with a fresh intensity each time they played it—not horrified by the sight of the man getting his head blown off—but distracted by something else on the screen.

The distraction:

A woman in black was standing in the shadows near the fallen president. She looked to be about fifty-five, a good twenty years or so younger than Jezelle herself, but her hair was jet black, the color of her dress. The woman's mouth was open like those around her, but she wasn't screaming. No, she wasn't screaming at all—in fact, she seemed to be laughing. She *was* laughing—Jezelle was sure of it.

Something about the woman in black; the shape of her mouth, the wildness of her eyes, made Jezelle think not of insanity—of which she had become well acquainted these many years in the Facility—but of evil. She had known plenty of evil in her lifetime—had, in fact, authored more than her share of it—but she had believed all that to be behind her now. These memories of wrong doing she had spent years meticulously burying deep within her subconscious through the mysterious and merciful workings of God—with not a little help from these numbingly bland olive walls and dull-stinking bedpans. And now the laughing mouth of the woman on TV had savagely ripped a hole in the thick scar of her brain where memories had been blissfully kept on ice for so very long.

Jezelle closed her eyes. "Forgive me, my chilluns," she whispered tearlessly. For it occurred to her at that moment that she had borne children at some point in her life—children she had given away. No— not given away; *sold.*

"Forgive me."

Sold to a devil posing as God, but sold: *sold, sold, sold.*

At first that was all she could remember. But she pressed her eyes closed tighter now, needing to draw from her own mind the reasons— the events leading to the event—

five thousand dollars

her one act of pure weakness and cowardice and hatefulness and, and, and . . .

s*old*
There had to be a reason . . .

_____

Nora White was seven when her parents left.

The war had ended months ago, but down here in Jackson things hadn't changed much for black folks. Truth is, Nora and her folks were one of the lucky black families of the South. The man who had owned them, Will Branson, always treated them kindly, more like kin than slaves. But all kind treatment aside, slaves is slaves and Mr. Branson didn't have enough money to put Nora and her parents on payroll, so technically slaves is what they'd remain if they didn't leave. They left Will a note thanking him for treating them well through the years and asking him if he would please take care of Nora while they searched for a new home up North. They knew that it would be dangerous times for colored folks traveling as free people through the South and felt that Nora would be safer with him at the farm.

They were right about the dangers. They never returned.

Will raised Nora the best he could, taught her right from wrong straight out of his family bible and treated her as a daughter. When Nora became a young woman, though, he treated her as a wife. Will and Nora were all each other knew after the girl's parents left—they relied on each other and loved each other quite a lot. Then one day, Nora became pregnant with Will's child.

Although Will loved Nora, he refused to marry her, having been raised of a strict and particular religious background. It was, however, a set of values that Nora couldn't cotton to.

Will would sometimes preach for hours to his sobbing, broken hearted love; quoting scriptures that he felt made clear the will of God in such matters, scriptures which illustrated God to be just and good but essentially racist. No, a marriage that mixed the races would only anger God, placing their immortal souls and the soul of their unborn child in danger of eternal damnation; it just couldn't be.

Nora was a simple girl and couldn't understand nor abide by a God who was angered by a love as true and pure as her and Will's. She could not understand or abide by it no matter how much evidence Will un-earthed in his trusty bible.

The baby was born in October. Nora named the tiny girl Jezelle because she liked the name. Jezelle was not even a year old when Nora leaned into her crib and kissed her on the cheek for the last time, said *goodnight, lovely child.*

Nora walked away from the big front house and walked out to the old slave quarters, now vacant, out back. She could not read or write, so she left her suicide message in the form of symbols.

In the little slave shack, by the light of three candles, Nora made her point:

With an axe, she split Will's beloved Bible neatly in two.

Then, calmly:

She knelt beside the table that stood in the center of the little shack. The table was a butcher's block. She lay her left arm on the table, all the way up to the shoulder. She lifted the axe with her right arm. She relaxed the fingers of her left hand. She did not cry out as she brought the axe down.

The cut was not clean, so she had to pull the arm free, veins and tendons snapping like wet popcorn.

Holding the severed arm by its elbow, she used it to paint the shape of a heart on the dirty wooden floor beside the butcher block. Like an artist, she meticulously placed the arm to the right of the blood drawn heart-shape, laying the first half of the Bible in its hand, wrapping the still warm and pliable fingers around its pages. To the right of the liberated arm and bible-half, she lay the other bible-half, plunging the axe blade into the heart of it.

To Nora, the arm was a symbol of strength, the axe a symbol of death. Come morning, when he discovered her, it didn't take Will long to interpret the message:

Love will overpower God, love will destroy God.

As Nora lay dying on the butcher block, the red life flowing from her wound, she made her final gesture to the God who she felt had betrayed her, the God who she had come to hate. On her naked belly she clawed the shape of an inverted cross. The message was eerily simple: the child of my womb is not of God, not for God.

Nora's terrible and sad death tore at Will's heart with a grief he could hardly bare. But deeper still cut a sense of terror; terror at his lover's flagrant renouncement of his God, a God he believed to be just and powerful but also vengeful and cruel. He could not deny his love for Nora yet he could not turn his back on God. Will was a lost man.

He buried Nora, but did not mark her grave.

Will Branson wandered around the big, near-empty house with the two sections of tattered, blood-specked bible in his hands, reading from them aloud, searching for answers, searching for guidance. But it was as if the bible had lost its power somehow.

He did not give up, though—searching its blood stained, beaten pages endlessly.

He raised Jezelle as well as he could under the circumstances.

He was determined that the girl not share the ignorance of her mother, that she not fulfill Nora's awful dying prophecy. He read to her from God's book diligently and, to his astonishment, the little girl's awareness and understanding of its teachings was downright scholarly; she had whole passages memorized by the time she was six. When Will was sure that he had pounded the savior's message indelibly into his daughter's heart, mind and soul, he decided that it was time to tell her the story of Nora; of her love for him, her ignorance of the ways of God, her untimely and blasphemous death. Will was truthful and left in every detail.

Jezelle turned ten years old on the day of the telling.

After hearing Will tell the story of Nora, Jezelle continued going about her chores, doing her father's bidding as usual. Her studies of the bible continued with particular fervor; it was as if she was searching within its pages for some sort of answer, some sort of explanation. Just like her father had done so many years ago following Nora's death.

But for eighteen days after the telling, Jezelle did not speak a word.

Then, on the nineteenth day, she snapped out of it. She became her usual blabby, bible-spouting self again. Will was relieved.

Jezelle stayed with Will until he died. She buried him, but did not mark his grave. That, she explained to herself, was the only way that her mother and father could ever really be together again.

She was forty-two years old at the time of his death, an old maid by anyone's standards, and knew nothing of the world outside Will's little farm. She was afraid—but left anyway, taking only the clothes on her back and one half of the family bible. The second half.

The half that her mother had left the axe in.

A little church in the city gave her shelter in return for a little old fashioned hard work; Jezelle kept the church grounds neat and trim and scrubbed the floors sometimes late into the night.

One of the gentleman in the regular Sunday congregation was a widower who had taken to regular church going after the sudden death of his wife. It seems that the man's wife just up and died one day; not a day sick, not an ounce of warning. He just woke up one morning and found her beside him not breathing. It happens that way sometimes.

He began going to the little church in Jackson County searching for answers; answers that were not evident or forthcoming. A seething bitterness began to swell in his heart as he gazed upon the blank stares of the stained-glass saints, but he continued his weekly visits to the little church just the same.

One day he noticed the handsome negro woman working on the church grounds. She saw him watching her and returned his glances with smiles. He asked her if she would like to go for a soda.

He continued his church visits, but began skipping the service, instead slipping away with Jezelle.

He became entranced with her, he fell in love. She became pregnant.

Michael Merle was a somewhat religious man, but didn't take the word of God quite as literally as Jezelle's father had. He did what he felt was the honorable thing.

He married her.

Jezelle did not love her husband, she had not ever. But by marrying a white man, she was doing her mother's bidding. She was going against God. She was getting even.

Nine months later, though, on the day of Ida Mae and Becky's birth, she knew it was God who would have the last laugh.

Michael and Jezelle's marriage was not a happy one.

Jezelle was convinced that the twins' deformity was a curse from God, punishment for her marriage to a white man, for her arrogance at thinking she could even the score for her mother against God.

And Jezelle recanted in horror; she renounced her mother, cursed her blasphemous soul.

She begged God's forgiveness, prayed for another chance, prayed that the twins could wake up one morning as two separate, normal little girls.

God sat stony and deaf in his Heaven.

And yet somehow, Michael never saw the horror in Ida Mae and Becky. He improvised clothing for them out of secondhand dresses and table cloths that he had sewn together and taught them to read and write—though they never could get a knack for arithmetic. He was gentle and playful and couldn't bear to punish them when they were bad, which was often. It was Michael who taught them to smile, told them they were beautiful and made them believe it. He even confided in them that he believed their mother was wrong; that they were not a curse but a blessing. The most wonderful and unique children that were ever born to earth, he would tell them.

But to Jezelle the sight of the twins only meant sorrow, and the love that Michael showed them only proved him blind.

She had to make her peace with God, and there was only one way. She had to sever the unholy union that had so angered God.

She took the twins, and she left Michael. She left no note.

Life with the carny was bad for the twins.

When the trailers were moving from town to town they were kept in a large steel cage, one meant for animals, in total darkness. When the trailers stopped they did not get to go outside and play. They were told it was for their own good.

Jezelle had made a deal with the carny master: the twins would be displayed in his Amazing Human Oddities attraction for free and in return Jezelle would be granted the right to preach to the gawking patrons while they were displayed. Preach about the evils of interracial marriage and the dangers of angering God in particular, using the twins' deformity as an example of God's awesome ability to punish. The carny master had a good sense for old fashioned hellfire drama and liked the idea. He instructed the twins to cry while they were on display for even more dramatic effect.

That, for the twins, was the easy part.

Jezelle believed that by paying penance in this way, God would send her some sort of sign, tell her what to do, maybe even undo his terrible curse.

The three of them traveled the carny circuit for four years, Jezelle waiting patiently for her sign from God.

Then one night, Jezelle believed, she got her sign.

After a three nighter in Charlottesville, the carny was packing up, getting ready to roll to the next town. There was a knock at Jezelle's trailer door.

The orange haired man's offer was blunt: he was working for a man who wanted the twins. They would be taken good care of, much better than what they were used to. The man's boss was willing to pay Jezelle five thousand dollars for them, not a penny more.

Jezelle's interpretation: The orange haired man was an angel, his boss was God. God was now willing to take back the girls, relieve Jezelle of her curse. In fact, He was so pleased with her penance that He was throwing in five grand as a bonus.

They paid Jezelle on the spot: in fifty crisp one hundred dollar bills.

The orange haired man and his associate, Paul Fish, left for Baltimore with the twins that night, at the bidding of their employer. Their employer, ironically, was not God at all, but a powerful circuit court judge back in Jezelle's hometown of Jackson.

Michael eventually tracked down Jezelle.

Jezelle informed him of the glorious news: God had sent an angel to take the twins. She explained to him that the angel had come in the form of an orange haired man with five thousand dollars.

Michael, incredulous: you *sold* them?

No, no, no, no, no, no, nononononononononooo!

And then he began his quest to find them. To find Jezelle's babies.

sold.

And Jezelle dissolved into madness.

And the madness allowed her to forget.

Until now.

The old woman in black bobbed in and out of the corner of the screen with that twisted mouth: laughing. There was something familiar about that mouth. There seemed to be some family resemblance between the woman in black and the orange haired man who had given her money for her children so many years ago. That resemblance must have been what had awakened her sad memories.

Forgive me . . .

Jezelle never spent the five thousand dollars. She painted black hearts on the back of each bill and put the devil's money some place where it could do no more harm.

In October of 1943 in a strange northern city called Baltimore, Michael finally did locate his daughters. They now lived in a small room on the third floor of a big house on St. Paul Street. To his surprise, they seemed healthy and content there; their door was not locked for they had no desire to run. Something was not right.

Upon this strange and happy reunion with his beloved girls, Michael realized that he could not simply leave this place with his daughters. Couldn't just walk away from the bad people who had purchased them from his disturbed wife. There was someone he had to see, something he had to do. He never explained exactly what these things were.

"Stay here," he said in the dark, cozy little room.

"Don't go, Daddy. It's not safe," Ida Mae said.

"I know, baby." He left.

And did not return.

That was the last time the twins would see their father as he was, of clear mind.

BALTIMORE, 1943

CHAPTER ELEVEN

POCKALIPPS START HEER

Route seventy is the only road from Maryland to Missouri. There is no turn off, no adjoining road, no detour. Sometimes the way is narrow; trees and scrub bushes hugging tight to the roadside. Sometimes the road is so wide and straight that you can travel at a hundred and ten miles an hour and feel like your going thirty. The stretch from here to there is so long that part of the journey must be light, the other dark. And the scenery changes: farmland to suburban neighborhoods to the railway torn, warehouse strewn city-backsides to miles and miles of trees that all look exactly the same. You have to fill your tank exactly three and a half times. A lot of things change on route seventy. Everything but one:

It's just one road.

One long motherfucking road.

It wasn't till the last two hours of driving that Ida Mae bothered to begin selling me on her little scheme. It was the least she could do, I mean, she was asking me to kill a man.

"Thing ta member izz you ain't killin' no regular human man. Elijah Truhart izza Devil in person, up from da boiling ground, poisonin' people in body and soul."

Elijah Truhart. That's just dandy. I'm not just committing murder, I'm committing a fucking political assassination.

Truhart was a U.S. Senator, no less. Recently appointed as chairman to a special committee investigating corruption and inefficiency in wartime spending programs—his scrunched up, bespectacled little owl face was popping up in the papers more and more, making things hot for the fatcats in Washington as well as some executive class army brass. He wasn't making many friends in high places but the American public saw him as a hero of sorts, the guy who was making sure tax dollars made it out to our brave fighting boys overseas and not into the pockets of greedy generals and politicians. Truhart had done so well for himself in the self promotion game that it looked good for him to go up against FDR in the next Presidential primary.

I'm gonna just walk right in there and shoot this guy. Right.

"*Do not* tell me you want me to shoot the next president of the United States. *Do—fucking—not* tell me that."

"He ain't gonna be no president. Cause he be dead and you da one gonna make him dat way. Nobody'll know you a hero Jack, but dass what you'll be. The truest hero izz always da one no one know about. And watch your language—I'm just a kid."

"Now c'mon, Ida Mae, don't sugarcoat this thing. It's fucking murder we're talking about and you know it. And it's not going to happen anyway. Truhart's an important man. There'll be security; lots."

"No matter. He's expecting you. Just walk right up to the front gate of his big old house and tell 'em you need to talk with Senator Truhart. Tell 'em your name, dey let you through. And watch your language."

Sure, he'll be expecting me.

"Like fuck they will. Ida Mae, this is all wrong. I don't know what this guardian angel pal of yours has been telling you, but this is all wrong. Whattaya say we go for a burger and a shake, see the sights of historic downtown Independence, call it a nice little vacation and head for home. How's that sound to you? Pretty good?"

"She gonna die."

"Who? Who's gonna die?"

"Pretty little wife. Yours."

"Now wait justa—"

"'Less you kill him, she die. Cain't tell you how I know but I know. Dat ain't all neither. Lossa people die. Truhart izza bad man, real evil bad."

"Okay. Let's say you're right about Truhart being a stinker. How do you connect him to Baltimore, to me, to those nutty theater freaks." Oops. Bad choice of words.

"Dokka Chollee work fo' Senator Truhart. Redd and Maxa work fo' him too. So do me n' Becky. Truhart is the center, the cause. He is the Devil."

I about turned the car around. What a damn crock. Instead, I gave her one more chance:

"Ida Mae, how do you know what you say you know? And don't feed me any mumbo-jumbo about guardian angels and just knowing, alright? Make me believe it."

She was quiet for a long minute.

"I can't."

"That's what I thought. We're going home."

Casually and quickly, she slipped the gun out of the glove box.

"Shut yer stupid white face and drive tha damn car. Just get us there. I'll do the talking, I'll do the shootin'. You just drive."

This couldn't be happening. I had to think fast.

"Okay. You win."

"What win?"

"I'll do it. Shoot Truhart, I mean."

I had no intention of doing any such thing. But I'd decided that I should try to talk to the man at least, find out if there was any connection between him and The Big Punch, find out if Ida Mae had just dreamt the whole thing up.

"You promise?"

"Promise."

Ida Mae was like me; didn't take much stock in promises.

"I don't know if I believe you, Mista Jack."

"I don't know if I believe you either, Ida Mae."

She thought about that for a minute. Then she put the gun back in the glove box. Forty minutes later we were in Jackson County. We did stop for a burger and a shake after all.

Then it was time for our little social call.

For a U.S Senator, Elijah Truhart spent very little time in Washington, preferring instead to stick close to home. Said it kept him in touch with his constituency; more likely it kept him close to the dirty little business ventures that he controlled out of the office in his mansion. I sighed with relief as we approached the uniformed guard posted at the gate of the mansion; there was no way this guy was going to let us through. Ida Mae was confidant though:

"Juss tell 'em yer name."

"No prob. King of Siam, coming through."

"Tell 'em yer name and don't lie. He let us through, all right."

We slowed to a stop at the gate, I rolled down my window and grinned at the stony faced rent-a-cop. He didn't say a word but asked me who the hell I was with his eyes.

"Jack Dellus to see Senator Truhart."

"You the killer?" Great, the fucker made me, I thought, wondering if the jail cells in Missouri were heated.

"Not exactly. Listen, it's kind of a long story—you gonna let us through or what?"

"Yeah, guess so."

"Guess so what?"

"Go through, killer. Boss' orders." Stone-face cracked a grin that matched mine: "The Senator sure does get himself a lively bunch of visitors through here. That surely is a fact."

"Yeah, I bet," I said rolling up my window and losing the grin.

We rolled up to the front of the house, parked it. I made to get out, said "Wish me luck."

"Luck," said Michael Merle with dramatic sincerity.

"Yer fergettin' sumpin'," said Ida Mae. She handed me the pistol. I stuffed it in the front of my pants.

"Thanks." For getting me killed, I thought.

I rang the bell and the intercom crackled on: a conversation similar to the one with the gate cop ensued. The door opened and an elderly woman in a green chiffon dress said, "Follow me."

I followed her down a long hallway till the hall stopped at a large, dark oak door. She knocked on it and said, "Wait here." Then she walked briskly, not quite running, away from the door. As if she were expecting the thing to blow up. Instinctively, I put my hand on the handle of the .38, ready for something to go wrong.

The door opened. By itself.

Truhart sat twenty yards or so away in the deep office, behind a desk, obliviously scribbling at something. "Come in, Dellus. Come in, come in." He spoke loudly, impatiently, without looking up.

I took two steps and stopped dead at the sound of cuck-click cuck-click, feeling cold steel rods pressed hard to both sides of my skull.

"Oh yes, that. You didn't really think you could just come in here and shoot a U.S Senator did you, Dellus?" Truhart looked up at me and his two goons. Looked amused.

"Nice and slow, shitheel." A voice to my left. I complied like a snail, using thumb and forefinger, tossed the gun lightly to the ground. The two pistol butts fell away from my temples. I looked at the two goons: one was fat, tall, old; the one who had spoken, called me a name. The other was just a kid—pint-size, nervous. Both wore rent-a-cop suits like the guy at the gate. The old grouchy one picked up the piece.

"Okay, fellas—you can stand outside the door. I'll holler if I need you." Exit Brick and Brack.

"What's on yer mind Dellus? Speak up."

"Excuse me?" I felt unprepared.

"You came here to shoot me. I'd like to know why. Talk, man."

"I ..uh..the girl told me, that is—"

"The girl? What girl?"

"Ida Mae, she—"

"Ida Mae, Ida Mae, Ida Mae! I should have known! You take a poor wretch like that in off the cold street, give her a nice home, a situation BY FAR better than what she was used to AND HOW DOES SHE REPAY ME? Ida Mae, Ida Mae. If only she had the good sense of her sister ... "

I didn't get it: "I'm sorry, I don't—"

"HER SISTER!" he shouted, "Becky! You know, the one you can't see so good, her head is, well.. "

"I know," I offered weakly. "I know about Becky."

"Well, Dellus, honestly." He seemed to be calming down. "You really oughta think twice before taking orders to shoot to kill from some damn little nigger freak. By rights you should be dead right now ... "

"I wasn't going to do it. I wanted Ida Mae to think I was, but I was only gonna come in here and ask you some questions."

"Well what if I told you I ain't gonna answer no goddamn questions? What then? Yer a pain in my royal butt, you know that, Dellus? You shoulda stayed in Baltimore, with Garvey and his men—you were safe there. Not here. I don't need no goddamn heat here in Missouri, don't need it not one damn bit.."

"How'd you know?"

"Huh? How'd I know . . .—KNOW WHAT?" He was losing his patience again.

"How'd you know to be expecting me? You knew. You were waiting."

"Yes, yes, of course I did. Whattaya think—yer playing with amateurs here? When you came up missing in Baltimore I got a call to be on the look out. I didn't know you'd come, but I knew it was possible. And if ya did come, I figgered it'd be with a gun."

"Why?" I was getting interested.

"Well, why WHAT man? Make yerself plain fer godsake."

"Why did you figure I'd be coming here with a gun? Even I'm not sure. Like I said, I wasn't really planning on using it."

"Well, surely Ida Mae told you something about me, gave you some kinda reason.."

"She did. She said you were the Devil." Truhart looked at me hard.

"Well. What about it if I am? Huh, boy? What about it?" He stood up then, turned away from me, faced the wall behind the big desk. The Senator let out a sigh, one that sounded tired, beaten: "I try to do right. I honestly do."

I jumped on the melancholy moodswing like a champ:

"Senator, I'm just a regular guy caught in a trap that he doesn't understand. If there's anyway I can help you out, I'll do it—I just need some answers. Someone's out to get me and I don't know why. I've been framed for a bunch of murders—I think the police are involved somehow, but it doesn't make any sense. I also have reason to believe that my wife may be in danger. Please help me, Senator."

"Janice ain't in danger, boy. She's the reason yer breathing right now. Dr. Garvey is an associate and good friend of mine; he doesn't want anything to happen that might upset his little girl and I guess he figgers she'd miss ya pretty bad if you turned up in a river somewheres. You're not in danger, son. Not now you ain't. Not from me at least. I know that you ain't the Bolton Hill murderer cause I know who the murderer is. I don't know who's framing you, but I will know. Somebody's playing games with old Senator Truhart. Whoever it is, I hope they're having themselves a good laugh because they're gonna have to pay for their entertainment."

"Why me? The frame, I mean."

"Because you're a scapegoat that can't be touched. If you take the rap, Garvey'll be pissed. If Garvey get's pissed then the whole operation is in jeopardy. No telling what he'll do. He's a good man but he ain't glued too tight if you know what I mean. Not when it comes to his daughter. She's his only child—since the murder of his boy, that is."

"Ronnie."

"Yes, Ronnie. Now, I think I've answered plenty of questions. It's time for you to cooperate with me. You're going back to Baltimore. You'll stay there till I clear up the matter of this little prankster who's framing you and making my life a hell. When that happens, you go back to your normal little life with Janice like nothing happened."

"I'll cooperate. I'll do whatever you say. But I need more."

"Believe me, boy—the less you know the better off you are. You know way too much as it is. I ain't sure it's such a good idea letting you out of Missouri alive. Shooting you is the only safe way to go, but I got reason not to. Be thankful for that and don't try and bargain with me. I may just change my damn mind."

"I don't need names. I already have all the names I need. I just need some whys. Then I'll stop poking around—you have my word on it."

The Senator took off his glasses, rubbed gingerly at his right eye. He looked tired. Then he said one word. One glorious word:

"Ask."

Truhart corroborated most of what Detective Black had told me about Janice's dad; the stuff about him going nuts after Ronnie's death and trying to find a cure for "rapist disease" or whatever. But Black had left something out—left it out or didn't know about it.

The year was 1934.

Garvey had come up with what he believed to be a working vaccine, a potion that successfully fulfilled and then *destroyed* the urge for violence in the animals that were treated with it. But in order to perfect the dosage for humans, he needed human subjects. And his subjects had to be sex criminals—of a particularly violent nature.

Very discreetly, but very widely, Garvey solicited state prisons across the country for "volunteer" death row inmates who fit the bill, vaguely explaining that his experiments could lead to the end of the sex—crime as we know it. He got a few cautiously interested call backs, but interest fizzled when Garvey fessed up to the fact that his experiments would more than likely prove fatal for the first dozen or so inmates that were involved.

No state prison wanted to be known as a human guinea pig farm who killed its inmates in the name of science. Covering up stuff like that could be tricky even for government officials.

Word of Garvey's failing quest for human subjects had reached Truhart, who was at that time a circuit court judge for Jackson County running for the Senate. Truhart was very curious about the nature of Garvey's experiments—for his own reasons, naturally. He contacted Garvey, arranged a meeting.

Truhart had a lot of say in the workings of The Missouri State Penn. He contacted the warden, a twitchy fella by the name of Asner who got a might twitchier when presented with the idea. He was fearful of the powerful judge though and agreed to help under the condition that utter secrecy be observed and protected. The experiments began.

To Garvey's frustration, the vaccine didn't seem to work on his human subjects. In fact, *none* of the inmates who were exposed to the serum even survived. The dying symptoms of the prisoners were unprecedented to any reaction he had seen in their animal counterparts. These symptoms included bleeding from the ears and eyes as well as extreme cranial pain brought on from a build up of blood pressure in the head. This unusual pressure in the skull was attributed to a grossly accelerated heart rate in the human subjects which, in turn, resulted in the actual cause of death: the explosion of the subject's heart. Garvey fooled with several variations of the drug, juggling around chemicals and potency levels, with not much variation in results. After twenty-seven inmate deaths, he had run out of death row sex offenders in the state of Missouri. It looked as though he would go home a broken man, his dream failed.

Then, a miracle happened.

The killer's name was Albert Fish.

Fish was a self-employed house painter. He hailed originally from Truhart's native Jackson County, having relocated with his parents as a young boy to Wilmington, Delaware.

Truhart recounted the killer's story to me with a relish that made me a scad uneasy. Here's the jist:

In 1898, Fish turned twenty-eight years old and got married. He had a total of six children by his wife before she left him for a man named

Trumbo, a sort of village idiot character, on the year of their tenth wedding anniversary.

Fish's anger and hurt expressed itself in the form of morbid pastimes: he began collecting news clippings about German sex killer Fritz Haarman, a man who lured teenage boys into sexual acts, killed them, and then sold them as meat. He began inserting needles into his fingers and scrotum. He began spanking himself with a nail studded paddle. He began telling his children that he was Christ.

Raising six kids can be a strenuous job for anyone, but Fish's weak and twitchy mind proved unable to handle the stress whatsoever. Some people take up knitting or fishing to relieve the pressures of child rearing. Fish took up murder.

He bought a small cabin in the woods not too far from his home, where he would lure young women and men, sometimes small children. Being such a kindly old gent, it was not difficult for him to inspire trust in his victims; a friendly invitation for lunch or, if it was a young boy, an offer of a little house painting job with him for ten cents an hour. They always went with the nice old man to his cabin in the woods.

Once in the cabin, Fish would go to work with his "implements of hell" as he referred to them at his trial; various knives, a wood cutting saw, a cleaver. Fish liked to experiment and would sometimes work himself into quite an appetite, devouring the fruits of his labor.

Although his own children knew about his self mutilation habits and obsessive religious bent, Fish managed to keep the little cabin a secret from them. Except for one. Fish's third child.

Young Henry would follow his father around without his knowing, as curious young children sometimes do. Henry found out about the cabin in the woods, would look in the window sometimes. He was nine at the time.

In 1928, a young boy by the name of Edward Budd placed an ad in the local newspaper. He advertised a strong back and a will to work. Albert Fish answered the ad, showing up at the Budd residence with his paint truck and plenty of hard work to do.

Fish befriended the boy's parents, Bert and Delia, and became so entrusted by them that they would sometimes let him babysit their four year old daughter Grace. One day, Fish told Grace that he had been invited to a birthday party; there were to be lots of presents and cake for everyone. Would she like to come?

In the cabin, there were no presents or cake. But Fish made himself a nice stew out of Grace's small, ravaged body.

He told her parents that he had fallen asleep while babysitting her, when he awoke she was gone. The case won national attention but no arrests were made. Fish was never suspected in the disappearance.

In 1931, Fish was institutionalized for sending obscene letters to a lonely hearts column. He was released after two weeks of observation.

Three years later, he wrote an anonymous letter to Bert and Delia Budd, apologizing for the murder of their daughter. In the note, he claimed to have not raped her. He left out the part about the stew.

The letter was postmarked St. Louis, Missouri. When Fish had moved away from Wilmington years earlier, he had told the Budds that he had relatives in St. Louis. They notified the authorities.

Judge Truhart could not believe his good luck. If he were the judge to convict and sentence The Grace Budd Killer during an election year, he'd be a shoe in for the Senate seat. He fought a Delaware extradition attempt on the grounds that Fish was linked to several missing persons cases in St. Louis and Independence. He won possession of his prize criminal, his ticket to Washington.

But Dr. Garvey wanted him, too. Needed him.

Truhart agreed to let Garvey have Fish—after he got his conviction. He figured that reheated extradition attempts from Delaware may take precedence after the trial and take the spotlight with it. If Fish died by Garvey's hands he would have at least died in Truhart's custody. It wouldn't be too tough to dress the death up to look like the result of some heroics on the part of the Missouri authorities. Fish was, after all, a mad child killer.

The trial was short and ugly. After the first day of Fish's confessions, women were barred from the courtroom. Five of Fish's six children testified that he believed his deeds would attain him heaven. Henry did not testify.

The jury bought his insanity plea, but voted for the death penalty anyway. In November of that same year, Elijah Truhart was elected U.S. Senator of the state of Missouri. The prisoner now belonged to Dr. Garvey.

Garvey revised his serum one final time.

Because Fish was sixty-four years old and in frail health, Garvey weakened the drug's potency, fearing that its so far violent effects may overcome Fish too easily. But Fish had no reaction whatever to the serum.

Garvey increased the potency of the serum to its normal level.

Still nothing. Fish had an unusual tolerance to the drug. Could it be that the more severe the dementia, the greater the tolerance to the drug's devastating symptoms? Garvey multiplied the drug's original potency by one and a half times.

This time there was a reaction, however slight.

Fish's blood pressure actually *lowered* by several points, his demeanor losing some of its tension. The hard stare that he had become famous for during his courtroom confessions softened slightly. Garvey interviewed his subject then, to see if there were any personality alterations, any change in his utter lack of remorse about his crimes.

Why did you murder those people? *I am Christ. It is my right.*

No discernible change in blood pressure or brainwave activity.

Why did you eat the remains? *Yum.*

Still no change.

Did you have any regrets or remorse about the children you killed? *Tasty. Gumdrop.*

No change.

Any remorse at all? *No.*

Nothing.

Garvey showed Fish photos of his victims; happy, living family photos first and then morgue photos, hoping for a reaction.

Fish thumbed through the pictures disinterestedly.

And then a thought occurred to Garvey.

He let Fish rest up for eight hours, then gave him another injection. This time the dose was at double the normally fatal level.

Still, Fish did not suffer the violent dying symptoms that the other prisoners had suffered. Instead, his body effectively shut itself down; pulse slowing to a crawl, respiratory all but stopped. He fell into deep coma and was put on life support. For all intents and purposes the man was dead; all vital functions now unable to work of their own accord—all but one.

His brain.

Fish's level of brain activity had run amok according to Garvey's equipment: doubled . . . then tripled. Garvey had the equipment tested for malfunction but everything checked out. Something very strange was happening. Something medically impossible.

Fish continued in his comatose state with high levels of brain activity for three days. And then he woke up.

Garvey once again commenced with interviewing. Same questions.

This time, when asked about the murders, at first Fish could not seem to remember having committed them. Garvey once again showed him the victim's photos—this time in an effort to jog the old man's memory.

When shown the pictures of his victims in life, Fish beamed uncharacteristically, occasionally making comments like: "Oh yes, John Waymark—a good boy, a hard worker" and "Joanie, what a sweet dear, always so polite to an old man. Dear girl." It was the first time that Fish seemed to be looking at his victims as people at all—none of the usual cold hearted comments; no yum, no tasty.

And then Garvey showed the old man the morgue pictures.

Fish began to tremble uncontrollably at the sight of them.

And then to sob.

"Dear sweet Jesus . . . I can't look, I can't look! I want to die, please God let me die. . . . what have I done? Dear God, what? *What* have I done?" Remorse!

The serum had actually worked. Garvey, desperately needed more subjects to try his new blend on, now more than ever. Seeing the dramatic urgency in the new developments, Truhart called in a few favors and within days death row sex fiends from neighboring states began to receive mysterious transfers to Missouri. All of them were subjected to the serum that had worked on Albert Fish. All of them died; bleeding from the eyes and ears just as the inmates before Fish had died.

With great frustration, Garvey diagnosed that in order for the serum to be effective, the level of dementia in the subject had to be *extreme*. Fish was the only specimen who had been twisted enough for the drug to work on.

So in order for Garvey to cure a "normal level" sexual deviant, he had to first bring the man's level of deviancy *up*—up to the level of Albert Fish. Only then could it be neutralized with the serum. He began work on a revised version of the drug that would suit this perverse purpose. One that would recreate in humans the murderous behavior that the original POP had inspired in animal subjects.

He had to come up with a strain that would take your garden variety sex killer and turn him into Jack the Ripper times ten. Then, theoretically, the madman could be cured completely with the original formula. Garvey eventually accomplished this special brew for humans. The same concoction that I had recently been infected with, then saved from with a little sex operation known as *chop chop*.

Albert Fish spent two years on death row feeling deep remorse and sorrow for his crimes. He attempted suicide four times.

During the permitted times, Tuesdays at four P.M., Fish was visited diligently by his third son. Henry was finally getting a chance to know the kind, gentle father that he knew existed all along but had never before met. The elder Fish told his son about Garvey's serum, about how it allowed him a taste of humanity, a chance to reclaim his soul. Henry Fish swore undying gratitude to Dr. Garvey, told the doctor that he would do whatever he could to help him complete his important research.

Finally, on January 16, 1936, Albert Fish was given the death that he had so longed for .

They had to give him two jolts, though—the needles that remained in his scrotum short circuited the electric chair.

Truhart informed me that myself, Ida Mae, Becky and their father would be returning to Baltimore by rail. Escorted. Immediately.

I complied with his demand—Missouri was starting to smell. But there was still something bothering me.

"Senator Truhart?"

"What now?"

"Ida Mae and Becky. You should see them as dangerous but you don't. They tried to have you killed and you let them go. Why?"

"Why, Mr. Dellus," the old man grinned, suppressing a laugh, "you really don't know, do you?"

I just looked at him; clueless.

"Punch is a front, my boy—there's no money to be made in the theater business. The local authorities are aware of it and tolerate it because they can see it's essentially harmless. But they don't really know what's going on. No, no—theater is strictly small time industry. Do I seem like a small-timer to you, boy?"

I told him that he didn't.

"Motion pictures! That's where the future is! That's where the money is! You think all this do-goody-good research of your father in-law's is cheap? Well, it isn't and he knows it. It costs money. Lots of money. And the research isn't nearly done—maybe a lot of years before he's got the cure he wants, maybe never. Gotta pay for all that researchin' somehow.

"Fortunately, there is a demand for a particular form of entertainment, a particular *illegal* form of entertainment. The illegality and sensitive nature of the movies that my little secret motion picture company creates, with the help of Garvey, Mr. Redd and their associates of course, comes at a high price—but there are certain wealthy patrons who are willing to pay. And getting back to your question, well . . ."

He let the laugh he had been holding cut loose a little.

"Ida Mae and Becky—they're our biggest attraction. Those little girls are stars."

I didn't get it and I said so.

"Hell, boy that girl's a natural! She don't even need Garvey's acceleration serum to help her along. She actually *likes* to hurt people. Likes to kill 'em. She's good at it, too." The twisted old fuck lost it then, ripping into peels of cackling laughter.

"You're crazy, you lying fuck. Ida Mae was right—you are evil." I made for the door.

"Hold it, boy. Don't go away mad." Truhart was making an effort to contain himself. "Before I set you and your little friends on that train back to Charm City, maybe you should see something."

I followed Truhart down the hall, into a large room with lots of chairs facing a blank wall.

A screening room.

Truhart called up to a little window near the ceiling, towards the back; "Frank! Roll reel seventeen! We have a special patron this afternoon!"

Frank rolled reel seventeen.

"You're a hundred per cent right, son," Truhart said after forty minutes or so, after the screen faded to black. "I should've killed that girl for what she done, for what she tried to do. But I can't, you see. I'd be losing the greatest little star that the snuff movie binness ever known.

"I'd be losing myself sure money, son, which ain't no common thing in this life."

The man who was to escort me, the girls and Merle back to B'more was Paul Fish, the sixth son of Albert and the driver who, along with Maxa, had picked me up off the floor of an alley on the fatal night of the diner incident. Besides his gig as a driver, Fish also functioned as a thug and a trigger man among other things for Truhart's Baltimore operation under Redd. Right now he was packing a .45 caliber hand cannon; not too subtly flashing its presence under his waistband to make sure I didn't get any ideas.

Once on the train, no words passed between me and Ida Mae due to the imposing demeanor of our new friend—but we did exchange a handful of icy looks. I figured she was dying to confront me about why I didn't ice Truhart, and I was hot to confront her about what Truhart had showed me in his screening room. Finally, Paul Fish went for a piss.

"You mess up sumpin' terrible, Mista Jack. We came all da way ta hell so's you could shake hand's wit da Devil."

"Yeah so he's a sick fuck, big deal, join the club. He ain't the Devil no more than you are—probably a lot less. At least he's out in the open about what he is." And then she knew. She knew that I knew about her little movie career.

We passed a long stretch of green pasture dotted by tiny cow bodies in the distance. Michael Merle pointed and said, "Lookit! Lookit cows! Moooooo!!"

"I know what you think you saw. But don't believe your eyes." The little girl's eyes were welling up.

Maybe she was right when she told me *right was wrong, up was down, evil was good*—all that jazz. I just didn't think to include her into that equation. The unimaginable was true; the little crying girl in front of me was a monster. And she had almost talked me into killing a man.

"I know what I saw," I replied flatly.

"I know what I am," she said simply, "I am not a monster. I am not a killer."

But she was. Didn't have to read the book. I saw the movie.

Michael Merle smiled goofy out the window.

"Moooooooo. . . ."

CHAPTER TWELVE

CUTE IN DREAMLAND, THE LITTLE MONSTERS

Whereas the drive from Maryland to Missouri takes roughly fifteen hours (if you're killing the speed limit which we had been), trains move a hell of a lot slower—there's no direct route—you gotta go all the way up to Chicago before you swing back down to planet Earth. The ride back home was shaping into a whopper; twenty hours if there were no delays which wasn't likely—probably more like twenty—five. After six hours of boring scenic panoramas, Ida Mae had fallen asleep against the shoulder of her father who in turn had fallen asleep against the window of the train. Of course, I couldn't tell if Becky was asleep.

I figured now was my best shot at getting some skinny out of Paul Fish. Never big on subtle chit-chat:

"So how'd you and you're brother get tangled up with this nutty crew, anyhow?" I acted like I didn't know.

"Who said you could talk, shitheel?"

Real damn friendly. Oh well:

"Hey, lighten up, will ya? It's a long ride—I'm starting to get a little stir crazy. Just thought I'd make a little conversation is all, but if you just wanna sit there like a statue for the next nineteen hours, be my guest."

He softened a little:

"Sorry, fella. It's just I didn't sign up for this shit detail. I guess it's got me a little edgy."

"Yeah, no problem. I didn't sign up for this crapola either, pal."

"Guess not." He smiled and then: "Dr. Garvey helped out our old man once. Me and Henry figure we owed him for that so we work for him pretty cheap. He's an okay guy, Dr. Garvey."

I decided to take a chance and tell him the truth about how Truhart had filled me in; I knew about his father, about his crimes, about the too late cure administered by my dear old father in-law. "I gotta say, Paul—and I hope you don't take this the wrong way—but it's hard to believe that you and Henry are any kind of chip off the old block. I mean, you guys seem pretty normal to me." Well, maybe *normal* was pushing it.

"Dad was sick. He couldn't help it. He was curable, too—but the cure came too late."

"Yeah, tough break. Good thing your old man's ..*condition* wasn't hereditary." Paul didn't answer right away and I figured maybe I'd pissed him off. After a long few seconds:

"It is."

I went blank: "I'm sorry—it is what?"

"Hereditary. It is hereditary."

"Are you saying that you and Henry are—I mean, you're telling me you guys. . . ."

"No. I didn't say that. I just said it was hereditary." He was starting to sound a little irate which made me uncomfortable considering the topic at hand. He continued:

"Dad didn't get sick until later in life. He was always normal when he was younger. Like me and Henry." Maybe this is what Garvey had told them—but I had reason to believe otherwise. I played along:

"You're saying that you aren't now but you will later?"

"Yeah, something like that. Dr. Garvey says we're like human time bombs."

I was beginning to smell a rat.

"And Dr. Garvey says he can fix you up when it happens, is that right?"

"He can. Like with Dad." A big rat.

"Look, Paul, I don't know how to tell you this but I think you and your brother have been hoodwinked by the good doctor. The kind of sickness your father had doesn't get passed down like eye color and height. Garvey thinks he's got himself some good cheap labor in you and Henry because he's got you scared. When you guys *don't* go bananas he'll probably take the credit. . . ."

"You're wrong. I can . . . I can't really explain it but I can . . . *feel* it. The sickness I mean. It's there in me. *Waiting.*"

Jeez, I thought; time to change the subject:

"So what kind of work do you fellas do for the doctor?"

"Henry does mostly odd stuff. He's a big guy so he keeps things in line at the theater. Me, I work out in the field. I'm a talent scout."

"Talent scout? What kind of talent you scout?"

"For the movies, the theater. I found the best stars we got. It was me spotted the twins in Charlottesville. It was me found Maxa. Found Francie, too—in a strip bar."

"Boy, sure sounds like you put the whole damn crew together, Paulie Boy." I was genuinely impressed. If what he said was true, then he may be able to supply some background on the supporting cast, which could lead to who knows what. "What girlie club'd you find that Francie broad at. She's a looker." I was betting that he didn't yet know about her getting croaked in the skinroom.

"Yeah, she's a cutie. Found her at Juicy Lucy's on Mount Royale Avenue. She liked to try different things so it was easy to get her started. On the drug, I mean. Once you get 'em started on POP you got 'em."

Juicy Lucy's. That was where the Dunn girl had worked. The first victim of the Bolton Hill Butcher. Probably not a coincidence. Could Francie have been the Butcher? She was sure strong enough and her POP addiction could have easily supplied the psycho element necessary.

"Ida Mae and Becky—they were easy, too. I check all the traveling carnies—the ones with the freak shows, I mean. The Senator says the customers with the most money always want to see freaks in snuff films—it's some kinda kinko thing. I thing it's kinda gross myself, but I ain't the one with the *dinero*, know what I mean?"

"I know, I know . . ."

"Anyways, their mom was a religious nut—real gone—and you know how those type are. If they smell a buck, suddenly they interpret the scriptures a brand new way so they can grab the loot without feeling bad. Truhart dumped a wad on those kids and the mother didn't bat an eye. Didn't even say goodbye when we came to take 'em. Turned out to be a good investment, too. But I can't take all the credit. No one coulda known how they were gonna turn out. Vicious," he said, eyeing the sleeping twins with an expression somewhere between distaste and fear. "Those little freak girls are vicious—there ain't no other word for it."

"Yeah, I know. What about Maxa? What's her story?"

"She's got a sad one."

"Don't worry. I got Kleenex."

"Her real name's Elizabeth Ann Short. She changed it to Maxa cause it sounds more mysterious. Plus her boyfriend's German—guess she thinks having a name like that will make him feel more at home."

I felt like a jerk for feeling a pinch at the word "boyfriend" in regards to Maxa. But I felt it all the same. Paul Fish went on:

"She grew up poor in a big family, like me. She had five sisters. I had five brothers—pretty hinky coincidence, huh?"

"Yeah. Hink-O-Rama."

"Anyway, she's from Medford, Massachussets. Moved to the West Coast though when she was just seventeen. Her family probably didn't notice her gone with all the pups running around. It was that way at my house, too."

"Why the move?"

"Same as all the pretty teenage girls. She wanted to be a movie star. Wound up hanging with hookers and lowlifes, though. Same as all the pretty teenage girls."

"Tough break."

"Not so tough, really. She hung with sluts but didn't become one—I guess you wouldn't figure it but Beth's a virgin. Still is. Plus, that's how she met me. I was out there looking for cronies for the boss' show in Baltimore—"

"Talent scouting Hollywood teen hookers. It's a rough life you have, Paulie."

"I don't complain much. Anyways, Beth is right up the boss' alley, right? She don't wear anything but black, she's into all this creepy stuff; voodoo, casting spells—witchy stuff. Plus she's a real kinko to top it off—likes to play rough, likes to play with girls, too—but won't fuck. So I says, to myself, I says: Paulie, this girl is wacko, she's paydirt."

"So she goes back to Baltimore with you to star in the freak show; then what?"

"No. She doesn't—not right away. See, she had this fella. An enlisted man she met in Dago. Right before they shipped him off he proposes to her—a lot of the enlisted guys did that—to make their girlfriends wait. So she's waiting on this fella and says she can't get involved in anything shady, even though I'm waving a handful of C-notes under her nose. Like hanging around hookers ain't shady."

"Dames are funny about stuff like that."

"I think she knew."

"Knew what?"

"Knew The Big Punch was a bust. She had good instincts in them days. Not no more, though."

"So why didn't you just plug her with your narco and move her along that way? Business as usual."

"I'm not sure why I didn't. I couldn't. Not with her."

It didn't take a rocket scientist to figure Paulie boy was warm for Maxa's form. Schoolboy crush, more like. What a schlep. I was anxious to keep the conversation moving:

"So she's waiting for this fella stationed over in Europe—"

"India. He was stationed in India. Beth figured there's no way he'll get hurt stationed where there ain't no action. But he bought it anyhow—they was doing some kind of aerial exercises and something went wrong with one of his plane's engines."

"Man, that's tough . . ."

"Yeah, poor kid took the news real hard. She wanted to leave the Valley because of the bad memories she had there but didn't want to go home to Mommy. She had kept my card and didn't have too many options. She gave a call. The rest is theatrical history."

"What about this German boyfriend? How does he come into it?"

"Oh—he's Truhart's Baltimore man. He's a real fanatic about that kinko stuff so the Senator took a liking to him. Anyway, the Senator's got a lot of German friends." Paul laughed—what he was insinuating was heavy-duty and he didn't care who knew it.

"You saying Truhart's in cahoots with the gerrys?"

"Not cahoots exactly. He doesn't think we'll win the war. Says it doesn't hurt to be friendly with the conquering army before the fact. A lot of the U.S. brass feel that way." If that was true, it was news to me. Me and the rest of the country.

"What's his name, this German boyfriend?"

"Dunno his real name. People call him Red on account of his hair. Bright orange."

"Redd," I said under my breath, thinking.

"Yeah, Red, Red—you hard of hearing or something?"

"No," I said, not really listening, "I'm not hard of hearing."

The fuzzy picture in my head was starting to crystalize. And it had looked a whole lot better fuzzy.

The jabber with Paul Fish turned strictly academic from that point on, the more touchy topics taking a rest with the snoozing Merle family. My forced escort had become my pal in the course of the long ride, which was good considering what I had in mind.

You see, knowing what I now knew—or at least thought I knew, I couldn't let him take me back to The Punch—and there was only one way to prevent that from happening. As the train finally reached the Maryland border at Frederick, I braced myself.

"Should be about twenty minutes more, pal," Paul said to me with a relieved grin. "Then it's dry land and dry martinis. I could go for a pizza—train food is the worst."

"Yeah, pizza sounds great," I replied, sizing him up, wondering if I could take him. Taking my catalog of injuries into consideration—busted hand, missing toe, no balls, multiple head-bumps, I decided that if it came down to a fistfight I'd get whooped. No, I had to be sharp—had to get that gun somehow. The element of surprise was my only friend.

Twenty minutes later the train was screeching to a slow stop at Penn Station. Paul Fish made a move to wake the twins, and I saw the danger in having too many active eyeballs:

"Ah, let 'em sleep a few seconds longer. We're almost there."

Paul looked at me hard, then cracked another grin: "Yeah, why not? They sure are awful cute in dreamland, the little monsters ... "

The train stopped and the doors to the train slammed open—

Paul turned his head at the sound, just for a second—

In one quick movement I reached into his jacket and pulled the .45 out of his waistband. Flushed in the cheeks at the realization of what was happening, he turned to face me—and by doing so rammed his right eye straight into the barrel. Opportunity knocks in the strangest ways . . .

I pulled the trigger.

The blast sprayed the train's interior with blood and brain goo, coating sticky gore and skull chips on several stunned passengers, also managing to bring the hibernating Merle family up and out of La—La Land. Ida Mae looked at me and hissed, covering her chest with all four hands—her first instinct was to protect her sister.

Not losing a second, I trained the gun on Ida Mae's forehead, cocked the trigger.

You see, too much knowledge had come my way—the kind that said yeah, the twins were just kids, sure—but they were also evil incarnate; deceitful, murderous and smart. It was a mercy killing that I had in mind.

"NAAAHHH!!! NAAAHHH!!! N—N—N—NAAAAHHHH!!!! NAAHH!!"

Michael Merle was freaking out at the prospect of losing his precious daughters, the girls he had given up so much to protect.

I looked at him and hesitated, Ida Mae still hissing at me like a serpent.

Then I let the hammer down easy, put the gun in my waistband. To Merle: "Okay. We're even."

I ran out the door of the train, no one on board brave enough to try and stop a man with a gun. On the platform there were no cops, no train security. Just a few redcaps with luggage carts.

Of course, by then I knew better than to be afraid of the cops. The cops were under instructions to protect, not apprehend me.

Pretty hinky, huh?

CHAPTER THIRTEEN

JESUS THE COOK, REVISITED

My new found fearlessness in regards to men in blue suits had me practically skipping to the one place I had previously seen as strictly out of bounds, namely, my own digs: 1216 Bolton Street. If I were an "ordinary" criminal on the run from an "ordinary" criminal justice system, the place would be staked out around the clock and the move on my part would be suicide. Usually, I really like "ordinary". Sometimes, though, "fucked up" can be real interesting.

I didn't even have a key to the place anymore, my peed in drawers left back at the theater house, all jangly contraband in tow. I busted in by tossing my battered little bod against the door.

The place had been ransacked.

But whoever had done the work was a neat-freak, having tried to put everything back where they'd found it—still leaving plenty of traces of the original violation, though. Like a dog who licks up its own vomit, just leaving enough for you to know what happened.

The post ransacking straighten-up campaign was superficially successful though—the place seemed eerily intact; almost exactly how I'd left it. I wondered what was missing—if anything. In fact, everything was so "ordinary" that I instantly slipped into my "ordinary" pattern of making a beeline for the fridge. There was a yellow sheet of paper taped to the ice box with Janice's loopy scrawl on it. Usually such notes said stuff like: "Cutie Pie—went to the store to pick up some milk" or: "Sugar Bear—having lunch with Daddy, see you soon, love you horribly ... "—that sort of thing. This note was a bit out of step with "ordinary", unlike the rest:

"My Dearest Darling,

"If you are reading this it means you are still alive. I am afraid for you and for me—there is blood and evil all around. I haven't been straight with you about Daddy. We have to talk right away, we have to leave, run, hide. Today is Thursday the seventeenth—if you are reading this today then it may not be too late. Meet me at Juicy Lucy's Showbar at ten tonight.

"Love horribly, J"

I felt a pull at my heart but something wasn't right. It was Janice's handwriting but it wasn't her tone. It was too thought out, too rational—it didn't have any sign of the little girl hysterics I had come to know and expect of my wife. Plus, a strip joint would hardly be Janice's first choice for a meeting place. She had written the thing, but the words weren't hers—some one had forced her. I was being set up. Again.

At least I was beginning to recognize the scenario.

I had to think.

I cracked the ice box hunting for grub. Two apples and a hunk of bloody roast beef stared me down. I grabbed an apple, then, as an afterthought, put it back, pulled out the roast, grabbed a knife. As I shut the door, I noticed three packs of something or other on the bottom shelf wrapped in plain brown paper. Probably fish. I hate fish. I let the door close all the way and sliced a hunk of the beef, ate it ravenously without bread, mustard or ceremony. The partially chewed meat knotted wonderfully in my previously empty stomach. I checked the clock: 8:45 PM.

That gave me an hour and fifteen minutes before trekking the four blocks to Mount Royale Street to keep my date with God knows what, armed with Paul Fish's .45 hand cannon, a blood taste on my pallette and the knowledge that someone or something meant to do me dirty when I got there.

Save for some sad-eyed jerk lounging behind the bar and a slow grind floosie on the stage wearing a veil and built to maim, the joint was empty. I was five minutes late.

I instinctively flipped to the possibility that the note had been legit and that something had happened to Janice. I focused: slow down big guy, check the odds—and the odds told me that it wasn't so.

"What'll it be, fella?": Sad-sack. Those eyes: they were familiar somehow . . .

"I'm meeting a friend." I wanted my wits about me, didn't need the haze of alcohol—later, but not now.

"One drink minimum, pal. Sorry, but you gotta buy something or I gotta ask you to—" I didn't need it spelled out:

"Gimme a jungle juice—go easy on the jungle."

As he mixed the thing, I realized I didn't have any cash. He gingerly placed the glass in front of me as if he had used nitro glycerine instead of vodka, said, "That'll be a buck."

"A buck?" I said incredulously, taking a quick, hard swig.

"Entertainment, mack," he said nodding towards the woman on stage who was down to her purple skivvies and a flowing head of jet black hair. She hadn't lost the veil.

"Uh, yeah," I said, trying to think of a good ruse to get out of paying and coming up blank. "Listen, I seem to have left my wallet in my other pants,—could you just,—that is—"

A voice to my left, like a Godsend: "Gotcha covered, Jack." The voice was familiar, deep, cracked.

"I can't break that, pal," said the barkeep, holding the hundred dollar bill up to the light, scrutinizing its authenticity. He turned it over. The back had been marked with dark black ink. A heart shape.

I turned to my left, saw the guy who couldn't be real but somehow was.

"Howdy, Padre," I said to the blind man. "Thanks for the spot. I owe you."

Jesus the Barkeep: "Looks real enough, but I still can't break it."

"That's alright, Harry," smiled the blind man, "let's just call it a tab that's paid in advance. I'll be calling on your services again. Calculate your gratuity however you see fit."

"Sure thing, Reverend Gary. Whatever you say." The barkeep, who was beginning to look terribly familiar to me,

fucking crazy shit. better clear outta here. pretty quick if you gotta brain.

was beaming at the old black man. Harry? Reverend Gary? These guys knew each other? Holy shit.

"You havin' another hard day, I reckon, son," Reverend Gary said to me with a smile, "gonna get harder. Then harder still."

"Yeah, things are hard all around, Reverend," I replied slow and easy, "but not for this boy. Not anymore. I've had it, I'm out. Cops won't touch me for some crazy reason and I'm taking advantage—I'm collecting my wife and I'm blowing town."

"You've been tricked, boy. You always gettin' tricked."

"Yeah, by who? You?"

"Now, that ain't no way to talk to a man juss bought you a drink. 'Specially since I placed the trust of my two great granddaughter' safety in your hands and you let me down. Let me down hard, waving a gun in Ida Mae's face and all. Meant to kill her, didja?"

Great granddaughter? I wasn't in the mood for this double talk so I kept my end straight:

"I did. She lied to me. She's not so sweet. She's a murderer and she tried to trick me into murdering someone, too. I'm starting to piece this sick picture together, see? I got some of the hows and quite a few of the whos but I'm still way short on whys and I'm starting to not give a shit."

Reverend Gary blew off my laundry list of accusations with a shrug; "Lotta people should be dead gonna live, lotta people oughta live gonna die, but I guess that's the way of God sometimes. Those two little girls of mine, well, I tried to save 'em but I guess I knew I couldn't. They'll be here with me soon—after they through with their binness on earth."

"Look, old man—talk straight or stop talking, okay? I'm getting a headache from trying to decipher double talk bullshit—"

"You know my story," his demeanor was patient—just barely; "I'm the father of Nora, name is Gary White. Me and my wife, Myra, we left that little girl with Mr. Branson when the war ended, thought we'd head up north to find us a little home, maybe some land to tend. When we didn't make it back I reckon Mr. Branson and little Nora figgerd we got killed by renegade rebels which was a pretty good guess. There was a lot of that sort of thing going on. You can't just take away a man's belongings and expect him to lay down for it and that's what the North done to the South when they liberated us colored folks. But not all the rebels were out for blood—some of 'em just wanted their possessions back.

"Slavery—" he said the word without bitterness, "just because you make something illegal don't mean it ain't gonna happen. Breaking the speed limit's against the law; so's murder. People do them crimes all the time."

"You're saying that you and your wife were abducted and kept as slaves?"

"Why, sure. And why wouldn't such a thing happen? You think they was Yankee forces stormin' every farm and field in the South just to make sure there weren't any slaves left?" Yeah, I guess I had—seeing how unreasonable the thought was.

"So the whole time you were holed up in some rebel field back in the slave business, " I said, incredulous. "Square one. And nobody knew, you had no way of getting help or even of letting your own daughter know you were still alive."

"Yeah, sure, thass right. But I wouldn't call it square one—it was much worse than square one.

"The folks who captured us, they wasn't like Mr. Branson. They was mean. They worked us hard and beat us regular. The old man took a fancy to Myra and had his way with her. She had a baby by that evil man." I could see his sightless eyes turn wet. "Little white baby. That made the old man's wife mad cause she couldn't have no babies.

She tried to kill that little white baby one night with a soft blanket, shoved it right at that boy child's little pink face. I woke up and saw what she was doing, hollered for her to stop. She got scared and ran back to the big house, told the old man some nonsense about me trying to rape her.

"He come back to the slave quarters to see me, holding a big shovel. He didn't come to kill me because he knew my back was strong and he needed me for the fields—hell, he probably figured out that his missus was lyin'. But he couldn't just let it go what with the her telling the stories she was telling and all.

"He hit me one time on the back of the head with that shovel, hit me so good I fell asleep for a whole day.

"I woke up the next night to the sound of Myra crying and stroking my banged up head." He turned his head so that I could see the scar of a gash where no hair would grow. "But I haven't seen the light of day since then."

"You lost your sight from a bang on the head?"

"It happen that way sometime, sonny.

"Anyways, Myra stayed on at the farmhouse tending to me. The old woman kilt herself not long after, guess she had her reasons. The old man started to soften up as the years went by, I reckon he started to feel bad about what he done to me and all since that little young un sorta made us all family, like it or not.

"It was a hard life being blind but I kinda got used to it. Being blind can help a man in other areas. You play the guitar better. You hear better. You think better. And you dream—*different.* You dream things that sighted people don't know nothing about."

I could tell him a thing or two about bad dreams, I thought. Hell, I had to be dreaming *right now.* "What kind of dreams? Nightmares, you mean?"

"No, nothing like that. In my dreams I could see things. Sometimes I seen things that already happened—but not to me, to other folks, stuff I had no business knowing about. Sometimes I seen things in dreams that was happening in the now but someplace else—I saw my little Nora growing up, I saw her fall in love and I watched her die. All in dreams.

And I seen things that ain't happened yet, too. I had dreams about you long before you were born, Jack. I knew there was this trouble coming."

"So how's it end? Maybe we can save ourselves a little time and effort here."

"The trouble's for sure, but the end ain't. That can still change. But not for my little girls. They as good as dead. Don't blame yourself, Jack. Your intentions was good—it's your instincts that are lacking. You got a good heart, boy, but you're not as smart as you think. And you unlucky."

"Yeah, well, don't rub it in."

"Sorry, son. Juss bein' honest."

"What happened to your wife—Myra?"

"She still alive. She ninety-eight years old now—and still waiting. Ought to be dead by now, I guess, but she cain't let herself go to God till things get straight with her kin. She stubborn that way."

"You say she's waiting. What for?"

"Not what—*who*. Someone coming to help her. Help her stop the thing our baby daughter started. She gotta stop this war on God. It's a war I couldn't stop. And it's a losing one. God fight us with our own blood. Fight us with our babies."

It was beginning to make sense but it didn't seem real; a scary story around a campfire. I had to ask the question that I was afraid to hear the answer to. The one that, in my heart, I guess I knew the answer to.

"The old man and his wife that captured you and your wife, enslaved you all those years after the war—what was their name?"

The old man faced me, his sightless eyes burning into mine. "Enough talk, boy. Time for this old bag of bones to move on. My work here is done."

"Hey, wait just—"

"You know what you need to know. Now do what you gotta do. I'll see you again, son. After."

"But—"

"Goodbye, Jack."

"*Hey, buddy!*"

The sudden bark of the bartender caused my head to snap involuntarily in his direction.

"Hey, buddy—this your newspaper? It's not nice to bring reading materials into a strip joint—makes the entertainers feel neglected."

"Nah, it ain't mine." I turned my attention back to the old man. His barstool was empty.

"Well, if you wanna read," continued the barkeep, "go to a library or a bus station, okay?"

"Look, I said it wasn't my—"

And then I saw the headline. And I knew that the barkeep was right. It *was* my paper:

"BOLTON HILL BUTCHER CLAIMS NINETEENTH VICTIM!!"

Beneath the headline was a picture of a man that I knew, or rather, a man that I had come across pretty damn recently. The caption beneath the mugshot photo read:

"BLOOD LEGACY: Ex—con Harold R. Fish, fourth son of the infamous Grace Budd Killer and nineteenth victim of equally notorious Bolton Hill Butcher, was a fry cook at The Maryland House on South Carey Street in West Baltimore."

I looked up at the barkeep who bore a whole lot more than a passing resemblance to the man who's picture graced page one. He was smiling.

"How's about another round, mack? According to this c—note you got about ninety-nine more of these babies coming.."

"Yeah," I said to the man who looked exactly like a certain dead fry cook named Harold Fish. "Yeah, I'll have another."

Jesus the Cook Resurrected grinned wide in my direction: "Friend of yours? Sorry, we don't serve his kind in here." He broke into a laugh and motioned to the barstool that had been previously occupied by the good Reverend Gary White.

On it sat a very large rat.

An orange rat, sitting up on its haunches, holding something gold and shiny in its mitts. It was holding its little prize out to me, looking at me sideways with one eye, twitching its whiskers . . .

And then I recognized the gold and stoneless ring that I had presented to my wife on our wedding day . . .

"That'll be a buck," said the dead man behind the bar.

"But I thought you said—"

"Just what are you trying to pull, mack?" The dead man's face lost its humor and that ain't all. Suddenly, the color was gone from it—except for a greenish hue. And his nose was gone—sliced off neatly. Dry, rusty looking blood clung to his lips and chin beneath the hole. "Whaddaya think, Redd? Think I oughta smash this deadbeat's brains in with this baseball bat" He was talking to the rat. Pal Rat.

But the rat was no longer a rat. It was an orange haired man. It was the man I had met at the theater house, the man Paul Fish had referred to as Maxa's boyfriend. Only difference (beside the fact that his hair was red now instead of brown) was that he wasn't making any effort to hide the German accent. "Oh no, Harry. He'll pay. He'll pay with this."

The orange haired man held my wife's wedding ring between thumb and forefinger, placed it on his tongue and then closed his mouth and grinned his little rat grin. I watched as he swallowed it, bringing peels of laughter from the dead man and the stripper, the latter of which had come down from the stage and was now standing to my right wearing nothing but a purple g-string and that damn black veil. But I recognized the laugh. I turned to face her and I recognized the lips and teeth that peered beneath the veil. And I recognized Maxa's sweet chocolate breath, too.

I reached for the gun that I'd planted in my pant waist. But it wasn't there.

"Looking for this?" said Maxa, inspiring renewed vigor in the laughter of her devil cohorts. She held the gun up and pressed its barrel against my pursed lips. "Say aahhh," she said.

I complied and she pushed its long barrel as far as it would go into my throat, pushing on that tickly part that makes a person want to vomit. Then, with her free hand, Maxa pulled off the veil. I had been wrong.

It was not Maxa.

Janice's eyes were red and teary as she cocked the hammer and said to me with profound, comic sadness: "Why hast thou forsaken us?"

My wife pulled the trigger and my world went bright red.

CHAPTER FOURTEEN

DEARLY BELOVED

My eyes opened on blackness.

Contrary to what I thought I knew, my skull had not been exploded by Paul Fish's .45.

My arms and legs were strapped tight to my sides, my head propped up by something hard like a cinder block introducing my chin firmly to my chest. I strained against the straps, the tiniest movement causing the bent up, cold metal table I was strapped to (only three legs of which contacted the floor at any given time) to rattle obnoxiously. I tried rocking back and forth on the thing—maybe if I turned it over the impact of my fall would break or at least loosen the straps. After a few fruitless seconds in this direction a loud *pop* filled the room. Then: an electric scratching noise.

Then:

"Hey, baby—you awake?" The voice was a whisper, but amplified, seeming to come out of every corner of the room—it was Janice's voice. I tried to answer, but the effort only informed me that my mouth had been sealed shut with the gummy finality of industrial duct tape. "It's okay, Honey Bun, don't try to talk. I wouldn't be able to hear you anyway. I'm just a movie." Her soft tone was loud in the room. Deafening.

And then a huge square of white light appeared on a blank wall before me. The white square turned grey and large numbers flashed one at a time in backward sequence, each number in the center of a circle divided into quarters by cross hairs, the numbers took turns going passed on the huge projection of grey, black and white light:

10, 9, 8, 7, 6, 5, 4, 3, 2, 1.

Every corner of the lighted wall became eclipsed by the image of a huge face. Janice's face.

The face spoke:

"I've always loved you. I loved you years before we met. I will love you long after you are dead. My love won't die.

The huge face smiled sweetly, sentimentally even, and went on:

"It began with a newspaper article," the face said.

"The date of the paper was August 5, 1918. The story was about a little boy only five years old, three years younger than me, who had done a bad thing in a sacred place—in a funeral home. You didn't think I knew about your past, did you Jackie? That's ironic, baby. It's your past that brought us together.

"The article said that the little boy was doing things to the bodies—to the female bodies in particular. Something about cannibalism, something about perversions, something about 'unprintable'. 'Very odd and frightening behavior for such a small boy', the papers said. And that's probably what the townspeople thought when they burned your father's business to the ground. But that's never what I thought.

"I always understood.

"And I knew then that there was someone who would understand me, too. Understand my secret feelings.

"I clipped that little article. I read it over and over again, I read it when I got lonely, I read it when I felt . . . *the need*—the need in my heart that I felt but was afraid to act on, the same need that you had. No one ever knew that I kept the clipping or that I'd even read it—it was my little secret to myself. I read it over and over again. I read it a million times."

She paused, expressionless, staring ahead for a moment, then went on.

"One day I smelled death in my father's house. I don't mean that symbolically—it was in the closet of Ronnie's little room on the first floor.

"A rat had died in the wall.

"Mommy thought it was sweet that I was beginning to go into Ronnie's room to play—she knew I didn't like the baby—what she didn't know was that I was going in there so I could sit in his closet and breathe the thick, sweet air. The smell stirred something in me, something forbidden and exciting. I would sit in there and stroke the wall where the smell was strongest. I stroked the wall so much that eventually the wallpaper there began to peel up. To my surprise the plaster behind the peeling wallpaper was crumbling apart. An exciting thought came to me.

"I decided to try to find the rat.

"For two weeks I pretended to go into Ronnie's room to play—always going into the closet to dig away with a little wire coat hanger and my fingernails. The hole got bigger and bigger.

"Once, mother came in and called for me. I came out of the closet and made a big tantrum about her spoiling my hiding spot—I told her I was playing hide and seek with Ronnie. She asked me how I could play hide and seek when Ronnie was asleep in his crib. Imagine that—a five year old who still slept in a crib! Ronnie was so spoiled.

"I started to cry when mother confronted me about the truth. That's what little girls do when they're caught in a fib. They cry. Mother said *there, there* and put me to bed. My visits to Ronnie's room continued and Mother never brought it up again.

"After two weeks I found the rat. As strong as the smell was, its body was hardly decomposed. It was as big as a cat and its fur was a strange color for a rat. Orange. I took his fat little body and I put it in a shoe box beneath my bed. Sometimes I would talk to the rat and I would imagine him talking to me, too. I even named him. I called him Redd.

"But I had found another thing behind the wall in the closet. Something glorious. I had found a whole other world.

"There was a staircase behind the wall, Jackie. A long stair case. It went down and down and down and down. I followed it and it showed me things.

"And then I showed Ronnie things."

And then Janice's tale took a sharp turn—I sensed she was leaving a hole in this odd confessional. I felt my heart pound as if it were going to explode . . .

"When Ronnie turned up missing there was such a fuss, I went to go hide in my room. But when I pulled out Redd's little shoe box bed so I could tell him all about the police station. . . . something bad happened.

"Redd wasn't in the little box anymore. He had disappeared.

"I cried for days after I found Redd missing, which turned out to be a good thing because all the newspapers and police and friends of Mommy and Daddy thought I was crying because of Ronnie being missing." She giggled at the irony.

I couldn't focus on the words as the movie spoke *at* me—it all seemed too much, a bad dream. I just stared numbly at the flickering image of my wife, wondering. About a lot of things—mostly about where all this horror was leading to, but also about myself in general. The thing that Janice couldn't understand was that I was not like her—not anymore at least. Somehow, I had changed when I got older, it was as if the evil person I had been as a child was a separate entity from who I had become. Somehow, mercifully, I had been allowed to leave the evil behind me as I made my way into adulthood, and yet my young doppleganger— my other, former self—had survived. But it had survived as a separate consciousness; an evil twin disembodied, still hungry for death. It wasn't me, though. Not anymore, it wasn't. My old evil—child self visited me in dreams, trying to seduce me with memories of my old bad habits, but the seduction had only repulsed me.

I couldn't focus on what the face on the screen was saying now, what she was trying to accomplish with this weird melodrama on film, didn't *want* to focus on it, but she went on, anyway:

"I waited for you, Honey Bun.

"I waited for you while you were in the bad boy's school. I waited till you were eighteen years old and got out. But once you were out, I was too shy to talk to you. I've always been so shy.

"I was watching you, spying on you the whole time. I just knew that you'd do something—something like at your father's funeral home. When you did I was going to be the one to catch you, and then I was going to tell you it was okay, that I understood. Then we would be soulmates. We would be like Bonnie and Clyde only we wouldn't rob banks.

"But you never did. You got that dirty job on the loading dock and you started drinking a lot but you never did anything. Well, you know— you never *did* anything. I was afraid that you'd changed. That you weren't the same little boy anymore, the boy that I had loved. Twelve years passed. I lived a dull and lonely life and so did you. I could never approach you—I'm so shy. But I watched you. And I began to believe that you really had changed, that you no longer had *the need*. I felt lost and out of love. It was like someone had died.

"Then the Bolton Hill murders started to happen and I was just sure it was you—and I fell in love all over again.

"All those killings must have been tiring for you—you began oversleeping and got yourself fired at the docks for showing up late too much. Then you got a job washing dishes and bussing tables at the Crockpit. It was my big chance to meet you. The man of my dreams.

"I became a regular at The Crockpit.

"Every time you came out to bus a table there I was sitting at the bar—and I always had a big smile for you. It took you two months to work up the nerve to ask to buy me a drink. I said, sure. One thing led to another—you were very romantic."

That's true about me, you know. I'm a real Valentino.

Her flickering face began to get smaller, slowly sucked into the center of the illuminated square, a reverse zoom.

Whoever was filming my wife's monologue was slowly backing away from her now, making her huge face smaller and smaller, slowly revealing her surroundings.

Her hair and neck entered the frame of light from the top, bottom and sides. I was able to make out a bit of her blouse. Then I could see that it was plaid and sleeveless. Casual. Smart. Practical. Something you'd wear around the house.

Now I could make out the top of her slacks. And the fact that she was standing next to a table. It was a surgeon's table—and there was a body on it, covered by a sheet. Beside the table was another smaller one that held a group of small cutting instruments. The black and white image didn't give up any information about the color of the instruments, but I had a hunch the thick gray would translate to a dull, rusty orange in a technicolor world. I thought I saw one of the instruments move by itself; the reflex squirm of a freshly severed rat tail. The camera stopped its retreat once I had a good view of Janice in her father's operating theater, standing by the body beneath the sheet.

Her pale, china doll face shattered into a million shards of laughter:

"It's funny really, don't you think?—about Daddy, I mean. He's not an evil man. He hates violence—and he's never been much for sex, either. He did this all for me. After Ronnie died—and yes, Ronnie died because I killed him, Jack. After they found the body and Daddy put the pieces together—quite literally, actually—he decided he wanted to cure me. Imagine that—cure *me!* I'm not sick. Do you think I'm sick, Jackie? Well, I'm not. And neither are you.

"You've been under the weather a little since that whore Maxa infected you. But don't worry. I can fix you. Things won't be the same, though. They'll never be the same again."

She began to pull the sheet back from the body slowly, exposing feet first. Two feet.

Nine toes.

"You shouldn't have talked to that black haired bitch, Jackie. Shouldn't have kissed her. She's a bad lady."

Two knees.

"And she made you sick with Daddy's drug. She stuck the needle in the back of your neck while she kissed you. While .. *you* . . . kissed . . . *HER* . . ." Angry now.

"Making you better will hurt—but it's the only way."

Belly button.

She began to touch the little knives on the smaller table. She brushed her fingertips over them, choosing, teasing. Then she picked one up.

I squirmed and winced as I watched. Hell, I cried like a baby. So would you, smart guy.

The simple operation of castration was performed quickly and professionally, there was not much blood. Janice, it seemed, had done this sort of thing before.

My dearly beloved picked up the severed red meat-marbles gingerly with one hand and walked away from the table that held the body of the sleeping man with nine toes. The camera followed her. Against the wall of the operating room was a shiny metal counter, on it an electric hotplate. It was plugged in.

She dropped the bloody bits onto its surface and I could hear a sssssshhhhhhhhing sound as they sizzled on contact. She sprinkled some powder from a shaker onto the pan, held the hotplate by its handle and rolled its contents around a little. Then she put the hotplate back on the counter. Picked up a fork.

She stabbed the fork into one of the fricasseed testicles and held it up, faced the camera again. Smiled. Spoke softly:

"*Gumdrop,*" she whispered.

I could feel tender hands at my temple then. Tender hands brushing my face. Tender hands removing the tape from my mouth. I was not surprised when the gag in my mouth was replaced with the barrel of a rather large hand cannon, tickling my tonsils.

Gun in my mouth? Another day at the office.

With all this distraction, I still couldn't take my eyes off the smiling image of my wife.

Chewing.

CHAPTER FIFTEEN

OLD SPORT

The screen went blank.

The gunsight knocked hard on my upper teeth as the barrel withdrew, the sound segueing musically with the *clipclop clipclop* of high heels in the dark—and then the clicking of a light switch. A fluorescent overhead bulb flickered momentarily like lightening before settling into a thick buzz of hard white light. I pressed my eyes shut in the glare.

Clipclop clipclop.

The heels and gun had a face. Maxa leaned over me with a weak smile. But she didn't look right. Her face was her own but it wasn't—it was familiar but strange.

like the strange way you recognize people in dreams . . .

And her hair was bright orange.

I had plenty to say to her. I kept my mouth shut.

"I thought you might be interested in seeing Janice's little home movie. You may have noticed she was a little pissed when she made it. You kissing strange girls and all—word gets around about things like that." The voice was deep with a German accent—a man's voice; the same man who'd swallowed my wedding ring at Juicy Lucy's not long ago.

This was Maxa. And it wasn't.

"I know your lovely wife wanted to be here, to be with you when you saw it. I'm afraid that isn't possible—she's predisposed right now. Couldn't make it. She's sorry. Real damn sorry. In fact, she's so damn sorry it's killing her." The German accent turned the word "killing" into "killINK". A giggle came out of the orange haired Maxa's mouth. It was familiar.

This was Maxa. This *wasn't* Maxa:

"She's a lost cause. Locked in the belly of this stinking pile of brick and wood. Flames should reach her soon. Dearly beloved. Poor, poor dearly beloved." That being said, I became aware of the faint odor of smoke in the room. A distant fire—but not too.

"Everything's gone just as planned," I watched as her lips spoke the hard sounding words that didn't fit the soft looking mouth. "Almost. Everything but one."

The thing that was and wasn't Maxa stroked the bridge of my nose with the butt of what I now recognized as a .45—real fucking popular caliber. And continued:

"This building is burning. All of its impurities will be burned with it. This place has been quite useful through the years but it's become a liability. It has to go. *C'est la vie, c'est la morte.* The fire? No, I didn't set it—but I won't stop it. Bet you'll never guess who did set it. Go ahead—guess!"

I thought it over quickly and came up with two possibilities—the only two men who had displayed an iota of decency since I had began this sad journey through hell. I took a stab:

"Garvey."

"Very Good! Sharp little fuck aren't, you? That's right—the esteemed Dr. Charles Garvey can add arson to his long list of accomplishments. And now for pop quiz number two, Mister Sharpfuck: *Why'd* he do it?"

Another educated stab: "Guess it dawned on him that all his work trying to cut the evil out of men's hearts was a dead end street. Guess it dawned on him he was only causing more evil. Now he wants out."

"Right again! But you left something out—something important. Something you should have figured by now." She (?) paused expectantly—but had stumped the band with that last bit of tune. I told her (it?) so.

The Maxa-thing's eyes burned cold grey as it went on:

"Something else dawned on the good doctor. It dawned on him that he wasn't just battling science anymore. Wasn't just battling nature. It dawned on him that he was battling God. Had been all along. Garvey was one of the Four chosen to set the Great War—the Apocalypse—into motion. Or stop it. He couldn't stop it, though—didn't have the stomach or the mind. Too much booksmarts, not enough streetsmarts. He was chosen for the same reason that the other three were chosen. He had committed an act so offensive to God as to be Unforgivable.

"God punished the Four Horsemen by putting the seed of evil in their unborn children. It is the children that will carry us to the Apocalypse."

I interrupted, a strong desire to cut to the chase:

"Who are you?"

"I am God."

"You lying prick. Who are you? *What* are you?"

Peels of laughter from the Maxa-Thing and then: "Okay, okay; God I'm not. Let's call me God's messenger, God's servant, God's little asswiper. Call me what you want. People around here call me Redd. Some folks say Satan or the Devil—but that's so dramatic. I kind of like Old Sport. Men always try to pit me against God in their stories. How unimaginative. Isn't it obvious that we work together? I'm an employee. Not exactly a favored employee; hence the steady stream of shit detail I get. Something about falling from grace, etcetera, etcetera—such a tedious business. But I've come to like my vocation even if I don't like my boss much. But, hey, don't hold that against me—can you say you've liked very many of your bosses?"

I couldn't.

"Well then, you see." Redd, Old Sport, whoever.. laid the gun on my chest and went on.

I didn't look at the gun. But I felt its weight on me, knew it was there, knew that somehow getting a hand free and on it was my best chance.

"The birthright of the children of the Horsemen was to commit atrocities. Atrocities that somehow pave the way for mankind's destiny, mankind's undoing. You are one of those children, Jack. You were the only apple in the bunch with enough balls—*oops*—bad analogy—sorry! Enough inner strength, let's say, to do something to stop the inevitable, to hurt me. But you weren't smart enough. Now it's too late."

I sensed that it wasn't. Redd seemed nervous—there was something missing in his grin, something that didn't quite add up for him.

I decided to bluff—act like I knew something that could foil things. Couldn't hurt.

"It's not gonna happen, Old Sport. I'm the one's gonna stop it and you know it. You could kill me but it won't help. It's over, you fuck."

His face blanked, then smiled: "Name your price, Dellus. We all have prices. But give it to me. I must have it. Don't and you'll be very, very sorry."

Keeping a poker face was tough—this was one bluff I didn't expect to have any luck with. I'm unlucky—remember? My mind raced trying to figure out what went right, what could I possibly have that this guy wanted. No time for that now, I reasoned with myself quickly, got to play some poker:

"Maxa and Janice—let them go now. I want a car with a full tank of gas waiting outside in thirty minutes. Then you can have what you want.

"Your sow wife is already dead—and what's she to you anyway? She ate your balls, remember? And Maxa—she belongs to me of her own accord. She too, was brought to this place for crossing God. She was a dabbler in the black arts—strictly a morbid curiosity for her at first—it always is. But when her fiancee saw flames and the unsmiling face of God as his plane went hurtling onto those mountains—she felt true grief, and more importantly, true rage. She began to use the forbidden spells—and she summoned *me*.

"She presumed that invoking me into her body would give her my powers and that once having secured such powers, she could bring some kind of revenge to the heavens. But she was wrong. When she brought me forth it was an invitation—and it was *I* who gained power. You see, I can take possession of almost any animal—a dog, a cat, a lion, or as you know, a rat. I can also take the form of inanimate objects—a set of rusty orange tools, for instance. But it is one of God's little rules that I can not enter the body of a human unless I am invited. You can imagine how seldomly that happens.

"Not so fast, devil. I saw you and Maxa in the room together, in the office ... " I thought I saw a hole in his tale. If he needed Maxa's body to take human form, then how could the two of them exist separately in the same room?

"Smoke. I was in your mind's eye just as I appear to many in dreams. But when I am in the body of this woman I am more than smoke. I can hold this gun. I am flesh. So, you see, I couldn't possibly ... "

"No deal. Kill me and get it over with, you sorry sack of shit."

"In due time. But don't fool yourself. I will get that paper. Somehow Lieutenant Black and his girlfriend got it to you. It's the only thing that can stop Elijah from fulfilling my dream. The only variable. But I'm not worried. You'll tell."

He was worried and so was I. The paper? Lieutenant Black? His girlfriend?

Then it hit me. . . .

Lieutenant Black was the cop that Maxa had told me about that day in the dark, the dirty cop who ran security for the Big Punch. And the "paper" Redd was showing such concern about now was the list of patrons that Black had been keeping as insurance. So, for at least a little while, Maxa had escaped the presence of Redd, long enough to tell me her fears, tell me about the Lieutenant's letter. Then of course Redd regained possession of her actions, that's when she turned considerably less attractive by injecting me with that rat poison, POP.

My salvation: he thought I was hiding the list somewhere. That explained why my place had been ransacked. But he hadn't looked in the one, most obvious place. He thought I'd stashed it, or sent it to someone—either action would have been intelligent, logical acts on my part. The truth was plain dumb.

I was lying on it.

Francie had stuffed a folded piece of paper in my pants pocket the day I fell out of the peach tree. I had been so distracted by the following hallucinogenic events at the police station that I'd never taken it out of my pocket, never unfolded it.

In fact:

I had forgotten about it completely. Hadn't give it a second thought. It was still in my pants pocket . . . It was beneath me right now.

But if it was the Lieutenant's list, then why did *Francie* give it to me—why did she seem to not want the Lieutenant to know what she was doing? And why give it to me in the first place?

Unless . . .

It was all part of their plan. Francie slipped me the list in a covert way so I would be afraid to open it in front of the Lieutenant, so he wouldn't have to explain it, so I wouldn't have to act on it until absolutely necessary. Until after the plan to destroy The Big Punch had been set irretrievably in motion. Sheer thought was causing actual physical pain in my nut until, mercifully, Redd broke my train—wreck of thought:

"Oh yes, you'll tell. Do you remember the little movie that Elijah showed to you—the one starring your little friends, Ida Mae and Becky? How would you like to star in their next full length feature?" Peels of cruel laughter. "Henry! Action!"

A bright flood light went on and I could see the nose of a large camera pointing down at me from a small hole in the wall directly above a closed door. The man filming I assumed to be Henry Fish, the man who had given me my initial greeting to this fucked up world. Henry was the other man, besides Garvey, who I'd figured to have a crumb of decency in his soul. I wasn't so sure anymore.

"Rebecca!" the Devil called Becky by her proper name. I wondered absently why he didn't shout Ida Mae's name as well.

The twins appeared in the doorway beneath the camera. Ida Mae's hands were at her sides and empty—but Becky's hands were not. Each hand held a long sharp knife. Long, sharp, rusty orange knives. Redd spoke:

"Now, Rebecca. I won't say another word. I want you to *play* with

Mista Jack. Do what the little knives want you to do—like always. Only stop if he tells me the one little thing that I want to know. Do you understand? "

One of Becky's hands responded by flicking an orange knife at the top of the twins' dress, severing the top button and exposing Ida Mae's bony chest. A face was drawn there, but it wasn't the smiley face that I'd seen there days before. It was a demon face; pointed teeth and cruel eyes—drawn with orange lipstick.

The twins took a step towards me.

CHAPTER SIXTEEN

IMPLEMENTS OF HELL

The twins scuttled towards me with a pronounced unevenness, not quite a limp. It was as if the front pair of legs—Becky's legs—were dragging the double body towards me without consent of the back pair.

And then I realized that the scowl on Ida Mae's face wasn't of malice but of pain.

She was straining against her sister's will. It was Becky coming at me with the knives. It was Becky who had committed the atrocities in Truhart's movies. Ida Mae had been unwilling then as she was now.

I ain't no monster . . .

Suddenly Ida Mae was not fighting her sister, the twins pushing forward with all four legs in the direction of the table that I lay strapped to. The double body made its way to my right shoulder side, Becky's little rump pressed to the metal table leg. Both knives were poised above my chest in ritual fashion—though I knew that such a mercifully quick death would not be to the taste of the monster that I'd seen in Truhart's snuff film. Redd cackled something in German through Maxa's contorted face and let out a laugh that could've passed for the rabid howl of a wolf. I braced for the stinging, slow tear of rusty knives. Prayed for death to not come too slowly.

Then things happened too quick.

Becky's hands were suddenly empty.

Both knives had been snatched from her. Redd let out a panicked shriek, realizing, or at least getting the general jist before I did, of what was about to take place. The hands that had stolen the orange knives belonged to Ida Mae.

Ida Mae plunged both knives into her sister's back, blood spraying like a hose into my eyes and mouth, smelling of stale urine, tasting of sea water. My eyes pressed shut in the sting of spurting blood—then I felt the seesaw of a knife pressing near my shirt sleeve and my left eye cracked open . . .

Ida Mae was cutting my straps. Before Redd had become completely hip to Ida Mae's coup, I was able to get an arm free and snatch the gun from its perch on my chest. Redd caught on pronto, intensified his shrieking and tried to get me in a headlock before I could teeter—totter myself from the table—the blood was too slick, though, and he couldn't get a grip—letting me slide to my desired destination: Floorsville, USA. On my way down I couldn't help glancing up at the little movie camera peering out of the hole above the door—it appeared that Henry wasn't missing a frame of the action. Upon hitting the blood slick floor, I absently stroked my hair into place. It's funny how people respond to cameras—no matter what the circumstance.

After my quick vanity check, I raised the .45 in the direction of what I figured to be the most immediate danger. And, hey, what better way to test Redd's claims of demonic immortality—at the very least I'd be doing Maxa a solid.

I squeezed one off right into the fucker's heart.

Fucker didn't fall down. Fucker didn't squirt blood. Fucker didn't even say ouch.

Fucker exploded.

But not into bits of blood and bone. The pieces that flew out of the explosion were little creatures—squirmy little bodies with heads and claws. Screeching mouths with chubby torsos and whipping tails. The blood drenched bodies of rats. Hundreds of them.

I looked down to see the one part of Maxa's ruined body that seemed to have survived in human form. Her head lay in a puddle of scampering gore—covered rats, screaming and hissing, eyes now bright yellow, tongue serpentine and forked, flicking rapidly: *in—out.*

Then I was blinded by a blow to the head.

"Mista Jack, look out!"

The stars cleared form my vision in time to dodge Becky's next kick.

Becky had not been mortally wounded by her sister's knife attack because Ida Mae knew that the twins shared a heart—she'd avoided piercing it for the sake of her own preservation. But as long as one survived, so did they both.

Blood was frothing from Ida Mae's mouth now—the injuries she'd inflicted on her sister had taken a grim toll on herself as well. She plunged the knives down again, this time into the area of Becky's back close to where her neck should be, near Ida Mae's own chest. She began a sawing motion with the blades at the ribs and spine, around Becky's shoulders.

"Mista Jack! Grab her feet! Grab Becky by the feet!"

Made sense to me—I didn't much like getting mule kicked. But Ida Mae had something else in mind.

Ida Mae had freedom in mind.

After I'd gotten a good grip on Becky's bony little ankles, Ida Mae dropped the knives clanking to the floor.

And she jammed both hands into the little gory openings around her sister's neck—the openings that she had just carved.

And pushed with all her might.

"Pull, Mista Jack! Pull hard!"

I complied, not knowing exactly why, yanking hard on the little feet. Ida Mae pushed hard on Becky's shoulders.

As Becky's head ripped free from Ida Mae's misshapen sternum there was a great sucking sound—but not nearly as much blood as you'd expect. Ida Mae fell backwards to the floor.

And Becky's head emerged into the light.

The skin that stretched across the tiny skull was veiny and burgundy in color with thin patchy hair like a wet coconut. The eyes were wide and staring but not squinting in the light like they ought to have. It's as if Becky realized she had seconds to live, seconds to take in the world around her with those infant eyes. She was willing to suffer the inevitable searing pain of light for such a taste.

Her eyes were familiar to me, her nose was a baby's, her forehead was a bit too large, her mouth was full.

Clenched in Becky's tiny baby teeth was Ida Mae's heart. Still beating. Becky's blinking eyes met mine and I placed the familiarity. Her eyes *were* mine. The eyes of the small boy in my dream. My own eyes as a child. When I had been a monster.

Becky's teeth bit down hard and the heart bled like a squeezed sponge. The yellow eyes went glassy and Becky fell to the floor, dead.

My attention turned to the liberated body of Ida Mae, minus a heart, but somehow not quite dead.

"I'm free." Through blood reddened teeth, she smiled.

I knew I wasn't free yet, though.

On my way to the door, I brushed off and pulled at the dozen or so chubby little rat bodies that were lunching on the scrawny flesh of my ankles.

I made a quick observation as I ran through the room's only exit; the camera above was now unmanned.

Common sense would have launched me to the front door of the big house, landing face first on the front lawn, screaming for help, curling neatly into a fetal position. I'm not famous for my common sense, though.

I ran down the steps. Into the flames and smoke.

Looking for Janice. The only woman I'd ever really loved.

CHAPTER SEVENTEEN

AND I HAVE LEARNED THAT SUFFERING MEANS NOTHING

I charged down the hall with a shoe-skidding slide-stop at the top of the first flight, where I proceeded to slam myself down the steps two at a time. But I wasn't so frantic that the larger points made in the last twenty minutes or so had gotten lost on me. It was plain to me now that most of the people and things that I had set out to save in the first place were lost.

It hit me on the way down that first bunch of steps that Janice really must be dead—almost had to be—and dead by her own father's hand, no less. Even if she wasn't, she might as well be.

Because if she wasn't dead then she was locked up tight in one of the cells awaiting the rapid approach of smoke and flames. I couldn't save her and I knew it—there were too many doors to check and the smoke was thickening by the second. Even if by some miracle I did locate her, I wasn't in any shape to be breaking down reinforced steel doors.

Still, something pressed me on.

It also dawned on me that the one thing Redd had feared, the one thing that he believed could prevent his vision of apocalypse, was in my possession. And it would perish along with me if I insisted on pursuing such a patently hopeless cause. To find my wife.

My feet carried me forwards just the same.

I leapt over the last six steps of the stairwell, the soles of my wingtips hitting hard on the landing, a shot of pain crackling like lightening through my stitched groin and my four-toed foot telling me to fuck off in no uncertain terms. I paused to survey the row of heavy steel doors lining the hallway. Naturally, all were locked.

I pounded on them all anyway—shouting Janice's name into the dark porthole of each one. Fully aware of the loopiness of my actions, I intended to repeat this ritual on every floor if necessary. After the last door of the first level yielded nothing, I ran back to the stairwell, taking the steps three at a time as I plunged to the next level down—aware of the pain in my body in a detached, aching way.

The smoke was very thick now. I commenced pounding on the doors regardless; gradually the metal that connected with my fists was getting hotter and hotter—cluing me to the tough little truth that the locked cells had become ovens. And the cells on the lower levels could only be hotter.

Janice was dead. Had to be.

Irrationally undeterred, I continued more frantically than ever, my shouts hoarsening with the smoke, my pounding fists growing tender in the heat. Even if I did have a mind to give up, I wouldn't have had the strength to climb back up to the ground level.

A thought: I'm sunk.

I didn't make it half way down the hall before I collapsed, falling to my knees, my whole body crippled by sooty poison filling my lungs. The smoke played hell with my eyes, stinging bad, forcing me to shut them tight, rubbing. When I opened them again the pain was only worse—I closed them again instantly.

"Eyes can be a nuisance if you need 'em to see. Me, well, somethin' stingin' my eyes I just close 'em up. See as good as always."

I recognized the voice of the old blind man. With eyes closed, I reached out in the direction of where I guessed him to be standing but touched nothing.

"Take me," I coughed, "take me to Janice. I have to see my wife."

"I'm sorry boy. You ought to know by now that little girl is dead. She's in a better place now. No more hurting. Not for her or anyone around her."

"If she's dead then I have to see her dead. Take me."

Reverend Gary sighed. "Never took you for a genius, boy, but I never 'spected you to be so all-fired stupid neither. You know what yer doin'? Yer diving head first into a mountain of flames lookin' for a particular ash when there's a world of livin' and breathin' babies that only you can snatch from the mouth of doom. Well, surely you are a fool. Yer heart and yer mind ought to sit down and talk every once in a while, boy. But at least it's the foolishness of the heart that you listen to. Your stupidity ain't never been motivated by selfish reasons—that's your saving grace. You don't have the brains to do good by no one, but you always mean to do right. Always have. That's your salvation. And the salvation of the world. That's how you shook loose the evil of yer kin, the evil that got stuck in yer heart before birth. That's how come you can look the devil in his yella eye an' tell 'em where to get off." He paused and then, chuckled. "I about split a gut watching you tell off Old Sport. He ain't used to that kinda gumption. You sure ruffled that old bird's feathers!"

I still couldn't pry my eyes open against the smoke, but I felt the presence of Reverend Gary grow closer, felt his gentle and weathered hand stroke my hair as I lay gasping. I wanted to speak but could only muster a croak. The ghost went on, seemingly unconcerned with my dying state:

"Well, boy, this is it. You won't be seeing the likes of this old ghost no more—'cept maybe in dreams. So I'll just be tellin' you what you need to know and git on. Here—put this over your mouth—makes breathin' easier in the smoke." I felt something cool and moist touch my forehead, grabbed for the wet rag and tried sucking air through it. It helped a little.

"Guess I knew dem little babies a mine good as dead, but you cain't blame a fella fer hopin'. I was thinkin' they might come around to good like you did. You was the only one managed to turn hisself around like that—that's why I been botherin' ya. Just trying to give you a friendly shove in the right direction is all. Well, it seems to be working out all right, me meddlin' and all. Up to now, that is. I mean here we are just about won out against the devil and you gotta drop the ball at the forty yard line with this crazy notion of killin' yerself and every hope the world ever had—tryin' to find someone thass already a goner. And that someone you lookin' fer done gave up the right to be alive long time ago anyway if you ask me."

"Who's asking you?" I knew he was right—Janice was a murderer and pure evil to boot if you added all the evidence up. And even though she robbed me of my beloved man—marbles and filmed the event for posterity, I couldn't let go of my feelings for her. She was the only one who really knew me—bad and good—and loved me anyway. Unconditionally. And if what Old Sport said was true about our evil being handed down through our parents, through some kind of curse or other, then well, maybe she wasn't responsible for what she had become.

"Sorry, boy," Reverend Gary said with a pure warmth in his voice, "I know you're sensitive. Plus, it ain't nice of me to rub it in, true or not. I got loved ones done bad things too, and now they're dead just like yourn. But I guess you figured by now that though they both done bad things, only Becky was a product of that curse. Ida Mae was always pure as snow.

(I ain't done dem things, Mista Jack . . .)

"You and Ida Mae a lot alike, boy. You had it easy, though—you left yer evil part in the land of dreams and memories. Ida Mae hadda go through her short little life with the jaws of evil clamped onto her heart." I could hear a terrible sadness creep into his rich voice, tearing at the edges of it. "Pure evil latched onto that little girl—seeing things and knowing things by no earthly means. Pure evil bossin' her little girl movements around, making her do things, causing death and pain that only Ida Mae could see, never explaining *why.*

"In this life, son, sometimes a man does a little dance with the devil. Sometimes he does something he oughtn't, something he regrets later, something that brings shame to his heart. But little children, little ones like Ida Mae—children ought never to dance with the devil. It ain't fair and it ain't right. They shouldn't be born with evil teeth nibblin' at their hearts, shouldn't be made to decide between dyin' and dancin'."

The Reverend's demeanor changed in a blink, the tearfulness left his voice and his tone became instructional.

"I guess you know things ain't quite resolved today. Ida Mae is free and Becky won't be causin' no more pain and you, Mista Nine Toes and No Balls, you got the salvation of the world in your hip pocket. How 'bout that. Funny story 'bout that letter—how it came to be. Lieutenant Black bein' a cop and Francie bein' a stripper I guess you'd figure them to be natural enemies like a snake and a rat. But they had one thing in common—POP. Garvey infected the Lieutenant so's he could have him some free police protection and Paul Fish infected Francie so she could be used in the underground horror shows. This led to that and not long after the two met they took a stone liking to one another, an understanding. They were both afraid, both made slaves by a drug that they hated. They wanted more than just to kick it—they wanted to end it; period. Black told Francie he was done with it no matter what the consequences, that he was going to the newspapers with his awful story, but that he wasn't sure how fruitful such an endeavor might be. Truhart's connections are far reaching and include members of the press, you see. He had a change of heart at the last minute, decided the press couldn't be trusted. He only knew of one person who was completely safe, untouchable, who had protection from Garvey himself. He chose you. He was betting that you had rabbit in you, that you were gonna blow town. Once out of town it would be safe for you to let the note out. He gave the note to Francie, who was to seek you out—which she did. It was that day you fell out of the peach tree.

"That letter includes details of the whole sordid story; the military and prison experiments, the abductions of children for the snuff movies, the whole POP mess."

"Military experiments?" I coughed. Here's a new twist, I thought.

"Hush up and listen, boy," he cut me off, and began talking faster:

"It also names and tells where a body or two is buried for the sake of verification. That letter could stop Truhart in his tracks before his time comes, before things is ripe for the kind of disaster the Devil has in mind for him to set in motion. Could take the Devil hisself down a notch or two as well.

"Well, anyhow, since you so intent on doing the wrong thing for the right reason and screwing up everything in the process, I guess I gotta introduce you to some acquaintants. Some folks who can maybe shed a little light you be needin'."

I felt the old man grab at my collar, lifting me up from the floor with the brutal grace of a pro wrestler. I cracked my lids, exposing my eyes once more to the burning smoke, just enough to make out a black, gnarled fist slam into the steel door I had been leaning against. The old ghost smacked it hard enough to knock it open; one punch.

What was on the other side of the door could not be real. The old man tossed me into this improbable world like he was tossing a muddy puppy into a bathtub.

Slammed the door.

I landed butt first onto a field of tall grass and dandelions made of purple and blue tissue paper. The dirt was moist and smelled like sweet chocolate mixed with manure. I rolled over on my back and looked up at a clear, yellow cloudless sky. There was no smoke. There was no heat or flames. My eyes saw clearly and did not sting or tear.

I looked around me. I was no longer in Charm City at all it seemed. There were no buildings as far as the eye could see and, in fact, there was only one tree—about a hundred yards off.

A peach tree.

I pulled the wet rag from my face and breathed in deep of the cool clean air. Dropping the rag to the ground, I recognized it on impact. It was a torn piece from Ida Mae and Becky's homemade red and white checked dress. The rag was wet because it was soaked in blood.

Three figures walked towards me from the direction of the peach tree, a man, a woman, and a child—all dressed in their Sunday best.. As they got closer I was able to recognize the man even though his hands and face were covered with fresh burns; black and red with streaks of purple that must have once been veins and arteries.

It was Charles Garvey and he was real, real dead.

The other two figures that accompanied him were equally dead. Garvey's wife Madeline and their son Ronald Scott also bore the markings of their violent ends—the wounds were as fresh as if they had happened hours ago instead of years.

The first to speak was the boy: "Hello," he said, "I'm Ronnie."

I couldn't reply—could only stare at his wounds, his cut face, smashed skull, broken fingers. The killer had been very thorough. A knot formed in my throat and I couldn't hold back the sobs that built there.

"There, there," said Madeline Garvey. Bright red noose burns trickled beads of blood around her neck like a string of red pearls. "Ronnie's just fine now, just fine. He doesn't feel anymore pain."

"Hello Jack," said Garvey. "I'm sorry I didn't have a chance to say goodbye. I wish this wasn't necessary but our friend the Good Reverend seems to think you may need some guidance. We'll have to be brief so pay close attention."

"Now I want you to take my hand, son", this from Madeline Garvey, "I'm going to take you back home. There's something there that you have to know about. Something you have to see." Before I could protest, my hand was in hers.

And Charles and Ronald Garvey were no longer there. Gone.

The strange little field we had been standing in was no longer a field. In fact, we were standing in the front yard of a house—the house I grew up in. The one with Dad's funeral home built into it, the one that had been burnt to the ground so many years ago by an angry mob.

There was thick black smoke coming out of the chimney. Thick black smoke and large white ashes.

The house was the same as I remembered it—but different. It looked *newer*. The street in front was paved with cobblestone instead of asphalt. Madeline tugged gently at my hand, guiding me towards the rear of the house, to the hidden area that was used to receive deliveries. Deliveries of dearly departed remains, that is.

There were no trucks or cars back there like there should have been—just one very large horse drawn cart. Two horses waited patiently at the reins while crusty looking men unloaded heavy looking canvas bags in through the back door. The number of bags was easily in the dozens.

"What have they got? What are they doing?" I said to Madeline whose demeanor had become grim at the site of the men. "That entrance is meant for clients—for *bodies*. Dad doesn't allow anything else in through there—"

"Yes." She interrupted softly. "Yes. Bodies."

We walked past the workers at the back door. *Through* the workers. Our bodies were like mist. We moved, unseen as ghosts, into the back room, observing the actions of the men. If it were bodies in the bags, some sort of mass burial, they would have to be taken to the crematorium. Two men were carrying an exceptionally large bag. We followed them down a short hallway, at the end of which they turned left. Madeline lead me to the right—in the direction of my father's accounting office.

"You never knew it, Jack, but your father had some financial troubles several years before you were born. He almost lost the family business, and this business meant everything to him—it had been started by his great grandfather almost a hundred years before. He would have lost it if he hadn't made a deal with certain government agencies. But it was a bad deal. Very, very bad. He should have let the business go, start over."

"What deal? What are you talking about?"

She said nothing, leading me to the closed door of my father's office—*into* and *through* the door.

Suddenly inside, I saw my father at his desk staring at some papers in front of him, gnawing on an unlit cigar. He was younger than I had ever seen him.

There was a man in uniform sitting across from him with his back to me and Madeline. He seemed to be waiting for something. Finally, my father spoke:

"Can't be done."

The strange man: "Has to be done. Will be done. Just like you been doing. Just like we agreed." The man's voice was uncultured and Southern—I recognized it immediately. "Don't be gettin' no thoughts about going back on a deal now, boy. You do that and you be fucking with the wrong sumbitch."

"Jesus Christ—" said my father.

"Don't bring him into this. This ain't none of his damn business. This is government business and it's gotta be carried out. *Military* business. Now, yer doing a fine job so far Tommy boy, fine job and I mean it. Juss get it done, get it done—"

"But the children—"

"*YOU KNEW THERE'D BE CHILDREN!* You were told about that in advance so stop crying about the goddamn children already. You got what you wanted, your business is all yours, clear and free. Now it's time to give Uncle Sam what he wants."

As he stood up I could see the man had lieutenant stripes, as he turned to face us I could see the face of a young Elijah Truhart chomping the stub of a fat Cuban, grinning.

"You'll do just fine, Tommy boy. Just fine." He let out a cackle of a laugh and walked out of the office slow and easy. Dad just sat at his desk looking at the same thin stack of papers.

It was a list of names—and next to each name were descriptive remarks of a medical nature; height, weight, afflictions, allergies, eye color, *age* . . .

He lay his face down against the papers and shivered. I'd never seen my father cry like that before. "Little children," he whispered.

Madeline tugged at my hand and we walked back into the hallway, passing the line of men who were carrying canvas sacks in the direction of the crematorium. Something fell out of one of the sacks and I looked down. A little girl's shoe.

"Never should have made that deal," said Madeline Garvey, "But what's done is done. Your father was the Fourth Horseman."

We walked out the back door from which we had entered but when we were outside everything was gone; the horse and cart, the men, the house—even Madeline was gone. I was back on the strange field again— blue and purple grass, yellow sky. This time I was alone—or so I thought.

Some one tapped me on the back.

I turned to face Ronnie. He smiled and said, "My turn!"

He touched my hand.

I was standing in a child's crib.

The decor of the room was mainly little boy blue; stuffed animals and tiny shirts littering the floor. A little blond haired girl of about nine or ten was holding a long candle at the far corner of the room, talking in hushed tones to a small boy who could have been Ronnie's twin—in fact, it *was* Ronnie. But this Ronnie was different from the one who'd touched my hand only a moment ago; this Ronnie's face was clear, sweet, unruined. No terrible cuts on his face, no caved in skull. The little girl opened the door of the closet and stepped in. Uninjured Ronnie hesitated—then followed.

I felt a small hand tug at the back of my shirt tail.

"Lift me out." It was Ronnie again, but not the Uninjured Ronnie I'd just seen. This one was the horribly disfigured one who had brought me here; Murdered Ronnie. I perplexed for a moment on the strange world of ghosts: two ghosts of the same person at one time?

"Lift me *out*." Insistent this time. I complied, pulling Murdered Ronnie out of the crib by his little armpits. He was ragdoll-light. Murdered Ronnie walked briskly—almost a skip—after nine year old Janice and Uninjured Ronnie. "Come on!"

I swung a leg over the railing of the crib, fell on my butt trying to get the second leg out. Murdered Ronnie giggled, "Come on, *doofus!*" I got up and followed Murdered Ronnie into the closet. We pushed our bodies through a small hole near the floor in the back of the closet with impossible ease. The small orange light of Janice's candle flickered crazy dancing shadows on the wall of an old metal staircase. We trotted down the steps in an effort to keep up.

As we got closer to the two I could hear a nervous quiver in Uninjured Ronnie's voice: "Jannie I'm afraid. It's too dark. Let's go back up, 'kay?"

"Okay," Janice lied, "but first let me show you something."

We went down what seemed like an eternal number of steps. Through the dim flicker I was able to recognize the strange architectural patterns of The Big Punch.

"Janice found a rat," whispered Murdered Ronnie. "It wasn't her fault what happened. She thought the rat was dead, but it wasn't. The rat never dies."

His words gave me goose bumps.

"The rat made her do it. Made her hurt me."

Janice to Uninjured Ronnie: "Come on slowpoke." Murdered Ronnie and I followed closely.

Finally, we reached the bottom floor. The air was damp, thick and unmoving. Stifling.

The room was large and empty except for a thick wooden table at the center; a table like a butcher's block. On the side of the table were little pegs upon which were hung an assortment of rusty tools. The tools were strange looking and unfunctional in any practical way as far as I could tell.

Janice to Uninjured Ronnie: "Do you believe in ghosts, Ronnie?"

"Jannie your *scaring* me. Stoppit!"

"Well, you should believe in ghosts because they're all around us right now. Lotsa people got killed right in this room. And they want revenge."

"*Stoppit!*" Uninjured Ronnie was near hysterical with fear.

"They want revenge on the one who killed them. They need a blood sacrifice. And it has to be innocent blood. Pure blood."

Uninjured Ronnie stopped yelling *stoppit* but kept making noise; sort of uhhuh huh huh huh huh—real shivery-like.

Janice blew the candle out.

Murdered Ronnie whispered at my ear; a broken record: "Janice found a *rat*".

As if that explained everything.

Uninjured Ronnie: "Jannie make the light go on, make it light pleeeeease—I'm afraid. I don't wanna play anymore.."

In the pitch black I could see nothing but knew somehow what was going on:

Janice found the boy's yelling head in the dark, pushed him down, kicked him hard, jumped on top of him, pulled his little shirt off and stuffed it in his mouth.

Pinched his nose shut until he passed out.

Uninjured Ronnie now officially *Injured* Ronnie.

A whisper in my ear: "Janice found a *rat*."

I stared into blackness as the sound of Janice's footsteps moved to the stairwell, began climbing alone in total darkness. Slowly, carefully. The room filled with the sound of Injured Ronnie's shivery breathing.

Murdered Ronnie: "*A rat.*"

What should have been a few minutes felt like an hour. A flicker of orange glow peeked around the corner of the stairwell: Janice returning.

This time she had brought an oil lantern instead of a candle. And she had brought some clothesline. She set the light and rope on the wooden table. On the butcher's block.

She walked over to Ronnie, picked him up off the ground. Cradled him like a baby. Took him to the butcher's block, tied him to it by the wrists and ankles.

Waited for him to wake up; when he did, she began.

For over an hour I watched as Janice work on her brother, transforming Injured Ronnie slowly, *very slowly*, into Murdered Ronnie. My movement had been paralyzed, I was only able to see—not to call out or intervene in any way. She used the rusty orange tools expertly; poking, tearing, stretching, gouging. Dying Ronnie screamed and cried pitifully.

Finally, Dying Ronnie lay almost still, unsquirming but still shivering; breathing irregular; wet sucking sounds. Janice stopped her work for a moment. Paused as if awaiting instructions. Then picked a long orange knife from the assortment on the tool pegs. She looked as if she were about to cut the ropes that held Dying Ronnie's arms and legs to the butcher block—then hesitated. Smiled.

Janice found a rat . . .

Used the knife instead to saw her brother's limbs off at the trunk. There were rivers of blood.

When she was done she brought the handle of the big knife down on his forehead again and again, crushing his little skull. Then dropped the knife to the floor.

Breathing heavy,
janice found a rat . . .

she shoved Dead Ronnie's head and trunk onto the floor with a bloody splat, leaving his four limbs tied to the table top. Janice turned then to face *me*.

"I did it for you, baby. All for you. Always for you."

I heard the *shick shick shick* of a child trying to suppress laughter; the laughter of a child who's just played a mean prank on a weaker child. I turned to face my escort, Murdered Ronnie. The face I saw was no longer his but my own.

My face as a child.

beneath jesus . . .

The laughter of the two ghostly children was unsuppressed and squealing; the sound of wailing, drowning rats. I closed my eyes and screamed.

I felt the sensation of falling; spinning head over heels through black, cold night.

When I opened my eyes I was laying in a field of tall grass, looking up at a clear yellow sky. The figure of Charles Garvey stood over me, sympathetic eyes peering through burnt ruined flesh. He bent down to me, hands reaching towards my face. His red and black hands smelled of bacon and I felt a wave of dizziness envelope me. He lay his thumbs gently on my eyes and said:

"This won't hurt."

He removed his hands from my face.

We were still in the field, but the field was different. The peach tree remained—but up from the ground had sprouted a house—*the* house. It was the house of The Big Punch minus St. Paul Street or anything else that should have surrounded it. No driveway, no neighboring houses, no cars—it was as if the house had been uprooted from its place on St. Paul Street and dropped in the middle of this wacky field. And the building looked different in the same way my father's house had—*newer*. Garvey took me by the hand and motioned me to walk with him in the direction of the house. He didn't seem fazed by the strange disembodiment of the building.

When he spoke his voice was clear and easy, defying the severity of his facial disfigurement, the horrible burns;

"Tell me something, Jack. You've walked through this big dung heap of a building. You've seen the house. You've been below in the hidden levels, you've seen the dozens of cells on each floor, the concrete walls, the wooden floors. Haven't you wondered about it? The building is fairly old—forty years or so. What could the original builders have been thinking when they built it that way? Who designed it, what was the purpose? Haven't you wondered?"

Of course, I had wondered about that quite a bit. But I hadn't a clue.

"Today in Germany there is a movement, as you know, called Nazism—National Socialism. To men, it is a political movement. To Redd, a mere vehicle for his work. Redd presents men with the opportunity to embrace great evil—essentially, that's the job entrusted to him by God Almighty himself. In Germany today, each man and woman must choose. On this very day there are thousands of German soldiers—good men— who are being faced with the question of whether to embrace their bloodlust—to participate in the extermination of an innocent race of people for so called political reasons. They also have the power to turn that bloodlust away. Unfortunately, such a noble decision would carry with it grave consequences, mark them as enemies of the state. Many have chosen to embrace the evil of the times—many more will do the same.

"The concept of Nazism is Redd's masterpiece to date. But forty years ago his darkest masterpiece took place in this very building, partly in collaboration with myself, I'm sorry to say."

We walked in through the front door, passed the entryway. A young and beautiful woman with black hair and green eyes sat in the living room upon a great wing-backed wicker chair, sipping at a cup of tea and staring out the window. She looked troubled.

"My love, my love," said Garvey with a deep sadness, and I realized the woman was a young version of his wife, Madeline. He stood stroking her hair as she continued to look out the window, oblivious to our presence.

"The year was nineteen hundred and three. I was a young man but highly regarded in my field—anesthesiology, the science of deadening pain. I had made significant progress in the study of pain, its causes, its cures—so on and so forth . . ." He didn't seem real impressed with his accomplishments. "I was an idealist—I believed that I could rid the world of pain. Dear Lord, had I only known that I was destined to be one of the greatest tools of the King Of Pain.

"Youth was my downfall—being so eager to please the first financial backer that showed any interest in my work, I jumped too quickly into a shady government research project that promised me unlimited backing in all of my future research. My colleagues backed away from the project—as I should have. I was by far more creative than they—but I sorely lacked their wisdom.

"My naivete and arrogance doomed me to become the Third Horseman.

"*Research* they called it. The army was developing some new war toys, you see, that required my particular expertise. It was believed that unfriendly nations in Europe were a few steps ahead in this particular area of weapons research. This fact, coupled with the threat of war that was stirring overseas, was making American brass antsy about being behind the times in the human destruction game.

"Naturally, when the details of their plans began to surface I, like my shrewder colleagues had done in the first place, decided to turn away from the proposition. But agents of the government can be quite persuasive. Solid financial backing was as hard to find in those days as it is now. I reasoned that if I could truly rid the world of pain with my *future* work, well, was it really too high a price to pay? Would it be truly wrong to cause a little pain in the present to achieve the absence of it in future generations? I know now how perverse it is to try to justify my actions. Especially with hindsight.

"I bit that apple, Jack. I was later to find out my own capacity for evil—and it was quite high. Quite high, indeed.

"The weapons project that was being developed was for chemical and germ warfare. Mustard gas, bubonic plague—perhaps you've read about all that . . . nasty stuff. Very nasty stuff. I was not only to be in charge of developing those weapons—I was to test their effects; *that* was the morally consuming part. You see, you can test weapons on animals that are meant for humans only up to a certain point if you want truly accurate results. And the army wanted details: what would be the effect of their weapons, at various dosage levels, on a three hundred pound man? A woman with diabetes? A healthy five year old child? How would a young boy react differently to his female counterpart? What would the effect be on an unborn child?

"A young lieutenant by the name of Truhart was the Army's head man in charge of the project, which was called Operation Big Punch. The name was an inside joke, a loose translation of the French atrocity theater called Grand Guignol. I believe Redd gave you a little oratory about that abominable place a few nights ago. If the research I conducted in Operation Big Punch proved satisfactory to the powers that be, Truhart was destined to make a necessary jump in his career.

"A necessary jump for Redd's interests, that is. You see, Truhart is Redd's ward. Each of the Four Horsemen play an integral in Redd's advancement towards Truhart's inevitable destiny, a destiny so malevolent and destructive that the effects on mankind would almost certainly be uncorrectable. But I get ahead of myself.

"This house was built to serve the purpose of Operation Big Punch. Above ground, an ordinary house, a front. But below; six floors of cells, each housing human guinea pigs of every imaginable race, creed, color, age, sex, and deformity. The army, as represented by Lieutenant Truhart, insisted on very thorough testing. Subjects were collected from the poverty areas on the west side, in particular the neighborhood know as Pigtown. Truhart's night squads worked quietly and efficiently in their selection of test subjects—the brutish soldiers spoke softly and carried big sticks, managing to scare the poor urbanites very effectively. So effectively that word of the abductions never reached the suburbs for fear of further visits, more abductions. More hell on earth for Pigtown.

"The torture and murder that took place within these walls was unequaled in modern history. Until just recently that is. The Germans have set up secret camps, you see—camps where *terrible* things are happening. But that's another matter . . .

"The question of disposal was something that neither the doctor nor the Army had much considered, though—and was becoming quite a problem. The Army could dig a good mass grave in a pinch—but that's battlefield stuff. This was a major city. One can't just dig a trench in some alley and start up a bonfire"—he paused then grinned with a disturbing air of nostalgia; "although I do recall some discussion of such a proposition. No, someone with expertise in the matter of body disposal had to be called in to assist—a private party. It was decided that Truhart would seek out a local funeral director who was suffering financial troubles, someone who could be persuaded easily with a cash payoff. Someone with private access to a sizable crematorium. The lieutenant found such a party, as my dear wife has shown you, a man who's family business was facing bankruptcy after generations of successful operation. A man who's feelings of guilt regarding that failure were eating him up. Lieutenant Truhart pulled out Uncle Sam's check book and made the man's troubles go away.

"This funeral director—he was told everything. He knew what he was getting into. He knew he was facilitating the deaths of hundreds, he knew he could have stopped it with a twinge of conscience—but didn't. And he did this dirty work for money. Sealing his fate."

I spoke then:

"You told me that you were the Third Horsemen and your wife told me my father was the Fourth,"—my knowledge of the bible is pedestrian at best, but I recognized his reference to The Book of Revelations. "Who were the other two?"

"That's not important now. The information I've been giving you is crucial to your understanding of how you came to this place. Now I must give you information that will give you a sense of your responsibility to undo the sins of the fathers. It is urgent that you understand and then act.

"There is a reason why Redd has bided his time, why he has let the pain of the Four Horsemen drag on for generations. The world's ruin could not be brought about by cannons and musket balls. Technology had to catch up to the evil in men's hearts—and now the time is ripe.

Explaining to you won't be enough for you to understand. I'm afraid I'll have to show you. Take this vision, Jack, take it and let it serve you. You alone possess the key that can stop the chain of destruction."

My body flushed with a wave of cold fear as the man pressed his thumbs once again to my eyes.

The things that I saw in those seconds were horror beyond imagining. Horror that made my recent few days tripping through hell look like a tiptoe through the tulips.

The vision:

There was an explosion. Two explosions. I saw cities evaporate into black dust, eyeballs melt from faces like chocolate covered cherries in an inferno blast, people buried alive, ignited instantaneously. Human skin transformed into a silver reflecting surface; human chrome. There were children. Thousands and thousands of children. . . .

"Now you see, boy." The voice: not Garvey, but Reverend Gary. *"Now you see."*

Suddenly whatever doubt that lingered in my body left me. I believed it all. I was resigned to the whole story, no matter how twisted or farfetched. My next words quivered from my lips, my natural trademark sarcasm gone fishing—it was the tone of a meek private requesting orders form a drill sergeant.

"What now, Father?"

Thumbs lifted from my eyes. Smoke rushed into them instantly, stinging.

"I ain't yer pappy, Slim. Upsy-daisy." Reverend Gary's voice had been replaced by yet another. A hand gripped my upper arm and yanked me to my feet. I tried to open my eyes but the slightest movement of my eyelids in the smoke brought pure agony. "Hold on," the voice said as I was hoisted onto the big man's shoulder like a sack of rags. The man was coughing as he ran, stomping up the steps two at a time.

As I clung limply to the man's suspenders, I placed his voice. I felt myself shaking violently and realized that it was not from fear but from shock; I was going into convulsions. A blinding light illuminated the thin red skin of my eyelids and cold, clean air filled my mouth—I was outside. But the air refused to enter my straining lungs—it was as if someone had stuffed a baseball in my throat. I realized I was in the process of swallowing my tongue.

Henry Fish tossed me to the grass outside the house, took one look at me, said,"Oh, shit", and leapt onto the ground beside me, burrowing a clumsy finger into my mouth trying to get some kind of grip on the swelling tongue that was blocking my throat.

"Christ, fella. Don't die *now*. Not after all this. Holy *shit*"

Suddenly I was very sleepy. I heard the distant sound of fire engines. I forced my eyes open and the October air felt like cold water. Henry's concerned and frantic look melted away, turned brown and cracked. His eyes clear and blind. His thick lips turned up at the corners.

"Sleep now, boy. You goin' home. Close dem baby browns. Sleep, Jack." Reverend Gary had returned once more. He began to hum an old spiritual that sounded as good as a lullabye to me.

My sleep was heavy and dreamless.

CHAPTER EIGHTEEN

GONNA MEET YOU AT THE JUDGEMENT BALL

Three days passed since Henry Fish, the son of Albert, pulled me from that burning building on St. Paul Street. Henry had driven my snoozing sack of bones, along with the newly separated, albeit dead, bodies of Ida Mae and Rebecca Merle, to a little farmhouse in Missouri.

As the old man's ghost had promised, Myra White had begun her long wait on the day Reverend Gary had become a ghost at the hands of young Albert—and had remained in waiting all these many years. Tending her little farm and waiting, waiting, waiting.

And now the wait was over.

At Myra's request, Henry buried the bodies of Ida Mae and Becky in a little plot beside their beloved murdered grandfather, the Reverend Gary White, the dead man whom I'd come to know under such odd circumstances. He lay them to rest out back near the old slave quarters where Nora Branson had left her angry and violent message to God so long ago. Henry accomplished the burial of the twins before I'd awakened from my extended nap—and Myra also had been busy while I slept, dressing and cleaning my wide assortment of injuries.

On the fourth day my eyes opened.

Myra White was ninety-eight and looked every minute of it; her face a web of cracks and lines, her hands deformed with calluses from the years of lonely, hard work. But beneath her scarred shell there lie a particular softness, the softness of patience. And in her eyes I saw the same playful radiance that I'd always seen in Ida Mae's .

Surprisingly, the first few days brought painfully little to say. The occasions that we did speak to one another usually centered on the weather, how it was shaping up into a chilly fall—that sort of thing. It was as if the words needed to ripen on some vine of the heart.

Finally the words fell. They fell from our mouths with the agony of birth, but they came.

Myra sat in blue silence as I told her what she had craved to hear for so long; news of her kin. I told her about Ida Mae's bravery, about Reverend Gary's visits, about Redd's plans for Apocalypse and our attempts to intervene. Myra listened dry eyed and intently until that last part—the part about saving the world.

"That old dead fool!" she said with a sad smile, tears welling up in reddened, radiant eyes.

"Excuse me, ma'am?"

"That *old dead fool!* He always meant well. But he never shoulda come to you, boy. Shoulda stayed happy in tha ground where it's safe. Gary's a gentle soul, son, but he been misleading you."

"I don't understand."

"Fools on earth can't mess with no Judgement Day. Not even the Devil can stop or start God's business. Redd is a instament of God, don't you see that? You can stop one bomb from dropping but not the next. You can delay today's catastrophe but maybe it be worse later if you do. Maybe better. Doesn't matter. It's God's business. It's s'posed ta be, at least—but now it's on you. You got a decision to make about that piece of paper in yer pocket and you just about got all the information you need to make that decision."

"What do you mean *just about* got all the information?"

"Well, come on, boy! Cain't you see day's holes in yer story?"

I thought about The Four Horsemen bit. Garvey was Three, Dad was Four. I had no idea about One or Two. I only vaguely understood where that Bible stuff was coming from, anyway.

"About the Horsemen. Can you tell me about that.?"

"I can tell you about anything you don't know, son. Just as long as you ask the right questions and my memory still workin'." She sat back in her rocker, looked hard out the window:

"The Horsemen just a bunch of ordinary folks. Ordinary in every way except they committed terrible crimes against God hisself. So terrible were the crimes of the Four Horsemen that God wrought a terrible vengeance down on them. God lay the burden on their eternal souls that their actions should set into motion the downfall of mankind. Start the Apocalypse. These four ordinary people made the little snowball with their abominations agen God, and God punish them by makin' their children keep that snowball rollin', gettin' bigger and bigger till it's a piece of ice so big can't no human heart melt it.

"The children of the Four Horsemen is innocent, you see. But they payin' for their parents sins. It ain't fair, but God never claimed to be fair."

I had to think on that. Bible talk never goes down smooth with me, it always feels a little shady.

"Okay," I said, "Doctor Garvey was responsible for the deaths of hundreds of women and children in the name of medical research—okay; huge sin. My father was responsible for accommodating the murders by destroying the bodies for a price—also a whopper. This made them Horsemen Numbers Three and Four?"

"Not hundreds of deaths, Jack; *thousands.* That qualified them to be the greatest mass murderers of all time—unless you include deaths from Christian war or inquisition which the Good Lord tends to look the other way on. Of course they had a little push from Redd and his no-good whipping boy Elijah Truhart—but that don't make them any less accountable for what they done. Iss their children that had to pay the real price, though. Sad, sad, sad—it surely is." Myra wrinkled her weathered forehead with dramatic effect. "That poor little wife of yours born with the taste of blood in her mouth—killed her own brother for starters as a child then got to killing folks so regular in adult life that she can't remember which victim's which, startin' to actually believe dat *you* done some of the killin'.

"And you." She cast a tender eye in my direction, "You born with a taste for death too—but you shook it somehow. All but the dreams—and your former self comin' to haunt you now and again ... "

With great effort, I said the thing that I had to put into words. I had to hear those terrible words even if they came from my own mouth: "Janice was the Bolton Hill Butcher. I know that now."

"Yes," she said with finality, "she was the only one coulda set it up to look like it was you. She put your driver's license in that dead man's car. But she didn't frame you out of malice, Jack. She did it out of love. She needed your love and she needed you to be *like* her—when she found out that you weren't, she had to *make* herself believe that you were. She loved you, Jack—just as much as you loved her. Ironic thing is that no one will ever believe she was the killer. All the evidence point at you and it always will. It's your word against the word of a lot of poor dead folks. Your a fugitive, Jack—now more than ever. You'll always be running, you got no choice."

"I loved her. I'll always love her." I felt a swell of emotion, fought it.

"Of course you did, child," Myra said softly.

"The Horsemen," I prodded, getting too much information to digest emotionally but wanting more, "Who were the other two?"

"The first was a man by the name of Samuel Fish. He and his wife, Allison, were the two that Gary done toldja 'bout. The ones who stole us back into slavery after the war.

"Gary also toldja bout Samuel coming into my room and havin' his way with me that awful night. That little baby was born out of this black body with pure white skin; pretty little thing. Samuel named that child Albert—after his own daddy. Yes, that boy of mine would grow up to be that child killin' monster you read about in the papers some twenty years back. They wound up killing my little Albert in the 'lectic chair, y' know. I read all about it in the paper." She paused as a tiny drop of salty water broke free from her left eye. The droplet ran like a guilty man down her face only to dangle helplessly at the dead end that was her chin. She wiped at the traitorous tear harshly and continued:

"Well, after I done birthed little Albert, Samuel's wife Allison—who just happened to be a barren old maid with a hart shriveled up tighter than a rat's ass—got it into her mind to kill that pretty little baby. She was a simple and petty woman. A vengeful woman. She thought killin' Albert would be a good way of tellin' the good Lord above a good what for. As you know, her murderin' ways didn't stick. Baby Albert lived."

Her face softened minutely as she went on: "Keep in mind, mosta these things I'm tellin' you qualify as normal trials and tribulations of poor folks in the south at that time, nothin' too special, I know. Sam and Allison was evil and mean for sure, but no more so than my neighbor or yours in the bitter days following that terrible war. What brought the hardest of damnations down on Sam's pitiful soul was a misconception he cultivated about God Almighty, one that advised him badly. He got it in his head that God had made his wife barren as a sack of stones out of spite, a mean trick played by big bully. And it was through this trickery that Sam was forced to spend his precious seed on a lowly negress like me. Couldn't see it for what it was; a divine blessing, a second chance for a man who didn't deserve to have a second chance. The chance to have a child. Nope, Sam twisted things up in his head so bad that he developed an unhealthy hankering for vengeance himself.

"Samuel's plan for revenge on God was more ambitious than Allison's smalltime child murdering schemes. It was his intent to murder God directly—or the next best thing. "It was a black October night when Sam Fish rode into town with several jugs of good grain alcohol and an oil lantern. The little wooden Baptist church on the edge of Jackson County was having a night service. The singing was so loud that the congregation didn't hear when Samuel nailed the big doors of the church shut. Splashed the grain alcohol on its walls. Lit the fire.

"The dried up building went up quick—there were no survivors. It was the first of many church burnings that would plague the Black South. Sam didn't mean the gesture to be against colored folks—he was mad at God. But he set the style for racial hatred with that little gesture of his, meaning to or not. Samuel's church fire was big news back in them days and it set a terrible trend among the bitter white folk of the South.

"God didn't cotton much to the idea of church burnings as a popular way to liven up a dull night in the Deep South like it came to be after that. God never forgot that little church burning, that first of so many.

"Samuel stood and watched it burn, feeling a tingle in his heart that he mistook for justice.

"He rode home with a sense of peace that night—and he let ride with him the dangerous belief that he had settled his score with Almighty God. This sense of having righted God's wrongs had a mellowing effect on Samuel, so much so that he took me, Gary and that little baby into his home as kin. To our surprise, he even began helping us raise that baby into a young man. Helped Gary learn to cope with his blindness, too.

"Samuel became a decent man after the church burning—funny how things work out that way sometimes. But God didn't forget. That burnt down church—what it meant and what it started in the South—is what put Sam in line to be the First of the Horsemen. And what doomed his own child—my child, too—to have that taste for blood. A taste for evil doin'.

"The peace that Samuel had achieved for himself brought no comfort to Allison. No, that bitter old woman couldn't help feeling injured every time she saw her husband's soul peer out through baby Albert's eyes. She made herself a little pie out of lye soap one day, died spittin' blood.

"After Allison's death, Samuel insisted on doing most of the fieldwork himself, what with Gary bein' blind and the baby needin' some motherin'. Me and Gary did most of the child rearing and, though it was risky, we would sneak the child Bible lessons while Samuel was out working the fields. Risky because old Sam still bore God a grudge and din't want no bible talk 'round his house. Gary took to learning how to play an old guitar that Samuel had piled up with a lot of other junk in the barn. Got pretty good after a while. Used to sing that little baby to sleep with that old guitar.

"And then Gary began to have dreams.

"He saw things in dreams that he couldn't tell anyone about, not even me. The things he saw in those dreams scared him—not because he was easily scared by bad dreams but because he knew that what was in the dreams was real. He didn't know how he knew this—but he did. They were not normal dreams, you see.

"So he kept them dreams mainly to himself. Didn't see how talkin' about 'em could help no one. Then little Albert started with his troubles—and Gary had a vision of the trouble getting worse. He thought maybe there was something he could do to change fate." She rubbed at her eyes and smiled. "Back then he was an old *living* fool.

"You see, Jack, that little boy had acquired strange urges—just like you, just like Janice—but worse. He had taken to doing bad things to stray animals he found on the farm; birds, squirrels, cats, whatever. Sam disciplined the boy but the beatings only seemed to egg him on. By the time he was fourteen he'd gotten so ornery with his animal murdering that Gary decided to speak with him about the dreams, tell the boy what those killing ways would bring him if he wasn't careful. He thought telling him might scare some sense into him. Well, it scared him alright. But it made him mad, too. It's a hurtful truth, but knowledge of one's own destiny is rarely a pleasing thing.

"Made him so full of rage that he picked up that shovel—same one that had taken away Gary's sight years before—and pushed it into my old blind fool's throat just below the chin. Little Albert knelt down beside his dying step daddy and lapped up his blood like a thirsty hound. Samuel walked in on this awful scene—and then he knew what the boy was.

"He knew that Allison was right in wanting to kill the child, he knew that God had one-upped him in the scoreboard department.

"Albert sprung on Sam like a wild animal, Gary's blood still sticky on his lips and chin. Tore Sam's throat out with his teeth. The boy ran into the woods. Never came back to this little farm.

"When the Sheriff came snoopin' around about the killin's, I made up a story about Gary and Samuel bein' attacked by a bear. Told him young Albert had run off in fear. It was assumed, when Albert didn't turn up right away, that the bear had gotten him too.

"Albert lived in the woods for several weeks like some kinda blood hungry savage. His bloodlust served him well in the wild, kept him from going hungry. He spent his days killing things to eat and thinking about what Gary had said to him about the dreams, about his destiny. He spent his nights wondering whether he should live or die. He decided he wanted to live.

"And then he walked out of those woods.

"He turned up in town one day and managed to find—with the help of God or the Devil—the doorstep of Samuels's second cousin, a bricklayer by the name of Wilson Truhart. Wilson had a wife, Sarah, and a young son about Albert's age, Elijah. Wilson took Albert in and the two boy's became fast friends; inseparable. They learned many things from each other. Elijah taught Albert how to play nicely in a sandbox. Albert taught Elijah how to peel the skin off a live puppy. The two boys were essential to each others destinies.

"Gary and Samuel were my two men and I took care to mark their graves well. I prayed to God for forgiveness and tended to the land with no help from no one. And I waited. Been waiting ever since. Up till now, that is."

Myra looked hard into the fire, her forehead wrinkled with frustration. I got the feeling that she found no satisfaction in her story's outcome. There was still one big hole:

"The Second Horseman," I edged gently.

"Ida Mae done already done told you in so many words. Think about it boy." She was right.

"Nora Branson," I filled in.

"My first born, by my husband." She looked on the verge of tears. "Her crime was small and innocent in a way, but not in the eyes of God. She presumed to mark her child as separate from and above the love of the Almighty. All because of a broken heart. A person shouldn't let a simple thing like a broken heart turn 'em against God." It made me think of Maxa, her deal with Redd to get even with the God who she'd believed killed her soldier fiancee.

"The penance that her child, Jezelle, my granddaughter, was doomed to pay was not the simple horror of being born with a taste for blood and death like the rest of y'all. God had something special cooked up for Nora's kin. Jezelle was damned to the agony of giving birth to a monster . . ."

I stayed in the main room of the farm house, sleeping on a sack of straw that Myra had made into a bed. The room was drafty but there was a fireplace and Henry Fish, who had made a home of the slave quarters near the little family cemetery, always made sure there was a log on. Myra had given me some fresh clothes to wear, my own lying in an unwashed heap by the foot of the straw bed.

I spent most of my time there thinking. But the thing that I should have been giving thought to was the thing that my mind seemed desperate to avoid.

I should have been thinking about what was in the back pocket of those rumpled pants lying on the floor. And what Myra had said about fools on earth not being able to change God's plans.

Somehow, delivering Lieutenant Black's letter to the proper authorities did not seem the obvious choice to me. Maybe it's because I knew, in my heart, that Myra was right, that it wouldn't do any good.

I thought a lot about my father. I continued to pine over Janice. I smiled when I thought about Ida Mae—I always will, I think.

I thought about the orange haired man who claimed to be the devil.

I thought about the unlikely heroes of this story; about Lieutenant Black and Francie the Amazon. And about Michael Merle. Francie was dead—but Black and Merle? They could still be alive somewhere for all I knew. The same could be said of the twins' mother, Jezelle—and even of Janice. I just had no way of knowing if any of these people were alive or dead.

Holes.

But mostly, I thought about Maxa.

I had assumed that Maxa had died when I shot her in the chest and she exploded into a hundred blood-soaked rats, but I had a gut feeling that that wasn't the end. The feeling that she was still among the living nagged at me for years. Then, in nineteen fifty-two I got my answer.

There was a big story in all the papers about a woman horribly murdered in Hollywood. The woman had been abducted and tortured for quite some time—possibly a week or more. Her body had been drained of all blood, sliced neatly in two at the waist and dumped in a field near an elementary school. The press called her "Black Dahlia" though she was later identified as Elizabeth Short. You might recall that as the name Paul Fish had called Maxa on the train ride back to Baltimore. I figured it for a coincidence till the papers released a mugshot of the woman. The photographs were clear and there was no mistaking—it *was* Maxa.

The LA Police had been desperate for leads in the case but too little was known about the woman. The things the police did turn up were almost comically vague; something about prostitution, something about wanting to make it in show business, something about coming from a big family, something about a fiancee who was killed overseas.

To this day the murder has gone officially unsolved, the killer never found. The only real lead the police ever got was a page in an appointment book found in the dead girl's apartment dated the day of her alleged abduction. It read: "meet Redd 4:30@ Sasha's". The detectives on the case later declared the lead a dead end.

I could have come forward, told them what I knew—and I thought about it. In the end, I realized that doing so would have been futile. Crank calls, I'm sure, had to be common in the Black Dahlia case—my story would have been in some pretty interesting company. And still the image of Maxa's disembodied head comes into my mind, squirming in gore and rats, still trying to suck air—and I wonder . . .

I guess I thought so hard and long about everyone and everything that happened to me in Baltimore and Jackson partially in an effort not to think about Lieutenant Black's letter. Maybe it was all that thinking that finally led me to my decision. I tried bringing the letter to Myra for advice, but she pushed the unopened envelope away without a word—all she had to offer was a sad smile that seemed to say: "This decision is yours. It can't be influenced by anyone, not me, not anyone."

So I threw it on the fire. The letter was never opened.

You see, the one thing I'd learned at The Big Punch was that true evil can't be stopped by simply doing the right thing. True evil has to be allowed to work itself out.

> *if ya thinkin' iss loose den iss probably tight*
> *if ya think iss wrong, well, iss gonna be right*
> *if you know dat iss black den iss sho' nuff white*
> *if ya bettin' iss left, son, ya betta be right*
> *backwards every time. . . .*

As you know, Truhart was elected vice president of the United States a year after The Big Punch burned down—and was appointed president in 1944 after FDR died. And he did drop exactly two atomic bombs on the Japanese cities of Hiroshima and Nagasaki, the same terrible explosions shown to me by the ghost of Charles Garvey that October night in 1943. These bombings constitute perhaps the greatest human tragedies of all times—but that fact got upstaged by Hitler's concentration camp atrocities. Understandable in a sense, but not really.

Truhart lives quietly in retirement to this day. He is remembered only as one of the greatest American presidents.

As for Redd, well, WWII was a good war for the Devil; Old Son got a lot of human misery accomplished. But even with all that death, I knew that Redd was somewhere wringing his fists, feeling beaten. His ultimate dream of Apocalypse hadn't been realized.

You see, mankind had gotten the shit kicked out of it in the Second World War—but was still intact.

I think maybe God himself had a hand in that. Could be that Reverend Gary was right; that the key was in Ida Mae and Becky all along. They were, after all, the literal embodiment of good and evil if ever there was one. And maybe like Ida Mae and Becky, Good and Evil are also twin sisters sharing a heart, one unable to live without the other.

It's nineteen sixty three now. Someone shot Kennedy last week. Hearing about it made me think of Maxa. I'm not sure why.

Life these twenty years has been peaceful for me. I'm still a fugitive—

as Myra predicted—but I don't have to run anymore; just hide. I've got a little job and a little apartment in a town far from Baltimore or Missouri or anywhere that someone might know who I am. And I have a little dog named Clara Bow who keeps me company when I'm sad.

Sometimes I see Reverend Gary in my dreams. In those dreams we sit around like a couple of old war buddies shooting the shit. He tells me I ought to take care of family, journey up to Liverpool, Ohio, tell my Daddy hello. Maybe I just will—after all, I'm not getting any younger and neither is Dad. Sometimes Gary picks up that old guitar of his and plays a verse or two. I guess what brought this story to mind is that last night, after twenty years, he finally played me the last verse of that old song he started singing back by the tracks at Penn Station. The one about the train.

That last verse went like this:

> Well, this train rolls through the night
> Its way is paved with light
> Some people say this train is bound for hell
> But I have been and back
> And I can ease your mind
> This train just goes in circles far as I can tell . . .